Praise for Can You Be

This is a delightful, intricately woven novel. *Can You Be* is a curious title and a simple enough question, yet the answer becomes deeper and more complex the more you ask it. *Can You Be.*

I became a champion for protagonist, Naina, a quirky introvert who struggles to discover her happy, authentic self. She questions the life she has chosen to settle for, and her self-worth in how she allows people to treat her. Upon finding a sticky note, a box, and an Angelite crystal, things get quite interesting. *Can You Be* evokes thought provoking insight into what the universe may be trying to share with us, if only we are open to the signs and trust in our own knowing enough to listen.

Naina's journey of self-discovery, friendships, and love is heart-warming and encouraging to anyone who thinks 'settling' is good enough. Through Naina's love for the stunning area of Charleston, the readers get to explore the beauty and history of the city, and beyond to Sweden, the Baltic states, and Finland.

Can You Be is filled with tangible messages that we need to believe in ourselves and respect all we can be, if we just allow ourselves to be.
> **– Mickey Martin, Award-Winning Author of**
> **The Given Series and The Victoria Collection/**
> **Mental Health & Disability Support Worker**

Can You Be is a captivating story following one woman's journey as she finds her place in the world. I love the spiritual through-line which is artfully woven into the author's exploration of trust, knowingness and overcoming conditional patterns of behaviour.

Can You Be is beautifully written in the unique style of the author – I was hooked from the opening line. The book is an informative and interesting read, providing great historical and cultural detail of the protagonist's trips through Northern Europe and the Baltic countries.

The part I loved most, was how this book has so many valuable life lessons and takeaways. I felt energised and motivated to make positive changes in my own life after devouring the final chapters. *Can You Be* is another wonderful novel from Sonee Singh. I look forward to reading more from this author.

– Lisa Benson, Author of Where Have I Been All My Life?

Can You Be

SONEE SINGH

Lusaris

Typeset in Adobe Garamond Pro 12/17pt

 A catalogue record for this
work is available from the
National Library of Australia

National Library of Australia Catalogue-in-Publication data:

Can You Be/Sonee Singh

ISBN:
978-0-9942850-1-0
(Paperback)

ISBN:
978-0-9942850-3-4
(Ebook)

To everyone who has ever felt they are different.
Our gifts come from being our true selves.

Author's Note

I tried to be as accurate as possible in describing the events and places in this book, although I have taken a few liberties to change details for literary purposes. For instance, the visit to the Hill of Witches between the Northern Fort and Plateliai may not be entirely possible to fit in the time that was described in these pages, but I felt it was important to include a visit to the Hill of Witches, as it provided Naina with a more mystical experience.

Also, I have mentioned real places, restaurants, and businesses, but the scenes that took place in them, as described here, are entirely fictional.

Much of the historical information included, particularly the portion that took place in the Baltics, was fact-checked. Even so, any errors, inaccuracies, omissions, additions, and/or inconsistencies in the manuscript, are entirely my own.

Warning: This book deals with the sensitive topic of suicide. If you or someone you know needs support, please contact:

Australia:
Lifeline
Call 13 11 14

United Kingdom:
Samaritans
Call 116 123
Email jo@samaritans.org

United States:
National Suicide Prevention Lifeline
Call toll-free 24/7 the at 1-800-273-8255 (https://988lifeline.org)
    You can also text HOME to 741741 for free, which offers 24/7
support from the crisis text line (https://www.crisistextline.org)

Chapter One

Naina was bothered by the sticky note on her computer monitor, especially the smiley face. "I hope you liked it Naina," the note read.

Who would leave her a sticky note? She hardly knew anyone. And what did they hope she liked? Naina barely dared to smile – ever – lest her face wrinkle, and the few people who knew her, knew this about her, so who would leave a smiley face? She touched her cheek, relieved she hadn't been tempted to smile back. At twenty-nine she had to be extra careful. She'd reached the ominous age when collagen decreased and wrinkles began to appear.

No one else was at work yet. Naina was always the first to arrive, and that morning was no exception. Everything else on the reception desk was as she had left it the night before. Oddly, though, the sticky note was the second item out of place that day. There had also been the box outside her apartment door.

That morning, events had unfolded as they typically did. Her alarm had rung at six o'clock on the dot, and she'd snoozed twice.

She had gotten out of bed at 6:18am and hopped on the Gazelle, the only machine she ever exercised on, for twenty minutes. She had bought it in college eleven years ago because, at the time, she had watched an advertisement in which Tony Little promised the machine was low impact. Naina used it because she dreaded hurting her knees. Any type of injury worried her, and while exercise was a necessity, she did it in the safest way possible.

She had showered, eaten a bowl of Special K cereal with 2% milk, and walked out of her apartment five minutes before eight in the morning. It took her less than five minutes to get to work. As she had stepped out of her apartment door, instead of walking directly to the staircase, she'd paused briefly. A box had been placed next to her door. It perplexed her but the confusion lasted only a moment. She hadn't placed any orders on Amazon – the only site she used for online shopping. Plus, her Amazon delivery day was set for Thursday. Someone must have misplaced the box. It irked her that they had chosen to leave the box outside her door.

As she searched the office for more irregularities, she worried her cherished get-to-work routine – one of many such routines – was in peril. She broke out in a cold sweat. Naina was already perspiring from the muggy 84°F Charleston morning, even though the 678-step walk from her apartment down Hasell Street and onto Meeting Street took less than five minutes.

Naina removed the sticky note. Where should she put it? She swiveled around in her chair. Normally, she would let her mind wander and concoct a story about the note, as she loved to do, but the real estate office needed to be set up by 8:15am and there was no time to spare. Naina hated disapproving gazes from Alice, who was forever on her case.

She still remembered the story she had come up with about

her when Alice had interviewed her for the receptionist job at the real estate office. At first glance, Naina had imagined Alice was the super-mom type, successfully juggling work and home. This was before Naina understood that Alice was the owner. Once Naina started the job, she had learned that Alice had founded the real estate company on her own while being a mother to three children. What had started as a one-woman office, Alice had expanded into a six-agent real estate business with an office manager and a receptionist.

On the rare occasions where Naina got to know the person she'd made up stories about, she was eerily accurate. But that Tuesday morning in early August, she didn't have time for any memories.

Naina had many routines, and the get-to-work one was particularly important. All she had going for her at the real estate office was her timeliness and efficiency. They were the only things keeping Alice from firing her.

Naina placed the sticky note in her wallet and tucked the wallet safely in her purse. She rushed to turn on the air conditioning and stood in front of a floor fan for a few deep breaths to lower her heart rate and dry out the sweat accumulating in her armpits. She read people, but she had never been good at foreseeing the future, no matter how hard she tried. But in that moment, she got the feeling change was imminent. The sticky note, despite its smile, felt ominous. Every event that had shifted – derailed – her life had come out of nowhere, shoving her in a new direction. The sticky note felt like a similar change agent.

She came back to the previous questions: Who had left the note? What was she supposed to like? And why the smile? She hadn't managed to calm herself as she walked into the pantry to brew coffee and slice the lemons to place into the water jug. Just

3

as she finished filling the jug with ice, there was a ring at the desk.

A gentleman stood by the entrance, smiling brightly. His eyes glittered and his teeth seemed like models for a whitening commercial. Naina could have sworn one of his teeth sparkled.

"Good morning, Naina. How are you?"

How did he know her name? She didn't say anything. She tried to come up with a story about him, but oddly found herself blocked. She shrugged it off, deciding it was just her being too stressed about setting up the office.

"Did you open the box?" he asked.

Naina was once again struck with a sense of foreboding. She took a moment to steady her voice. "I haven't checked for packages yet. I'm still setting things up."

"I mean the one I left outside your apartment door early this morning."

"Oh." She chided herself for not having looked at the box more closely.

"Naina, please tell me you saw it." He was still smiling.

She couldn't think of what to say. She had seen it, but it was out of place. She didn't know anyone who would have left her a box – or anything for that matter – and assumed it had been left there by the neighbor, and thus, the neighbor would take care of it.

"It contains what you've been needing, it's about who you can be." He winked and broadened his smile. "I'll see you after you open it."

Huh? What could he possibly mean? "How will—"

The mysterious man walked out.

A roller coaster of questions sped through her mind. Who was he? For the first time ever, she drew a blank. No story had come to her, still. She usually connected a story about a person within

4

seconds of meeting them. She couldn't think of a single scenario about who this guy could be.

She had more questions than answers. How would she contact him? How would he know when she opened the box? How did he know who she was? Or where she lived? What was in the box? How could he possibly know what she needed? Wasn't she already who she was? Who else could she be?

Those questions hung in her consciousness. If *she* didn't know what she needed, how had he figured it out? She hadn't ever felt her life was complete. Could she be different?

Naina had spent most of her life letting circumstances (and people) decide what happened to her. She followed the path of least resistance – the one that would send her into the least amount of spiraling. Life had been unpredictable, and making sure all remained immutable was her priority. But none of it gave her a clue of what she wanted, much less what she needed. Nor of who she could be. She knew the sticky note had been ominous.

Naina's morning routine was key for her holding on to her job. She'd had it for seven years and didn't want to risk getting fired. For the first time since she had started working at the real estate company, she was late setting up the office, and she didn't care. She couldn't wait to get back to her apartment. She had to make sure the box was still there. If she could have, she would have left immediately, but Naina was well aware it could be just the act Alice was waiting for as a justification to fire her. Naina sighed loudly and quickly set up the rest of the office. She had brought her packed lunch, as she always did, but maybe that day, she would eat it at home.

Chapter Two

Naina walked back to her apartment for lunch. In her eagerness to get to the box, she forgot how intense the muggy August midday heat could be. She usually avoided being outdoors at that hour – the morning and evening walks were bad enough. Her phone indicated it was 91°F with 94% humidity. To her it felt like 111°F. She saw heat waves rising from the asphalt.

Summers in Charleston were meant for the indoors. She didn't understand why people ventured to the beaches when it was so hot, especially to Folly Beach or Isle of Palms when they were so crowded. She only liked the beach at Sullivan's, despite the darker sand. It was quieter, and although there were still a number of people, tourists didn't flock to it as they did the others. She preferred to go in the fall, nearing her birthday, when the heat wasn't as intense – and when there was a lower risk of getting caught in a hurricane.

When she stepped into her apartment building, she was still sweating profusely. She smelled her armpits and made a mental note to wipe herself with a wet towel before heading back to work. She didn't usually wear any scents, and today wouldn't be an exception.

When she reached her apartment, she was relieved to find the box was still outside, but it was now placed squarely at the front of the door instead of being off to the side, as it had been in the morning. She squatted down to read the label. Her name and address were listed, but there was no indication as to who sent it. She had hoped to see the sparkly toothed man's name, and even learn more about him, like where he lived.

"Hi there," a male voice said.

Naina jumped back, reaching for the wall behind her.

"I'm sorry. I didn't mean to scare you." A tall slim Indian man held out his hand. He wore white shorts and a dark blue polo shirt, tucked in. His hair was cut short yet it was clear if he grew it out, it would twist into curls. His toes were perfectly groomed in his flip-flops, as if professionally pedicured. He appeared to be in his mid-thirties.

He was attractive and Naina was tempted to smile but stopped herself. She shook his hand, envisioning he was a start-up entrepreneur who'd set up his business in one of those new loft offices appearing on upper Meeting Street.

The man laughed. "I meant to help you get up."

"Oh." She hid her face in her top, which made her remember to wipe herself. She might need to change her top.

He held his hand out again but Naina didn't reach for it. She stood up by herself. "I'm fine, thank you."

"I'm Raiya, your neighbor." He pointed to apartment 206.

Naina looked at her own apartment, 205, as if to confirm.

"I haven't seen you before. Have you lived here long?" he asked.

"I was one of the first tenants in the building after they converted them into apartments."

"Wasn't it like ten years ago?"

"Twelve."

"Wow. You look so young …I mean, not like someone who's been living here that long." He laughed again.

"I moved here before starting college. I'm turning thirty this year."

"You go, girl. I would have thought you were still in college. You look way younger than me. I'm thirty-two."

Heat rose around Naina's neck, and she started to sweat again. She was growing increasingly nervous. Yes, she'd have to change her top. She stumbled on her feet.

Raiya placed his hand on Naina's shoulder to help her steady. "What's your name?"

Heat rose around her face and she stepped away from his touch. "Naina."

"Naina … and you have the eyes to match the name." He winked.

Naina was surprised Raiya pronounced her name perfectly. It was evident he knew what it meant. Naina didn't like her name. It meant beautiful eyes in Hindi. It's not that she didn't appreciate its meaning, but she didn't like that people couldn't pronounce it properly. It was neh-na but people called her na-ee-na like hyena. She hated it. She usually spent the first few minutes of an introduction correcting the pronunciation of her name, and she didn't let it go until she made sure the other person got it right. "Neh-na. Neh-na," she'd say repeatedly, ignoring the discomfort it caused.

She didn't think her eyes were beautiful. They were large and round and she did her best to hide them – without using makeup, of course. She was proud of her smooth, pore-free skin – she did have pores, but wouldn't admit it. They were still there, but they were invisible unless under a magnifying glass. Her skin was the only part of her body she truly loved. She considered it her only accomplishment. If her personality were outgoing, and if she liked people, she could have been a skincare model – the face of Neutrogena. And perhaps if she made more of an effort to look presentable. And be less simple, which is, after all, what Alice had wanted. The irony is if she had done as Alice requested, Naina wouldn't have remained at the real estate office.

"Do you need help with the box?" Raiya asked, bringing her back to reality.

"No, I think I'm good." Naina picked it up. It was a perfect square, six inches on each side. Naina wasn't good at estimating weights but she was able to toss it easily from one hand to the other.

"I hope there's nothing fragile inside."

Naina stopped playing with the box, in case Raiya was right. "It's padded inside."

"You can tell, or you know?"

"I don't know for sure. It seems that way."

"And the contents definitely won't break?"

"I don't know." For a second, she wondered if Raiya had given her the box. "Do you?"

"I have no idea. Isn't it addressed to you? Were you expecting it?"

"Yeah, but I don't know what's inside."

"When you open it, you'll know, won't you?"

"You're right."

"You're not going to open it now?"

"No, I'll wait until I'm inside."

Raiya nodded. "We must be the only two Indians in all of

Charleston."

Naina was surprised by the change of conversation. So, Raiya had clearly not sent her the box. How did he know she was Indian? Then again, she rationalized, she looked quintessentially Indian, no matter how little she knew of her culture. "There is a small Indian mart in West Ashley," she offered.

"India Spice on Old Towne Road? I've been there. You don't see many brown people around here, right?"

"In downtown? Not really. The only ones you see are tourists."

"Right ... I've got to get back to work." Raiya pointed toward his apartment.

"Your office is in there?" Naina raised an eyebrow.

"I moved here to head up marketing for a start-up. I am working from home until they earn enough to rent an office space. It was nice meeting you. I hope to run into you again." He walked away smiling.

Chills spread through her body. She hadn't been right about him being an entrepreneur but she accurately predicted he was part of a start-up. This time, Naina allowed herself to relish in that she was rarely wrong in the stories she concocted about people.

Even so, she didn't want to run into him again. Friendships were something she had ruled out long ago. Boyfriends too. Even as a child she'd kept to herself. It was easier than to have to deal with the risk of being abandoned. Naina also didn't like talking about herself. Invariably, the subject of her upbringing came up and she hated the looks of pity she would get.

She entered her apartment. She didn't bother warming her lunch and ate it out of the Tupperware while staring at the box. She shoved the food down as quickly as possible, and after she cleaned the container, she stared at the box again. It was a nondescript, brown cardboard box. The only marking was the label with her name and address. She was no closer to figuring out what was inside. Her only option was to open it. She had ten minutes to get back to the office.

Naina changed her blouse and came back to the box. She shook it slowly and a muffled sound came from inside. There was definitely something padded within. When she had mentioned it to Raiya before, she wasn't completely sure, but now she could clearly hear a heavier object thudding against a softer one.

She took a deep breath and grabbed the scissors she reserved for cutting into tape – the adhesive rendered them useless for anything else. She knew there were scissors made just for cutting tape, but she didn't like them. She opened the box and found a purple silk bag. Inside the silk bag was a spherical light blue and white crystal with thin red threads woven throughout. She held it in her hands for a few moments, and, once again, got a sense her life was going to change.

First the sticky note, then the man, then the box, and now this funny crystal. Or had it been the box, the sticky note, the man, the friendly neighbor, and now this funny crystal? Either way, none of it belonged. All of it was out of place. And she didn't like it one bit.

Chapter Three

After work, Naina walked to the Charleston County Public Library with the crystal sphere in her purse. That Tuesday evening, in August, it took her ten minutes and thirty-three seconds to walk over. She knew the streets of downtown like the back of her hand, and she often counted either the steps or the time it took her to get from one place to another. Naina created personal challenges to entertain herself, slowing down or quickening her pace to ensure she reached her location in a predetermined time or number of steps.

She walked down Meeting Street, making a right when she hit Marion Square, and headed down Calhoun Street. The library, sadly, didn't have the same historical quality of many of the buildings in Charleston. In fact, the first library in the city had opened in 1930 and had been located in the current Charleston Museum. As the needs expanded, it had moved to Rutledge Avenue, then to King Street, and had found its current home in 1998.

Still, she loved being in that space and she often spent her evenings there. Libraries had always been a haven for Naina. They had supplied her childhood's fondest memories. The public library in Charleston was expansive, larger than her home and office, and most importantly, it was quiet. She didn't mind the homeless who hid in cool comfort from the sticky heat, or the bow tie wearing older gentleman sporting a walking stick who jetted in on his golf cart to read the day's edition of the *Wall Street Journal*. People there kept to themselves, like she did, and it suited her.

Naina stayed until closing at eight that evening as she did every time she went to the library. But she didn't do as she usually did. She didn't peruse the most recent release in history, look up the latest romance from Nora Roberts, the recent *In Death* series Nora Roberts published under the pseudonym of J. D. Robb, or the latest in the *Jack Reacher* series from Lee Child.

She identified with Jack Reacher because he had no ID, no family, and he came from nowhere – granted it was because he moved around so much. Jack Reacher served for his country. He was brilliant, and he disappeared easily. He had a clean record and he was a "ghost" because he had no driver's license, no residence, no credit cards, no credit history, no PO box, no cell phone, and no email.

Naina hadn't moved much recently but she had as a child, and although she had an ID, she often felt like she didn't belong, except maybe to Charleston. She definitely had no family, no one she was close to. She spoke to her father only a few times a year. The only times she was certain he would call was on November 11, her birthday.

Naina would take the day off from work if it wasn't a weekend so she wouldn't have to worry about missing the phone call. She hated that her father didn't give her a time in advance. It was the only day in the year she kept her phone in her hand, making her feel as normal as everyone around her. She glanced at the screen every time the phone beeped or buzzed, even though she'd set a special ringtone for her father. She even took her phone with her into the toilet.

The conversation was always brief. He'd wish her happy birthday, ask after her work and health, and confirm she was still receiving the $2000 monthly deposit to cover her rent and utilities. If it hadn't been for the recurring wire, her receptionist salary would not have allowed her to live in the heart of downtown. Naina's father had secured the lease when Naina enrolled at the College of Charleston, reasoning she needed her own space. After graduation, she stayed on. Neither questioned why he continued to pay the rent when her salary couldn't afford it. Or why she didn't get a more affordable place. Or why she didn't seek a higher paying job.

Reacher wouldn't have stuck to the same job as she'd done. He was unlike her in terms of personality, and it's why she admired the character so much. She loved that he was invincible, he could tackle any scenario. And she wished she had the same ability, his agility and the same where-with-all.

That evening, she didn't look for the latest release with her favorite characters, and she didn't hide the book she was reading in between the stacks so she could find it when she went back – Naina didn't take any books home; she didn't want to bring the germs in.

No, she didn't do any of that. Instead, she needed to learn about crystals. She used *The Crystal Bible* by Judy Hall to compare the crystal that had arrived in the box to all the images in the book. The only two blue and white crystals depicted were an angelite and a blue lace agate. She then compared her crystal with all the crystals in *Crystal 365* by Heather Askinosie. From those descriptions, it seemed clear her crystal was an angelite.

A tinge of excitement awoke within when she learned angelites were found in India, among other places. Angelites facilitated a connection with the angels.

She searched around her for angels but saw none. Sighing, she continued reading.

The books said angelites brought a sense of peace and helped to heal from pain. The shapes of crystals carried their own significance, and spherical crystals increased self-awareness and integrated the mind, body, and spirit. They were used as windows to the past or the future. Naina stared at the ball hoping to see something. Beyond its opaqueness, there was nothing.

Orbs were signs spirits were trying to interact with the person who sighted them, and they helped people feel they weren't alone. She looked around again and there was still no one around her.

When Naina found *The Book of Stones* by Robert Simmons and Naisha Ahsian, chills ran through her. The subtitle claimed to explain stones by revealing "who they are and what they teach". The picture of the angelite in the book didn't look like the crystal she had received, but the description resonated with her in an other-worldly manner. It said angelites represented the energies of a guardian angel, guide, or spiritual entity.

The stones fostered a feeling of serenity and facilitated communication with beings in other dimensions, and they did so clearly and concisely. The book said angelite was the perfect stone to bring in more love and benevolence, and a deeper connection with angels.

Chapter Four

The next evening after work, instead of going to the library, she braved the busy evening King Street. As locals and tourists commingled to shop, visit art galleries, bar hop, and/or delight in culinary eateries, she snaked through the crowds down to Cornerstone Minerals to see if someone at the shop could confirm the sphere was an angelite. The shopkeeper held the sphere in his fingers and took it up to the light, and in mere seconds assured it was an angelite.

"Does it do anything special?" Naina asked.

"They bring about inner peace and people say they let you connect with angels. That's why it's called an angelite."

Even though the shopkeeper didn't offer any other insight, Naina was grateful the twenty-three-minute walk wasn't a waste of time. Still, to make the best use of her evening walk amongst the crowds, on her way back home, she stopped by the Earthbound Trading Company for a final confirmation, more to make her effort feel worth her while. It took the lady a quick glance to also confirm it was an angelite. She offered no new information and recommended the books Naina had already consulted at the library.

While Naina cooled off under the full air conditioning and ceiling fan in her apartment, she stared at the sphere, hoping for it to speak to her or bring about the promised sense of peace and connection to the divine. Maybe that was the change she longed for. Alice had told her she would feel differently once she turned thirty. Apparently, everyone did. Naina didn't know how she would feel but hoped turning thirty would somehow help fill the emptiness of her life. She didn't have high hopes. She expected it would be like any other birthday.

Her biggest indulgence was a yearly hair trim. Every November 11, she would go to the Urban Nirvana on Market Street and book with Caroline at 12:15pm. Afterwards, she would pop into Café Framboise and order a croque monsieur with a side salad and a slice of opera cake to take away. There were a number of French-styled eateries in Charleston, which wasn't surprising, given the city had a long history of French immigrants, starting from the Huguenots who had fled prosecution and settled in the city during the late 1600s, creating one of the oldest French quarters in the south. French immigrants continued to settle in Charleston after the French Revolution and even as a result of the Haitian revolution.

The weather on her birthday was usually perfect. Day times were typically a comfortable 72°F, ideal to spend a day at Sullivan's Island, which she would do, armed with her lunch. By then the crowds would have withered, and she would lay out her towel on the soft sand, close to the dunes and oat grass. She would eat her croque-monsieur on the beach. Afterward, she would walk on the harder sand closer to the water, letting herself soak in the soft waves. She would feel particularly lucky if she spotted a bottlenose dolphin.

Naina loved Charleston history, but she didn't like to think of it much on her birthday. She wasn't a native of the city but she wished she was. Knowing all about the city's history made her feel she was a part of it. Charleston was one of the oldest cities in the United States, founded in 1670.

There were darker sides to the city's story and she knew those as well. About 50% of all people who were enslaved in the United States made their way into the country through Charleston, particularly, through her beloved beach at Sullivan's Island.

Many could argue Charleston thrived because of slave labor; not only did they provide the workforce for the plantations (rice, tea, indigo, and cotton, among others), but from the business of buying and selling the enslaved. And where South Carolina had been a proponent of maintaining slavery (nearly half of the population in the state were the enslaved), they had also been a proponent of freedom from British rule. The first shot in the fight for American Independence occurred in Charleston.

But Naina refrained from thinking of those things on her special day. She would enjoy the three-mile sandy stretch of the island, and, after she'd had her fill, she would head back home.

Naina would take out one candle and sing herself happy birthday. It was her yearly ritual. But she no longer made a wish when she blew out the candle. She had spent many years wishing for her mother to come back to her, and it never worked. Even Naina wasn't naive enough to think she could come back from the dead. Her mother had joined the 1,700 other souls who found their death by jumping off the Golden Gate Bridge. There was no coming back from that.

Naina was pleased the box of twenty-four birthday candles she'd bought at Harris Teeter when she first moved to Charleston had lasted this long. She liked items with a long shelf-life.

Can You Be

Magic happened around her. Not to her. Others lived in happiness and togetherness. Others had families and friends. What Naina considered to be magical were those things most people seemed to have so easily; those things others took for granted.

She believed in other types of magic as well. Maybe the crystal would come alive when she wasn't paying attention, or when she wasn't around. She stared at it some more. She held it in her hand, hoping she could see a spark. There was nothing. She imagined it would take flight, coming alive like the snitch in Quidditch, zipping around her apartment. Maybe it would happen when she slept. After all, *The Book of Stones* said angelite was a good stone to use for dreams, especially in understanding and interpreting them. Maybe this meant it would come alive at night.

She decided to test it. Before going to bed that night, she plucked a hair and laid it carefully on top of the crystal. Naina sneaked a quick glance at the crystal before turning the lights off to confirm the hair was still there. When she woke up the next morning, she was disappointed her dreams had not stood out from those she had any other night. She didn't feel she understood them any differently.

The angelite sat on top of its silk bag in the box on the counter, just as she had left it. The hair hadn't moved.

What was worse, she had learned about the powerful attributes of angelites, but this crystal seemed to be doing nothing. What if it was a dud? What if all she read was bogus?

How could the angelite be what she needed or show her who she could be?

Chapter Five

A knock came from the door the next morning. It was Thursday. She froze in place. No one other than her landlady knocked on her door, and she only did so after emailing Naina asking if she could come by. Naina wanted to make sure the knock was not on her neighbor's door. She waited and sure enough it came again. It was definitely hers.

She enjoyed living in her apartment. She spent hours staring at the exposed brick wall and hardwood floors. They had been there since the mid-1800s. When the building was converted into apartments twelve years ago, the owners kept the exposed piping in the high ceilings. It made her one-bedroom apartment feel spacious. She loved living there even more when they installed a double stacked washer and dryer in the unit. She cherished no longer having to spend time going back and forth to check on her laundry or mixing her clothes with that of the other tenants'.

That morning, though, she hated that her door didn't have a peep hole and she couldn't see who was knocking. She opened the door slowly, peering with one eye through the door crack before committing to engaging and fully open the door.

"Hey there, neighbor. Remember me? We met yesterday." It was Raiya. He was smiling.

Naina was unsure of what to do. She opened the door.

"Hi," Raiya said.

"Hi," Naina said back. Again, she waited.

"Can I come in?"

"Oh." Naina weighed her options. The last time she had visitors was soon after she had moved in. Her father and stepmother didn't stay with her. They stayed at the Belmond Charleston Place across the street, and walked over to see her place before they took her out to dinner at Halls Chophouse. They had not come back to see her again.

"Can I borrow some milk?" Raiya asked.

"Will you give it back?"

"I can bring you some back when I go shopping next?"

"Ok." She walked towards the fridge and was surprised Raiya had followed her in.

"I thought you said you'd lived here for a long time. This looks so bare ..." Raiya looked at her white walls.

"I don't like to own a lot of things." She had the bare minimum and it was enough. She had what she needed.

"How come? Do you travel often?"

"I don't like to travel. The last time I got on a plane was four years ago."

"Oh. I love to travel. I did e-commerce for a hotel company in New York City and I was on the road constantly. Since joining the start-up here, I haven't gone anywhere. I miss it. But then again, it's my first time in Charleston and I am eager to explore. It's a challenge because I don't have a car."

"Neither do I." Naina didn't like that Raiya picked up the Special K and read the ingredient list. Or that he opened the cupboards until he found a cup, and helped himself to the milk before Naina got a chance to pour it for him. He was clearly in shape, his defined arm muscles protruding through his fitted white T-shirt.

Raiya looked at Naina as if waiting for an answer.

"I like to know I can pack up and leave on a short notice. I haven't had to do it in years, but I still don't like to own much," she offered.

"How odd. Are you on the run or something?" He chuckled.

"I'm not on the run. I like to be ready for anything. Life can change at a moment's notice."

"Huh … Right … So … I've been dying to have oysters at 167 Raw. Want to go with me? Maybe Friday after work?"

"I work until five," Naina said, hoping it would deter him. Yes, he was attractive, but she also didn't want him to think she was into him. There had been no one in her life since Kevin, and she didn't want a repeat experience.

Was he asking her out on a date? Naina wasn't sure. He gave her a friend vibe. But then again, he was so friendly and forthcoming. If Raiya was into her, how would she handle it? Kevin had liked her, but he too had disappeared. What if Raiya did the same? He lived next door, but that didn't mean he would stay in her life.

What would she wear? She always wore black slacks and a white button blouse during the colder days, and a black sleeveless dress that fell right below the knees for the warmer days. She had five of each, one for each day of the week. On weekends, she wore black yoga pants and a white t-shirt. She didn't have anyone to go to for advice. Alice was too patronizing.

"Great. Let's meet back here after. We can walk over together," Raiya said, interrupting her thoughts.

Just like that Raiya walked out of her apartment with a cup of milk and a promise to meet on Friday.

Chapter Six

Growing up, Naina had felt invisible, which was odd since she was unlike anyone around her. She was mostly surrounded by white girls, and mostly all of them were blonde. There were a few other types of girls, but they were only a handful of Asians, blacks, and other shades of brown girls. Naina was the only one with toasty brown skin and sleek silky black hair that reached her waist.

She considered her invisibility to be her superpower. She was unique, yet she didn't want to be seen. She chose when to blend into the background, when to become part of the furniture, and when to have someone notice and say, "Oh, hi! I didn't see you there."

"No, you didn't because I didn't want you to. Until I did. Only then were you able to notice," she wanted to say. But she didn't. She merely nodded in acknowledgment, her secret power safe with her.

At times she wondered if she wasn't distinctive enough. Or, if she was so odd no one wanted to see her. But she didn't allow herself to be distracted by those thoughts for too long. Her invisibility was her armor when she wanted it to be so, and her defense when it so required.

It's then she started creating stories about people. She would sit in her invisibility and dream up scenarios for the people around her. She had imagined the girls with their perfectly pulled back ponytails were part of a secret society that met at night in clandestine meetings where everyone was clad in black robes. She'd imagine they would draw circles on the ground and participate in seances to commune with the dead. She wanted to think that, in their blandness, they were quite exotic.

Naina thought her invisibility was the reason she hadn't been picked on while attending Candor Boarding School in Charleston. Yes, she hadn't been able to make friends, but she had also been content to be on her own. She felt sorry for those who had been teased, segregated, or alienated, but also grateful she hadn't been one of them. People left her alone.

Naina preferred the company of books. With them, she travelled without ever leaving her chair and got to know fascinating characters, and even some despicable ones. She drew inspiration from the stories she read to make up her own. There were people who had it better than her and it gave her a sense of hope, a feeling her situation could change. There were people who suffered more than she did and was comforted her life was not as terrible. She learned about other countries, world events, and history, and understood that prejudice led to conflict and compassion to resolution.

She was hooked on reading from the first time Mrs. Azuero, a librarian at Green Ivy School for Girls outside Albany, New York, introduced her to *The Berenstain Bears*. Naina had attended Green Ivy for a few years before moving to Charleston. Back then, Mrs. Azuero gathered the few girls who stayed behind on the holidays and talked to them about books. There were only a handful of them who didn't get picked up or flown out to their parents, although they were foreign students and they stayed behind because it was too cumbersome for them to fly to their home country. Naina was the only American who didn't fly home.

On these special days, Mrs. Azuero hosted reading time. Papa Bear and Mama Bear loved Brother Bear and Sister Bear, despite their fibbing, and they forgave them even after throwing tantrums in the supermarket. They didn't send them away and instead encouraged them to tidy up their rooms or gain courage to visit the dentist. The stories showed Naina it was possible to make mistakes and still be loved and wanted.

Naina devoured all kinds of books from that moment onward, wanting to be exposed to all kinds of families and all kinds of friends. When the school had hosted a reading challenge to encourage the girls to read, Naina won by a landslide. She was only allowed to take out five books at a time, which she did every day, eventually reaching two hundred and fifty books by the end of the school year. The person who had read the second most amount of books had only reached forty-five. Naina was awarded a pin from her school and it was one she still kept with her. But the school stopped hosting the reading challenge, explaining the sheer volume of books Naina read, discouraged the other girls from reading instead of encouraging them. No one, apparently, read as much or as quickly as Naina did.

"They will never be able to read as many books as you and it's not motivating for them," Mrs. Azuero had explained. "And soon I won't have any books left for you to read."

Naina didn't get to read all the books in the library before her father shipped her off to Candor Boarding School in Charleston, and to this day, Naina regretted she didn't get the chance to prove Mrs. Azuero right.

When she moved to Candor, she once again spent a lot of time in the library. It was where she knew she would find kinship, and she did when she discovered *The Babysitter's Club* series. Through them, Naina learned true friendship took many forms and although all the girls who were in the Babysitters Club were different, friendship involved accepting someone for who they were.

Books also gave Naina a sense of invisibility. She could disappear from her current situation, no matter what was going on, and escape into another world. When she wasn't concerned about getting to know one of the characters, she would imagine she was one, and as such, she was living the experiences the words transported her to.

What she took away from the time she spent at school was that she could live on her own. She didn't know if she was better off on her own but she knew she could do it. She hadn't thought she would ever have to live a solitary life. It had never occurred to her that her father would alienate her for so many years. She wasn't sure but she had hoped he would eventually invite her back home. Of course he hadn't and she had survived. She had proven to herself she could make it on her own.

She had also learned to seek refuge in books. Books were a form of entertainment, but they were also an escape for her. She imagined she was one of those protagonists who lived life on her terms, who had the courage to see the world. In the case of romances, she wanted to believe she would eventually find someone who would take care of her. It didn't have to be someone romantic, she didn't necessarily want to be in love, but she wanted to be cared for.

And the last thing she learned in school was she could do what she set her mind to. She hadn't been overtly interested in studies.

She did them because she had to. But she wasn't dumb, she was smart. She didn't get the highest grades, and most of the time she just got middle of the road grades, and she managed without trying too hard. She had it in her to figure out any topic or any subject, and that was a skill she kept with her for the rest of her life.

Chapter Seven

Naina now knew her perceived invisibility as a child hadn't been a superpower, but she was grateful she had been left alone. She inferred it was because she was odd, the kind of odd people choose to stay away from.

But she hadn't been able to outgrow her love for libraries. After consulting all those books, Naina had learned more about angelites and spheres, but they weren't able to tell her who had sent her the crystal or why. The crystal hadn't done anything. No matter how much she stared at it or held it in her hands, nothing happened. She hoped it would show her the future, like the psychics she'd read about in so many novels. Maybe she would see how to handle this date with Raiya.

Naina left work that Thursday afternoon and ran into the same mysterious man who had stopped by the real estate office. He was waiting for her at the corner of Meeting and Wentworth. He ate a vanilla ice cream in a cone and wore the same off-white linen suit and dark brown loafers as he had two days before. Naina disliked people who wore shoes without socks. There was no way to clean sweat from shoes, and she was sure when he removed his shoes, his feet would stink.

"Hey there, Naina," he greeted as she approached. His skin was glowing with the same pearl-like quality she'd noticed on Tuesday, contrasting with his dark brown wavy hair. There was an ethereal quality to him, like he wasn't really tangible. She wondered if he might be her angel but reasoned he was flesh and blood and thus, clearly from this dimension. He looked young still, although clearly older than her.

She couldn't quite place his age. She wanted to think he was in his forties but he appeared youthful and yet old with wisdom. Once again, she was disappointed in herself because she couldn't come up with any story about him.

"Hi," she said. She stopped two meters in front of him and clutched her purse, as if he were about to steal it. She might have appeared like she was protecting the contents of her bag, but really, she was stopping herself from touching him. Naina had not seen skin so perfect on a man before. It was too tempting. She had to keep her hands holding onto her bag or her instincts would get the best of her.

"I won't hurt you." He gave her the tooth-whitening smile.

Again, Naina could have sworn his teeth gave off a twinkle. She said nothing and didn't smile back. He certainly appeared to be in his mid-forties and there was a fatherly quality to him. She thought maybe he was an actor and that's why he looked so perfect, but he didn't look familiar. She squinted at him, scrunching her nose and her forehead, and narrowing her large eyes.

"You shouldn't squeeze your face. You're more likely to wrinkle," he admonished, still smiling. He truly belonged in an infomercial.

Naina straightened her face. She couldn't believe her lapse in judgment. She had let herself get carried away by the musings of the man and had forgotten all about her skin. That hadn't happened to her before. "The sun is too intense."

"Easily resolved," he said. He walked under the shadow of the tree at the entrance of the Grand Bohemian Hotel.

Naina followed, wondering why she had taken to following strange men without question. There was something about him that felt nurturing and safe, in an odd light-hearted way. "Did you send me the box?"

"I simply made sure it got to you."

"You didn't send it?"

"Nope." He smiled again.

"There was no label."

"That's not important. Tell me what you found out about the crystal."

"It's an angelite?"

He nodded in confirmation. He ate his ice cream cleanly and efficiently. Despite the heat, there wasn't a single melted drop. She was impressed. She only indulged in ice cream while indoors, exactly and precisely to make sure there was no mess, which was a near certainty in the muggy heat.

"What do you make of it?" he asked.

"It's meant to protect me somehow or connect me with angels, but I haven't heard anything and the crystal hasn't done anything."

"It's not meant to do something tangible. It won't come alive in the middle of the night or when you're not looking – like in *Toy Story*. Its energy has an effect on you. We are affected by everything around us. Everything carries energy. Crystal energy is subtle, yet potent."

Naina didn't confess she was already attached to the crystal. Over the past two days, she had carried it in her purse whenever she left her apartment, taking it out only in the safety of her home.

The mystery man licked his ice cream and stared at her intently, as if peering into her soul.

It unnerved her. "Why did you give it to me?"

"As I said, I didn't give it to you. I'm merely the delivery man. Continue carrying it with you, Naina. Trust. It is for your good. I'll check in another time." He patted her on the shoulder and walked away.

Naina was surprised his touch didn't cause her to tense. She was unaccustomed to people touching her. Her mother had been the affectionate one. The last time her father hugged her was before he shipped her off to boarding school.

She was filled with a sense of ease as she watched him walk away, continuing to lick his ice cream.

At that moment, she called him Holy Man. At least in her head. For some reason, she felt like celebrating. If she couldn't come up with a story about him, at least she'd come up with a fictional name. That alone was reason to celebrate. He gave her a sense of security she hadn't felt in years. She hadn't asked for his name and she wasn't sure she'd gather the courage to do so.

Naina walked further down Meeting Street and picked up a chocolate mint ice cream sandwich from Piece Pie before heading home. It wasn't her cheat day, but she didn't care.

Chapter Eight

"**R**aiya means treasure," he explained.

Raiya and Naina were sitting at the bar at 167 Raw. The dinner crowd hadn't yet packed in and it was quiet enough for them to hold a conversation. It was a warm evening, and Naina wore her only choice of clothing – the black dress she'd been wearing for work. Her hair was down, and she had no makeup on, as always.

"And Naina, you are true to your name. You've got beautiful large eyes," he continued.

"Oh. Thanks." Naina got warmer still and looked down at her hands. She hoped she wasn't going to reek of sweat.

"I'm not trying to flirt with you. I'm gay." Raiya placed his hand on her arm, reassuringly.

"Oh." Naina recoiled against the touch. She felt foolish. She had worried so much about getting ready for the date and it wasn't even a date.

"Don't be embarrassed. I'm strangely flattered. I would have hit on you if I were attracted to women."

"Why did you ask me out then?" Naina asked, clearly irritated.

"I didn't realize you'd think it was a date, but looking back, I should have clarified. I'm new to town, you seem nice, and I thought we'd have a fun time together."

"That's it?"

"There's something about you I find intriguing. You're weird, the good kind of weird. I like that about you. I think we can become good friends."

Of course Raiya noticed she was odd, everyone did. She had wanted to be invisible as a child, but she hadn't been. She had released the childish notion, and needed to remind herself of it again, just then. How did Raiya know they could become good friends? Sure, she figured out he worked at a start-up, but she didn't know the first thing about Raiya. She couldn't tell if he was weird or not and, if so, if he was the good kind. All she knew was that he dressed well, got pedicures, and intruded into other people's apartments. "Ok."

Raiya laughed. "You don't say much, do you?"

"I don't know how to make a new friend. I haven't had many. Even my boss tells me I'm not personable."

"I'll be your friend." Raiya smiled.

The dinner crowd had started coming in and the hum of conversations was rising. Had she heard him correctly? "Did you say you'll be my friend?"

"Yes, as I said before, I think we can be good friends."

Naina was surprised he was up for the challenge. Had the tables been turned, she'd have walked away right then and there. Why hadn't he done so already? Why hadn't she? An evening on her own seemed much more tempting than this. It had quickly gotten too loud and too crowded for her and she longed for the comfort of her loveseat and blanket. She would have loved to curl up and watch James Bond. She couldn't believe Raiya would enjoy getting to know someone as reclusive as her.

As if he'd read her mind, he said, "I'm not messing with you. Don't cut me out because you thought this was a date. I didn't mean to offend you. I genuinely just want to get to know you and have a fun time. The little I've seen makes me believe we'd enjoy each other's company. Plus, I'd love to explore this city with someone, and I've had a hard time meeting people."

She had to lean in much closer to him to hear him. "I don't know what to say."

He leaned in as well, and he practically screamed now. "How about we start by getting to know each other?"

"I feel really awkward now."

"Let's push through. How about we ask each other questions. You ask one. I ask one."

Naina had no idea what to ask and searched around her for clues. Holy Man waved at her from the sidewalk outside the restaurant while sipping from a plastic cup of iced bubble tea. She touched her purse to make sure the crystal was inside. Its roundness comforted her and she let out a deep breath she hadn't realized she had been holding. She focused on Raiya and ignored all else. Somehow, the loud voices around her lowered into a manageable background noise.

"What's it like being gay?" she asked.

Raiya laughed loudly. "You don't beat around the bush, either. See? I knew we'd get along. I like people who are direct."

He told her he had always known he was gay, and his mother had as well. He was lucky his parents were open-minded, a rarity growing up in India, where having homosexual sex used to be a crime. He had never had a problem expressing himself or sharing with others who he was, including his friends and family, due mostly to his mother. She had encouraged him to express himself as he was.

"Yes, I have experienced prejudice, but my mother instilled in me it wasn't because of me. It took me maturing to learn that other people's expression of homophobia has more to do with their lack of knowledge and their insecurity than with me. Other people's stigma is not a true reflection of who I am."

Naina was surprised he spoke so openly and was at ease with himself. Despite his intrusive behavior in her apartment, she felt comfortable with Raiya. Her annoyance at misinterpreting this as a date dissipated. It must be inevitable for people who meet him to feel at ease. There was a sense of familiarity about him. "I can't imagine someone would find you antagonizing."

Raiya placed his hand on his heart. "I'm touched."

The two dutifully exchanged questions and answers for most of the night. When Naina wasn't sure what to ask, Raiya provided the questions. It was easy to speak to Raiya. He told her about going to Cornell University for his MBA. He specialized in marketing, and he loved anything and everything about it.

She shared her experience at boarding school, where everyone ignored her. She hadn't been worthy enough to be picked on. In college, it had been easy for Naina to keep to herself. The years she'd worked at the real estate office were when she'd had the most interactions with other people.

"Why do you bother with that job? You don't sound enthusiastic when you talk about it," Raiya said.

"I think they're more bored with me than I am with them. Alice doesn't hide she regrets hiring me. I don't mind the work, but I don't love it. I'm grateful it allows me to live where I live." Naina hadn't intended to work for seven years as a receptionist at the real estate office, but the job suited her. It wasn't high paying, but she was easily able to follow her routines. Then again, routines were not an effort for her. She enjoyed them. They gave Naina a sense of control and she had convinced herself they helped maintain her health. She enjoyed the stability they provided because they made her feel safe. They gave her an unparalleled sense of structure. She imagined if she had been part of a family, if she'd had love, nurturing, and warmth from others, she wouldn't have needed her routines. But in place of that love, she'd been forced to fend for herself. Except, she didn't know the first thing about fending for herself, and so had created her routines.

"They pay you well?"

"No. My father helps me out."

"I see. So, what do you love? Clearly not your job. What would you truly love to do?"

"I'm not sure." Naina knew she could have grown into selling real estate, had she had an aptitude for dealing with people, but she didn't. She liked her quiet life.

Holy Man was no longer there. She regretted not waving back to him earlier and she hoped he wouldn't be offended.

"What have you thought of doing?"

"I used to fantasize about becoming a lawyer, like my mother, although I don't know what kind of law she practiced. It was long ago in India. By the time I grew curious, my mother had passed." Her father had dismissed the question when Naina had asked, but she didn't share this with Raiya.

"I'm so sorry to hear, dear. My father passed as well." He held her hand.

Naina tensed at first, itching to pull her hand away, but the genuine warmth in Raiya's eyes, allowed her to keep the touch. She'd never met anyone else who had lost a parent at a young age. There was compassion in his eyes, a shared grief, and not the usual pity she saw from others.

"Why don't you look into it? It's never too late, you know?"

"Look into what?" Naina asked.

"Studying law. If you are interested in it, you should pursue it. I believe we should all work on something we love."

"I thought of it once. I googled the different types of law, and the choices were overwhelming. I can't do it." She didn't have it in her to appear in a courtroom and much less to argue a case.

As they walked home later that evening, they were surprised by a sudden rain shower and walked into Cane Rhum Bar for shelter, deciding to have a drink while they waited for the rain to stop. Raiya came back to the topic of Naina's profession.

"I have never known what I wanted to be," she confessed.

"There has to be something you love."

She thought about it for a few moments. "Skin. I love everything related to skin."

"Your skin is flawless," Raiya complimented.

Naina shared her routine. She used Dr. Bronner's Castille soap for her body and hair. She cleansed her face with coconut oil, wiped off the excess with calendula hydrosol, and moisturized with a mixture of jojoba and rosehip to prevent wrinkles. She dabbed lavender essential oil on spots and also used the oil to heal and disinfect cuts and insect bites. She wore zinc-based sunscreen only if she was planning on spending more than five minutes outdoors, which was rare. She did not put anything on her skin that wasn't absolutely necessary. She had studied this well, pouring over herbal healing products and natural skin care books at the library.

Can You Be

They sat at the bar until 11pm, far beyond the rain clearing up. It was the latest Naina had stayed out since college. She couldn't believe they had been able to keep their attention on each other for that long. Raiya was so different from her, and other than being part-orphans, they had little in common.

Back in her apartment, she patted the crystal, wondering if it had transferred some of its courage to her. Maybe it was working.

※

Later that same night, Naina was unable to sleep. Maybe the angelite wasn't working hard enough. Maybe she needed to wait longer. Did she really have it in her to study law? She momentarily considered asking her father once again about her mother being a lawyer but then realized she couldn't.

Naina wasn't in the habit of questioning her father because when she had done so in the past, it had led to life altering results. He resorted to changing her environment, as if that alone would provide a solution. In Naina's experience, it never had.

When she asked how she would live without her mother, her father had brought in a stepmother. When she asked how to get along with the stepmother, he sent Naina to boarding school. She didn't know if it had been her father's decision to send her to Green Ivy School for Girls outside Albany, New York, or if he had done it under her stepmother's insistence. They'd clearly shipped her off without a thought.

When Naina asked her father how to get people to like her at school, her father got her transferred to Candor Boarding School. That was how she ended up in Charleston, South Carolina. When she asked how to make friends, he arranged for her to live with a boarder, with whom she stayed for three years.

Naina went to and from school and only attended school related activities. She didn't go out for other reasons. She kept mostly to herself – except for the brief time she knew Kevin. Instead of speaking to people, she came up with stories about them in her mind. She dreamt up scenarios of who they could be and what their lives were like. She didn't ask them questions. The only kind of investigation she did was to read, which she did avidly, researching the history of the city. It made her even more of a recluse, but there was little of Charleston she didn't know.

Even in the boarder's house, she only came out of her room to eat meals. She didn't make any other friends, and Naina learned there was no point telling her father. She knew he would never ask her to come back to live with them, which is what she had always hoped he would do. But she was continuously disappointed. Home was something she'd had to create for herself, and she had attempted to devise a haven in her current apartment, which is where she had lived since she was eighteen.

Still, Naina was afraid to ask her father about anything; he would make her move again. Or worse yet, he would stop paying her rent. That apartment was the most secure place she'd ever had. During their yearly phone call on her birthday, Naina asked after her father and his health, and with a quick tightening of the jaw, she asked after her stepmother. The last time she had spoken to her was the last time she'd visited them in Marin, California over four years ago. Her stepmother had criticized her for something Naina no longer remembered. Instead of arguing back, she kept herself in the guest room until the time came for her to fly back to Charleston. Naina hadn't had a room at her father's house since she'd been shipped off to boarding school at the age of eleven.

Chapter Nine

The next morning, Naina prepared to have a day to herself. She grabbed her copy of *The Iliad* and sat on her love seat. *The Great British Baking Show* played in the background. She wasn't watching but having noise around gave Naina the sensation she was sitting with company, something to bounce off the walls and echo within, allowing her to forget there wasn't another living soul with her.

The only two books she owned had belonged to her mother, and those were *The Iliad* and *The Bhagavad Gita*. She hadn't known they belonged to her mother, but on the last visit to California, her stepmother had given them to her.

"Take these with you," she'd said, shoving them into Naina's hands.

Naina was at a loss for words. Her stepmother hadn't gifted her anything – ever.

"They're not a gift," her stepmother said, as if reading her mind.

"What are they then?"

"They belonged to your mother."

Shivers ran throughout Naina, and she immediately packed the books. She hadn't, until recently, begun to read them. She did not touch them because she wanted to preserve them. But she yearned for a connection to her mother, and finally, it had led her to read the books.

Naina considered taking a photo of the cover of *The Iliad* and posting it on Instagram to share how she was partaking in a book challenge. The book satisfied condition nine, which was to read a book she hadn't previously finished. Naina was meant to have read *The Iliad* in sophomore English, but she had only read the portions she needed to complete the assignments. Back then, she hadn't known her mother had owned a copy. Had she known, she would have made sure to finish it.

She had erroneously thought *The Iliad* told the whole story of the Trojan war. She had only just learned it merely covered a few weeks within the tenth year of the war.

Just then, there was a knock on the door. She took a moment to make sure it was on her door, and after the knock came again, she got up, swung the door open, and faced Raiya.

"What are you up to?" he asked, walking right in, without waiting for an invitation.

Naina tensed. She hoped these intrusions were not going to be a regular occurrence. "Reading *The Iliad*."

"Why on earth would you be doing that on a Saturday morning? Or any other time, for that matter?" Raiya sat on the love seat, picked up the book, and flipped through the pages.

Naina's jaw tightened. "It's part of a reading challenge. I was going to do an Instagram post, but I backed off from the idea." She couldn't come up with a witty caption, and she realized it wasn't eventful to be reading a book. Yes, it was eventful to her because of its ties to her mother, but how could she explain that to others? She had no idea why her mother had owned the books.

"If you were reading one of the current best-sellers or had some smart insight to share about *The Iliad*, perhaps people would be interested."

The Iliad hadn't been as interesting as she had hoped. She had read *The Bhagavad Gita* first, and although it was also a war poem, it provided less of a description of the conflict than *The Iliad* did, and more of a perspective on life's purpose and duty. She had enjoyed it, no matter how disconnected she felt from her own purpose and duty. It gave her a sense of hope because it dealt with what a person should be, making her believe she would one day figure it out. And it had made her feel connected to her mother.

"Read any other books recently?" Raiya asked.

"*The Bhagavad Gita*."

"Heavy. Was it also part of a challenge?"

"No, it was just for me." *The Bhagavad Gita* had also been easier to read than *The Iliad*, and it provided more depth and sparked more thought. *The Iliad* was also about a war being described in verse, but it was the war related portions she found off-putting. Naina had already had too much conflict in her life and hadn't realized how much she disliked it until she read the book. The only sections she enjoyed reading were about the meddling Greek deities.

"Well you're not very talkative this morning ... Want to try some of the back-and-forth we did last night?"

"I can't think of anything right now." Naina decided she would definitely not post about *The Iliad*. It would confirm she truly didn't have much going on – at least not something exciting. Who would care this was the last condition of the twenty-two she needed to complete the book challenge? The post was likely to not to get more than a couple of likes.

"It seems to me you have plenty going on in your head right now. I'll leave you to it." Raiya walked out of the apartment, and before closing the door behind him said, "Have a magical day."

How had Raiya known to say that? Naina had always wanted to experience magic, to see lights sparkle, glitter twinkle in the rain, flowers twirl in the sky, and talking gnomes skip in her garden. Most of all, she yearned to communicate with every sentient being, from a fern to a dolphin. She wanted to speak to them and have them speak back to her. She wanted to have a connection with everything and anything, a bond she had always felt had been missing from those in her life.

Every now and again – when she remembered – she got on her knees and prayed, her whispers projecting out to the moon, extending up to the sun, across the oceans and rivers, and down deep into the core of the earth. She asked for evidence of the intrinsic connection she felt to the animals of the land and the trees of the forest. She wanted proof that the simplest of crystals – as Holy Man attested – held the energy of surrounding events and transmitted messages. She wanted to reignite the unconditional love, the truest of all loves, which she had felt from her mother. She wanted it to still be there, to still be a part of her life, to still be with her. She prayed despite knowing, in the most profound aspect of her being, that she felt it to be true. This knowing, somehow, wasn't enough. She searched for tangible evidence. Ironically, instead of following the scientific method to find such proof, she prayed.

To her dismay, her prayers had gone unanswered. Naina felt betrayed. It seemed life was giving her the opposite of what she had been asking for. Limited by her abilities, she was unable to make the simplest of connections, even with herself. And, in recent years, she had broken all the connections she once had. A sinking feeling had taken hold of her and it twisted into a sense of loss, as if she had been forgotten.

Naina had hoped reading *The Bhagavad Gita* or *The Iliad* would somehow awaken the magic she yearned for, the connection she yearned for with her mother, the connection she yearned for, period. She had hoped reading those books would help her find a sense of belonging, provide an indication she could be loved for who she was, who she could be.

Naina had never been the type to have social engagements every week, or meet up with a group of friends to go partying, but when she had been in college, she realized that despite her love for solitude, there were times when being out with people had energized her, making her feel full and like she belonged. She would still need to recuperate in the quiet of her apartment, but being among people now seemed like a burden, although Raiya seemed to be changing that for her. But would he stick around? Would Naina want him to?

Now, she felt encapsulated by her 800-square-foot one-bedroom apartment. The open kitchen and four-person dining table constrained her, the world closed in on her as she sat surrounded only by walls.

The space had always felt grand to her, and she used it to the maximum, moving around as much as possible. She sat on the recliner when she read and on the love seat when she watched the wall-mounted TV. She had managed to accommodate a small desk against a wall that looked upon the world outside, and she sat there when she journaled or worked on her laptop.

She hoped reading might offer as much of a subtle comfort as the crystal orb. If the angelite had a subtle way of working, maybe reading would as well. And if the books hadn't helped her connect with her mother, maybe the crystal would. Maybe the crystal would help her connect with her mother's ghost.

Naina had always been fascinated by ghost stories. As far as she could tell, every culture had them. The spirits of the dead, the departed, or whatever other names there were, were energetic forces tethered to the tangible because they didn't want to let go. They felt attached to a person or a place because it gave them a sense of belonging. They were a part of something. They had a reason for being. They had a reason for staying with the living.

She wished she had a way to communicate with the dead, the departed, the lingering spirits. If there was a talent she truly wished she had, it was that one. Yes, she did wish she was more courageous, but she knew she could eventually overcome her fears, if she set her mind to it, she knew she would get there. Communing with spirits, though, wasn't something she was sure she could learn although she wanted it more than anything. Hopefully then she could connect with her mother. Maybe her mother could give her guidance.

Chapter Ten

After Raiya left, Naina couldn't go back to reading *The Iliad*. On that Saturday morning in early August, Naina needed time to herself. All she had experienced was too new, too different, too outside her beloved routines. She was eager to go back to the comfort of her solitude. She didn't want to wonder about crystals, run into Holy Men, think of questions to ask, or have to answer to anyone. Raiya asking her about work distressed her more than she had previously realized. She didn't like being a receptionist. But she didn't know what else to be.

Although Naina had been biding her time for the right friend, the right person to open up to, she didn't want to wonder if this was Raiya. She wasn't sure if she was ready to share her life once again.

The cure for her melancholy was James Bond. While romance novels entertained her, James Bond invigorated her. It was similar to the feeling she got by reading *Jack Reacher* books. She had also read every *James Bond* novel, from the first one by Ian Fleming published in 1953 to the most recent one by Anthony Horowitz released in 2018. She owned all the James Bond movies, including the *Casino Royale* spoof from 1967 where a supposed celibate James Bond, played by David Niven, was promoted to the head of MI6 after a hiatus following the death of his beloved Mata Hari. The new 007 was played by Peter Sellers and Woody Allen played James Bond's nephew, Jimmy Bond.

The only Bond film she hadn't watched was the first ever film showcasing a Bond character released in 1954. It was the American made-for-TV version of *Casino Royale*, but James Bond was an American spy working for the CIA. Naina settled down on her love seat once again but her mind kept on drifting. All she could think of was her need to be alone. Where did it come from? How could she simultaneously yearn for company and for solitude?

Naina had grown up all by herself. It may have been considered a privileged upbringing by many, but rather than the white-gloved nurtured attention of her classmates, Naina felt like a kid who had been dropped off at 160 Calhoun Street. It was known as the Charleston Orphan House but not all of the kids were orphans. Back in the day, poor white parents were allowed to drop off their kids because they didn't have money to feed them.

The Charleston Orphan House was the first public orphan house in the United States and was operational from 1790 to 1951. The orphanage was self-sufficient, the children contributing with the daily operation. Girls sewed and washed clothes, and boys milked cows and chopped wood. Food was grown within the grounds.

In 1952, The Orphan House was moved to North Charleston and renamed Oak Grove. The building at 160 Calhoun Street was sold to Sears-Roebuck and demolished. It was a department store for a number of years, and the same site was now the bookstore for The College of Charleston. Some believed the ghosts of children who once lived there ran around in the building erected in its place. It wasn't the ghosts, though, keeping Naina away from the building.

Any time Naina happened to walk in front of 160 Calhoun Street, her heart filled with a wave of sadness with such strength she was afraid it might sweep her into its rip current. Her father had plenty to feed her, but he had dropped her off at a boarding school anyway. Naina wasn't poor and wasn't an orphan but felt equally discarded and unwanted. She never knew why her father shipped her off. He never told her. It was as if she was meant to be forgotten.

She didn't want others to suffer as she had, but didn't know how to go about reducing the suffering of others. So, she placed a small donation every year on her birthday, to the Lowcountry Orphan Relief. And, she vowed if she ever managed to earn enough money, she would adopt a child and raise them with the utmost love, care, and dedication she could muster. No matter how hard her life got, she would never, ever give that child away.

She again tried to focus on the movie, but this American remake didn't bring her the same comfort the other James Bond movies did. James Bond was similar to Jack Reacher since both characters were heroes. They knew how to get out of difficult situations, often impossible. They had courage, valiance, and the physical ability to beat the odds, and because Naina knew she had none of those qualities, she relished in James Bond and Jack Reacher to make up for it. They brought her a great source of entertainment. She knew she would never be as daring as them, she knew she would never travel around the world as they did. She didn't consider she would get the chance to leave Charleston. Not only could she not afford it, but she couldn't think of where to travel.

A James Bond movie would have been the perfect distraction. She enjoyed living vicariously through his adventures. The predictability of the movies soothed her. The "bullseye" covered with blood in the opening credits gave her a sense of safety. She loved to mouth along as James Bond got called to see M, flirted with Moneypenny, and was shown special gadgets by Q. It gave Naina a sense of comfort like no other. She fantasized about having a James Bond type of person come into her life, a real-life romance blended from the passionate and courageous Bond qualities.

That day, however, she didn't feel the same sense of calm after watching the American movie. It didn't have any of the predictable features of other James Bond movies. Also, there had been too much going on that shook her to her core. She didn't like it. That sense of impending doom she had felt since she found the sticky note on her computer at work hadn't left her.

Naina wanted badly to feel tethered in some way, to regain a sense of safety and security. Her apartment, no matter how stark, had always offered her a stability unlike any other. Her walls may have been white, but they protected her. Her furniture might have been sparse, but it comforted her. Her closet may have contained the same few pieces of her clothing, but they defined her.

Naina wondered if the crystal would give her courage. She glanced at the angelite on the coffee table in front of her more than she cared to admit. Did she have it in her to be as daring as James Bond? She wanted to follow in her mother's footsteps, although not completely. Naina's mother had stopped practicing law after she'd married. Naina's parents moved from India to San Francisco and somewhere along the way, Naina's mother lost her sense of self. Naina held on to the wisps of memories of her mother. Her father never spoke of her. And he pushed Naina away.

It's not what Naina wanted. She searched for something to give her purpose and meaning, to make her feel whole and complete.

Can You Be

When Naina thought back to what she wanted to be growing up, nothing specific came to mind. The thought hadn't occurred to her much when her mother was alive, and afterward, she definitely didn't think about it. She hardly wanted to ponder upon it when her future often seemed uncertain. It was easier for her to dismiss the thought altogether, thinking more about the personality traits she wanted to have. Thus, she read books and watched movies and thought about the type of person she wanted to be. She wanted to be independent, she wanted to be able to fend for herself. She wanted to make sure she didn't need anyone, and she always found a way to achieve what she wanted. She also wanted to make sure she was honest, she never lied, and was upfront when she said something. She didn't have to be outspoken, but when she did open her mouth, it had to be the truth. She wouldn't abandon someone. If she committed to them, she would stay, including a marriage and any children she may have.

She mostly still felt the same, but she could no longer keep herself so isolated. It had worked for Jack Reacher and James Bond, for the most part. Even they got attached at times. But it definitely didn't work with what she wanted. She really needed to change her approach to her isolation and need for independence. While it was okay for her to want to fend for herself financially, she needed to shift her perspective to recognize that not only did she need a support network, but she wanted one. She wanted family, she wanted friends, she wanted people on whom she could rely, and she wanted to stand by those people as well. She wanted to be happy and she wanted to be in a community. For this, she definitely needed to shift.

Chapter Eleven

The next evening, Naina was reading *The Iliad* after dinner and, without realizing it, fell asleep. Thirty-three minutes later, she woke to the sound of a "Hey."

The sound was clear, yet the tone was soft and gentle. She didn't know if she had heard the word in her dream or if it came from somewhere within her apartment. It sounded like her mother's voice. Had the angelite finally worked? Had her mother's ghost finally made an appearance? The more she considered it, the more it became clear that the word had been uttered somewhere in the apartment. Could she have heard Raiya? She had never heard her neighbors before. Had he found a way to get in? No, there was no way.

Naina lay on her recliner, petrified. Her eyes were open but she dared not move, not even to look at the time. It was dark. Very dark.

Her ears acutely tuned to listen for more clues as to where the "hey" could have come from. Nothing came. No sounds. No more voices. The loudest sound was her heart beating inside her chest. She tried to calm herself, taking deep breaths. She tiptoed to her bed and lay down without changing into her pajamas and without brushing her teeth. She didn't want to turn any lights on, and it seemed easier to continue her presumed sleep without further interruption.

Except, she wasn't able to sleep for the rest of the night. Her apartment had always brought her calm and comfort, but that night, it didn't. Although she was used to insomnia, this was different. She was too nervous to move, fearing even the slightest ruffle of her sheets would block out another "hey" and distract her from any clue that might alert her as to where it had come from.

She stared at the walls, noticing how empty they were, wondering if the voice came from somewhere within them.

She tried not to move a muscle until dawn, when the sun rays peered through the blinds illuminating the interiors.

※

Naina got out of bed, her body was stiff as she moved gingerly around the apartment. Despite the sun, it was still early. She stepped as lightly as possible to minimize the cracking of the wooden floors. Some wood cracked anyway – it was inevitable.

She found no clues. Nothing at all. Everything was as it had been the evening before she'd fallen asleep. She sat on her love seat and waited for a sign. Was the "hey" the magic she had been yearning for? The magic she had dreamt of as a child but since forgotten? What role did the angelite play in awakening or re-awakening her dream? Was her mother finally communicating with her? Or her guardian angel, if she had one of those? Was the angelite doing its magic?

As more day light streamed through her windows, her hunger overcame the need to figure out where the "hey" came from. Naina ascertained that everything in her apartment was untouched, no one had broken in, and she was most certainly alone.

She prepared coffee and set out her milk and Special K, hoping to regain a sense of normalcy. She scrolled through Facebook on her phone while she ate her breakfast. On most mornings, she had her set routine, but that August morning, she had gotten up so early she had plenty of time to waste on social media.

One of her college classmates had posted photos of himself in Iceland, which according to the post, was the seventy-seventh country he had visited. Naina wondered how he had managed to travel to so many countries while she hadn't even gotten on a plane in four years. She had only ever gotten as far as her favorite tree, Angel Oak, on the outskirts of Charleston, which was a mere twelve miles from her front door.

Her classmates seemed to live a life that felt so foreign to her. For them, there seemed to be a party or social gathering almost daily. In the past seven years, since she'd graduated from college, she hadn't attended a single gathering. Sure, she'd gone to a few work events, holiday parties and such, but nothing social.

How had she come to live such a quiet life? Her home was sparse, and even her kitchen counters were nearly empty. She hardly owned anything. Her apartment looked like a furnished space no one lived in. Naina sighed loudly, wishing it wasn't so obvious she lived there all by herself. Could she be more lonely?

She had been the one to set it up the way it was. She was the one who had chosen this quiet life. She had asked for this. Really, she had wanted this. Yet, Naina's jaw clenched and the fire rose from deep within. Her face flushed as she recalled the friends she'd once had.

Can You Be

Naina stopped scrolling on social media and put down her phone. She knew Facebook didn't represent reality, and people's lives weren't as full or happy as they wanted them to appear. But she didn't even have material to pretend to have an interesting life, no matter how hard she tried.

Was Raiya coming into her life an indication it might all change? What about Holy Man? And the angelite?

꙰

Naina'd had friends, but not many. She preferred her own company, welcoming the silence, the isolation. Her time was her own. She was accountable to no one. She yearned for seclusion, preferring to do without people before they were able to do without her. If she'd kept them around for too long, she would have to cut people off before the relationship grew too close.

The girls at Candor Boarding School called her dull and boring. Once her father had moved her to the apartment with the boarder, Naina didn't mind. It was where Naina learned to like her own company.

People in college were different. Ellen, for example, a classmate from the College of Charleston, asked Naina to work together on an assignment for history class. Naina agreed and eventually found it helped to have someone to bounce off ideas. They worked together on other school assignments. After some time, it was clear Ellen never expressed any desire to see Naina outside of class. Naina wished she'd had the courage to ask Ellen about it, or perhaps taken the first step to ask Ellen to hang out for a coffee or something, but had fallen short with words. Instead, Naina kept her thoughts to herself, pulling away gradually until she refused to continue working with Ellen.

Naina did attempt to hang out with Caitlin, whom she'd also met at college. Caitlin was a party girl and after going out with Caitlin once, Naina realized she had no interest in loud music and drunken dancing. Still, they met for iced chai lattes, lunch, or afternoon coffee. Caitlin gossiped about the other girls in class, described her dating life in gory detail and painstakingly described the latest rave she'd attended. Naina labeled these times as "Caitlin's verbal diarrhea hour". After some time, Caitlin's offloading monologue grew intolerable, and Naina stopped going out with her. She also stopped returning Caitlin's calls and emails.

The third friend Naina'd had was Elie. She was from Italy and her name was Elena, but everyone called her Elie. During the four years Naina was in college, Elie was her most regular friend. They had met while they'd both waited for the library to open. Naina liked to go in early to make sure there were fewer people, and it turned out Elie was the same. They bonded over books and reading.

Naina loved to hear about what it was like to live in Europe, and Elie's large family. Elie was the youngest of five and Naina prodded Elie to share her latest family stories, including all the gatherings, quarrels, bickering, and recipes. Elie seemed happy to have someone who would listen to her.

While Naina and Elie were friends, they explored every nook and cranny of downtown Charleston. The two also shared a disdain for the Charleston heat and enjoyed walking around downtown at night, when the air was cooler and not as sticky. Naina wouldn't have dared walk at night on her own, but having someone with her made it okay. Company made darkness less menacing.

What she lacked in family stories to share with Elie, she made up for by divulging stories about Charleston. Their school, The College of Charleston, founded in 1770, was the thirteenth oldest higher learning institution in the country. Thomas Hayward Jr., Arthur Middleton, and Edward Rutledge, three of the founders of the school, had also signed the Declaration of Independence. And three other founders, Charles Pinckney, Charles Cotesworth Pinckney, and John Rutledge, eventually signed the United States Constitution.

There was always some type of ghost story for Naina to share, and Elie readily lent an eager listening ear. Naina told Elie about Lavinia Fisher, the first convicted female serial killer in the United States, who poisoned guests – mostly men – who stayed at her motel. She was now meant to haunt the Old Charleston Jail House. And there was the ghost of the headless Civil War soldier who appeared in Battery Carriage House, or the various ghosts of the actors at the Dock Street Theater, the oldest theatre in the United States that opened in 1736 but was now the Planter's Hotel. And about the ill-kept pirates jailed at the Old Exchange and Provost dungeon's whose moans could still be heard.

As they walked the streets together, they had often wondered what it would have been like to live in Charleston in the old times, in the golden age of Charleston when there were so many riches, and those riches had built the city. What they had never wanted to see, though, was slavery. They were grateful they lived in the city after those torturous times were over.

There were many old charms, though, they loved to explore. It was with Elie that Naina discovered some of the secret alleys throughout the city, including the Unitarian Church Graveyard, Bedon's Alley, Longitude Lane, Philadelphia Alley, Price's Alley, St. Michael's Alley, Stoll's Alley, Unity Alley, and Horlbeck Alley. She loved those times they spent together, and many of the discoveries they made remained among Naina's favorite spots in the city. Naina would have maintained her friendship with Elie, had Elie not moved back to Italy after graduation.

After that, Naina kept to herself. While others considered her as weak and meek, she saw herself as biding her time. She might have been more assertive and more outspoken, but her quietness wasn't about being timid, it was about speaking only when she knew she would make sense. Only when she knew her words made a difference, and only when she knew they would have an impact. Yes, she was rustic and needed practice learning how to speak to others but she would get there. They misunderstood her and that was on them, not on her. All she could be was herself.

Chapter Twelve

"**N**aina, your simplicity negatively affects the company's image."

Naina didn't reply. It was three days after she'd heard the "hey" and she was having her yearly performance review with Alice.

"That, coupled with your quiet demeanor and lack of friendly approach towards the clients."

This wasn't the first time they'd had this conversation. Naina knew exactly where Alice was coming from. Alice was itching to be rid of her. She hadn't said so, but Naina sensed it. For years, Alice had expressed discontent at Naina's appearance.

Alice, on the other hand, was impeccable. Like the other women who worked in the real estate office, Alice's long blonde hair was styled into perfect curls. Alice had fake eyelashes that extended nearly an inch off of her face. Her nails were long and manicured. She had at least three shades of eyeshadow, always coordinated with her outfit and jewelry: a lighter shade as a base, a medium shade of the crease, and a darker one for the outer corners. On top of foundation, Alice carefully applied pink blush, orange copper bronzer, and a soft ivory highlighter on strategic areas to contour her face.

Four years ago, Alice had said, "It takes me at least two hours to get ready every morning. I get up at five with the timer set on my coffee machine. If I'm not up already, the smell of coffee brewing serves as my alarm. I don't ever miss it. I pour myself a cup and take it with me to the bathroom."

She slept with her hair rolled up and covered it in a shower cap when she showered. She had a standing appointment at the hairdressers every Friday, and that was the only place where Alice allowed for her hair to be washed. In the morning, all Alice had to do was unroll her hair and touch it up in places with a flat iron. Then she applied the various layers of makeup and dressed herself meticulously, ensuring even the finest accessory coordinated with her look for the day.

Four years ago, Alice had said, "I can see your large eyes staring back at me, Naina. I understand this would be too much for you." Alice motioned her hands toward herself, as if she were a show piece. "Can I suggest you wear a bit of makeup to be more presentable?"

Naina had gone to the Sephora on King Street where an obtrusive lady armed with a belt full of brushes whisked Naina onto a makeup chair, pulling out a dizzying array of shadows, eyeliners, lipsticks, bronzers, primers, foundations, powders, and mascara. It was there Naina learned all about makeup application, the only bonus from the experience.

After the makeover, Naina looked like a clown. She wondered how it was that Alice and the other ladies in the office wore so much makeup and didn't look as ridiculous as she did in that moment. She bought one eyeshadow, one lipstick, pressed powder, mascara, and lip gloss.

Alice seemed pleased when Naina showed up at work the next day with a soft and natural look. Naina would have continued using it if she hadn't woken up the next morning with teeny tiny whiteheads spread all over her forehead and cheeks.

"There is makeup that won't make you break out," Alice had said.

Naina had shaken her head vigorously, refusing to try it. She wouldn't risk her skin's health.

"How about jewelry?" Alice then suggested. "Try earrings."

Naina's ears had been pierced at the hospital in San Francisco when she was born, but she'd stopped wearing earrings at age seven soon after her mother died. The piercings sealed up, with no visible remnants of scars. Naina had purchased clip-ons, but they hurt and invariably fell off before the end of the day.

Finally, Alice had said, "Why don't you do something with your hair?"

Naina's hair was sleek and thick, and fell down to her waist. "Like what?"

Alice had looked like she was analyzing Naina's face. "Bangs, perhaps?"

"Cutting bangs seems like a big commitment."

"Naina, you've got to try something. If not, how can you be the receptionist? The sign outside may have my face on it, but you're practically the face of the office. You're the first person people see when they walk in. You've got to make some type of effort, darling," Alice had said.

It was clear, even back then, that Alice was threatening to get rid of Naina if she didn't try to do something. It was either bangs or coloring her hair, and chemicals were definitely not something

Naina would consider. So Naina tried bangs, but her forehead broke out. She realized she would have to wash her hair every day to prevent the oils from her bangs clogging the pores on her forehead. It hadn't been worth the effort, and Naina'd had to wait for several months before her hair had become even again.

That Wednesday morning in early August, Naina knew Alice was bailing on her. "It isn't just my demeanor, though, is it?"

Now, it was Alice's turn not to reply.

It was clear the rift between them was irreparable. When Naina first started working at the office, Alice had invited Naina to spend time together. They went out to lunch or afterwork drinks. Alice dropped off Naina at the Whole Foods in Mount Pleasant once a month for Naina to stock up on her supplies of essential oils and Dr. Bronner's. Naina would take a Lyft home. It had been several years since Alice had asked her to a coffee or had driven her to Whole Foods.

If Alice fired her, she would be lost and she would be forced to tell the truth to her father. Although he paid for her rent and utilities, she depended on her salary for all her other expenses, including her food. She would have to call her father to ask for more. What if it meant he would finally ask her to move out? The thought appalled her.

And what would she tell her father? She didn't dare confess that she'd been let go for not having good people skills. Her father had always told her this was her biggest obstacle: not knowing how to maintain solid relationships in her life. She didn't want to increase the rift between them or show him he was right about her.

She would need to figure out what to do. She needed to think of an alternative before the inevitable happened. But what could that be?

Chapter Thirteen

Most people who spent time with her eventually went away. Strangely, Raiya hadn't lost interest and had, instead, been persistent. Over the last week, Raiya had shown up at Naina's apartment every day. He made himself at home in a way no one had ever done before, as if Naina had always been his. Naina was dumbfounded. Raiya left a dent on her loveseat, as if the spot had been waiting to take the shape of him. He had even picked his favorite mug to drink coffee, making a habit of knocking on her door in the mornings, while still in his pajamas.

Naina was surprised to discover she enjoyed these visits. She wanted Raiya to stick around. On that Sunday morning in mid-August, Naina was towel-drying her hair, which, given its length and thickness was a thirty-minute affair, followed by four hours of air drying. She didn't dare use a hairdryer to prevent damage to her hair, and she stayed in the coolness of her apartment to prevent the Charleston humidity from turning her hair too frizzy.

Naina had kept waist-long hair since she was five-years old. Her mother used to trim Naina's hair every few months to cut off the split-ends, and put on coconut oil twice a week, braiding Naina's hair so the oil wouldn't seep into the pillowcase. It was a cherished memory Naina recalled every Saturday night as she applied coconut oil to her own hair, in preparation for washing it on Sunday.

Raiya came over that morning, hoping they would have brunch. It had been a week since Naina heard the "hey."

"No," she said to Raiya.

"Why not?" he asked.

"I can't go out until my hair is dry."

"Fine," he said, and walked away.

Naina's heart sank. The time had finally come for Raiya to leave. Rather than wallow in sadness, she reasoned it was better to get rid of him sooner rather than later. His departure was inevitable. It was unbelievable how easy it had been. She unrolled the towel from her head and grabbed the angelite, holding it in her palm, and settled on her sofa to watch reruns of *West Wing*, pushing away tears.

Thirty minutes later, there was a knock on the door.

"It's me, Raiya."

Naina's heart beat so fast, it threatened to jump out of her chest. When she got to the door, Raiya had take-away from Millers All Day. He'd even brought biscuits – her favorite – with an extra helping of strawberry whipped butter, exactly as she had ordered the last time they had gone together.

Naina didn't know how to respond. She leaped into his arms, surprising even Raiya.

"It's just biscuits," he said, smiling brightly.

Naina flushed and smiled back. For the first time in many years, she did not care at all about her wrinkles. The feeling didn't last long, though, as guilt filled her and she massaged the creases out of her face.

She set the angelite on the coffee table as Raiya served the food neatly on her plates – again, exactly as she liked it. He settled down to watch reruns of *West Wing* with her, not questioning her choice. It dawned on her he had never questioned any of her routines, or her quirks, or her eccentricities, as others called them. This had not happened before.

Naina considered telling Raiya about the "hey" but held back, afraid to further rock the boat. She also hadn't told Raiya about Holy Man. She even considered talking to him about her career. He'd prompted her to think about becoming a lawyer. She now knew it wasn't for her. But maybe he could help her figure out what she could be. She would ask him, for sure, but not that day. That day, all she wanted was to enjoy his company.

"Show me your beloved Charleston," Raiya said.

Naina agreed, eager to spend more time with him. She figured the more they got to know each other, the easier it would be for her to open up to Raiya. She also wanted to show him her favorite places and share her beloved ghost stories. She hadn't had an opportunity to do so since Elie had left Charleston.

And so, on the following Saturday in mid-August, they set off early to avoid having to wait in line like the other tourists they often encountered in downtown. They reviewed the details of their itinerary over breakfast, which they had at Poogan's Porch, a restaurant haunted by the ghost of a stray dog that had been fed by the owners of the house, prior to it being converted into a restaurant. The stray dog, named Poogan, had been buried on the property upon his death. It was believed the dog's spirit visited the various tables hoping to gather fallen food scraps.

Naina ordered chicken and waffles, eating the chicken first, then pouring the syrup over the waffles as if they were dessert. "That's not the only ghost in this restaurant, you know?"

Raiya was oddly silent, distracted by his phone.

But Naina wasn't deterred. "The other ghost is that of Zoe St. Amand. The St. Amand family owned the house some time before it was a restaurant, and the ghost knocks over glasses and dishes and can be heard calling out for a sister who passed away before her."

"Right," Raiya said, without much enthusiasm.

It became clear to Naina that on that day, she wasn't going to be discussing many ghost stories.

"This city's been around for 350 years, so clearly, there's plenty to see. What have you narrowed down for us to do, Naina?"

"I'm going to take you to my cherished spots." Naina was excited for the day ahead, despite the density in the air – it was expected to rise to an intolerable 92°F. Charleston was for Naina all she was not, historical, cultural, and exotic.

"Oh, really? Like all the back alley nooks and crannies? I was hoping to see all the big touristy spots."

Naina's heart sank. She wanted to show off to Raiya the city she knew so well and had originally planned to share her subjective collection of personal favorite locations, but discarded the idea. Thankfully, she had downloaded the Historic Charleston Foundation app as a back-up to feel like a real tour guide. Naina, of course, knew the city inside and out but she wanted Raiya to get the full experience. She took her job as a guide seriously and was nervous because she hadn't walked around the city since her nights with Elie. Given Raiya's lack of interest in ghost stories, it was clear the app would be their primary guide for the day. The app provided information on the most notable sites in the city, complete with an accurate account of historic events.

They started at the City Market, walked by the Powder Magazine, and stopped briefly at St. Philip's Church, reading the names off the graves on the cemeteries outside. They entered the Heyward-Washington House, named so because Heyward was a South Carolina delegate who signed the Declaration of Independence in 1776 and because President Washington stayed in the house in 1791.

They posed to take photographs by the free-flying, three-story staircase in the Nathaniel Russell House and in the dungeons of the Old Exchange and Provost and, after a sobering visit to the Old Slave Mart Museum, they shared a basket of fried okra and green tomatoes at Jestine's Kitchen. After a walk around the Waterfront Park, they finished their day by having spicy shrimp and grits at Magnolias.

They ate so much Naina grew nauseous and when she rested at home, clutching her angelite in gratitude, she thought about her friendship with Raiya. Naina didn't understand why Raiya wanted to spend so much time with her, seemingly asking her for nothing in return. He often paid when they were out together, as if he knew their activities were beyond her budget.

Naina was comforted in a way she hadn't expected. Her life had felt like it had been stripped to gray, yet there were now accents and colors she had never seen before. She pushed away her disappointment at having to keep her ghost stories to herself, and of not being able to showcase the secret alleys most tourists missed but Naina loved. Still, she felt grateful. She had made the first friend she'd had since college. Could the angelite be working its magic? Naina clutched onto her crystal as one did to the handles of a rollercoaster. And she enjoyed the ride.

Chapter Fourteen

The first time Naina walked into Raiya's apartment, she was struck by the smell of spices wafting throughout the space. He claimed to not be a good cook. In fact, he said he didn't cook at all.

Naina and Raiya hadn't connected in the way she had hoped while they were playing tourists, but that evening, she hoped to discuss the angelite, Holy Man, and her potential career opportunities. She wondered what his perspective would be. Maybe he could provide some of the clarity or insight she was missing. Maybe he could help her figure out what she could be.

But the scents distracted her. The smell came from clear decorative jars filled with whole raw spices: nutmeg, star anise, cinnamon bark, black peppercorns, pink peppercorns, Szechuan peppers, and many others unrecognizable to Naina.

"I love how all of these look in clear jars. I'm not an herbalist or anything, but it makes me feel knowledgeable to be surrounded by so much that came from the earth," Raiya said.

Can You Be

"I can't believe you don't cook," Naina said, carefully eyeing the shelves. The kitchen had open cabinets lined with even more clear jars filled with dried flowers and herbs, carefully arranged in alphabetical order, giving Naina the impression she'd walked into an apothecary. The living room also had shelves but those were filled with books. When she looked closer, wondering if they were books she could borrow, she realized they weren't. The books were mostly coffee table books – more for decoration than for actual reading. No wonder Raiya hadn't been impressed she was reading *The Iliad*.

"The only thing I know how to make well is a good cup of masala chai," Raiya said.

Ironically, the spices he used for those, he kept in well-sealed tin cans. He couldn't afford for the scent of those spices to escape. Like most of his family, he treasured his chai, and drank it twice a day. He had a cup first thing in the morning before he walked over to Naina's to get his coffee. And then he drank a cup in evening, around 5:30pm. He told Naina his two cups bookended his workday.

That Monday in mid-to-late August, Naina had come over after work and he made chai for her. Naina seemed to have forgotten there ever was a library. Even though she was spending so much time with Raiya, she still hadn't gained the courage to have a heart-to-heart conversation about the recent changes in her life. That Monday, Naina watched him quietly, wondering if her hesitation was because Raiya himself was part of the newness.

"I start with fennel seeds, clove, and crushed cardamom seeds," Raiya said, placing the three spices in a pot with water, and turning on the gas stove.

As the water came to a simmer, he said, "The key to bringing out flavor is crushing fresh ginger to a pulp," and he did so in a mortar and pestle, which he then added to the pot. "Pounding the ginger helps me release aggression," he added with a wink.

When the water simmered, Naina thought this would be her chance to open up to Raiya. "You remember that box I got—"

Raiya held up his hand. "Don't interrupt me. I'm not good at multi-tasking."

After the water had been simmering for three minutes – Raiya timed it – he added milk. "This is when you have to keep your eye on the pot. We don't want to lose any of the precious liquid as it rises to a boil."

It was clear to Naina she'd have to wait until after the tea was ready.

After that, Raiya added the tea. "I prefer Earl Gray. It's not traditionally Indian, but I like the taste of bergamot." Three minutes later – again timed – the delicious goodness was ready.

He had set out gold-rimmed turquoise porcelain cups and saucers. They had pink and white roses throughout. Raiya put out Biscoff cookies on a matching tray, giving Naina the feeling she had been served a fancy afternoon tea.

She loved the milky cup of tea with the biting taste of ginger and the subtle hint of warm spices. Naina was reminded of her mother's cooking, but the sensation was fleeting. Vague glimpses of the food flashed in her head like a slideshow, but she wasn't familiar with the names. Raiya seemed to be drilling holes into the vault of her memory bank and pulling at the threads of long-lost treasures.

"What are you thinking about?" Raiya asked.

"I remembered eating a *roti* rolled up with ghee and sugar that my mom made for me. She made it often as an afterschool snack, and I ate it greedily as my mother prepared a *roti* for herself, except hers was filled with mango *achar*. I remember trying it once, but it was far too spicy for me. I preferred the sweetness of the crunchy sugar."

"That's really sweet."

"My mother didn't make chai though. She made us bright red Rooh Afza." The memory came back to her so clearly, she still tasted the sickly-sweet rose essence on her red-stained tongue. Naina suddenly needed to shift in her chair. Raiya had antique-like furniture, making the apartment look like it was on display in a museum. Naina found it hard to relax. She couldn't curl up with a blanket on his chairs as she was able to do at hers.

"You don't eat much Indian food, do you?" There was a tender expression in his eyes.

"The closest southern food I've found that tastes anything remotely like the Indian food in my memories is Hoppin' John. It's my favorite." The black-eyed peas and rice reminded Naina of her mother, even though the taste wasn't as spicy as the dishes she held in her memory. She didn't tell Raiya how much she regretted feeling that her Indian heritage seemed lost to her.

"It's too bad I don't cook. I can't help you much there. I wish my mother could ship us some food. She's too frail to fly." Raiya's parents had been in a car accident when Raiya was a teenager. It had left his mother bound to a wheelchair and his father in a persistent vegetative state.

"I wish I had grown up with my parents, as you did with yours," Naina confessed.

"I was lucky, and I grew closer to my mother after my father passed. My mother became even more supportive of me when it was just the two of us. If it hadn't been for her, I wouldn't have come to college in the US. I would have stayed back home with her, but she wouldn't hear of it. She pushed me to come." Raiya'd had to delay attending college for a year because his father had been confined to a bed at home.

"When I realized my father no longer recognized me, my world imploded. He was the one person who knew me to my core and who loved me unconditionally. His loss was the strongest desolation I'd ever felt."

Naina put her hand out to Raiya, who held it tightly. Raiya continued to relay how he and his mother had tended to his father every day, taking turns sitting with him. Raiya had pretended he didn't notice his father's vegetative state and went on speaking to him as if his father was fully responsive, and told him about his day and his conquests and who had visited and what they had said.

But as the days progressed, and Raiya realized there was no acknowledgement registering back in his father's expressions, Raiya felt hopeless. He struggled to figure out how to act around his father, so he'd played his father's favorite music, hoping this still sparked joy in him. Raiya hummed along, not feeling comfortable to sing at full lung capacity, as he had once done. Towards the end, Raiya read *The Jungle Book* by Rudyard Kipling out loud. Raiya had never been much of a reader, but his father had read him *The Jungle Book* stories at night before going to sleep when he was a kid. Raiya thought it was the best way to honor their time together. And so he read it, in his honor, just in case he registered something. A few days after Raiya finished reading the book, his father passed.

Naina wiped away tears from her cheeks as Raiya showed her his copy of *The Jungle Book*, the only piece of literature in his living room bookcase. She wished she'd had a chance to be with her mother when she passed, and that her father had held on to her and supported her like Raiya's mother had done with him. At least she too had her mother's books.

She was filled with emptiness until she noticed the love radiating out of Raiya from his thoughts and memories. He looked up at her then and seemed to extend the same love to her. She realized then they'd been holding hands all that time.

"How did your mother pass?" Raiya asked.

"Let's leave that story for another day. We've had enough sadness for today."

She'd also have to leave the conversation about angelites, Holy Man, and her career for another time. Or maybe, she needed to figure it out for herself.

ॐ

"Who are you?" she asked Holy Man that same Monday evening. She'd left Raiya's apartment and needed to clear her head before having dinner. She wanted to think about her career options. She'd never envisioned being a receptionist, and much less for this long. But what could she be?

As she'd posed herself this question, she had run into Holy Man. She was making her second loop around Colonial Lake, and he matched her pace, walking alongside her.

He didn't answer.

"Why do you continue to come to me?" Naina had continued to see Holy Man. He had popped up regularly, always wearing the same white linen suit and sock-free brown loafers. He had waved from the window when Raiya and Naina were at the bar at Felix and he'd winked as he walked by when they sipped coffee at Bakehouse. He had jogged past them when they stared out at Charleston Harbor from the Battery. But she wasn't any closer to finding out who he was, why he had delivered the angelite, and why he kept hanging around. Apart from giving Naina the impression he was her own recurring character on her own personal commercial, as if he had been made exclusively for her – like her personal Gecko or Flo – she had no information about him.

"Why do you think I come to you?"

"Are you the angel sent to me through the angelite?"

"Would that make you feel more comfortable with me? Is my presence really that disconcerting?"

"Yes. I don't know anything about you and this is the first time we've had a conversation since the day I saw you eating ice cream."

"And how have you felt when we've encountered each other?"

This time, Naina didn't answer. But, she couldn't deny that every time he had appeared, Naina felt he was encouraging her, letting her know she was heading in the right direction, making the right choices, motivating her to continue. She even felt that now.

But she still wasn't any closer to figuring out what she needed, and much less, what she wanted or what she could be. As she inched closer to thirty, she had begun to wonder if there was more to life. What if she dared a little? What if she tried new things? What if she explored, for herself, the options that were open to her?

That evening, she'd failed to get insight from Raiya, but she needed to release her confusion. She had been content with her life, complacent even. But it no longer seemed enough. Seventeen years of this monotony no longer seemed satisfying. She would be turning thirty soon, only three years short of the age her mother had been when she'd jumped off a bridge. She was filled with dread, as she realized that really, what she yearned for, was change.

As if reading her mind, Holy Man said, "Often, we experience our first true rite of passage around the age of thirty. Most people believe it happens when we turn eighteen because that's when we become adults. Or when we turn twenty-one because we can drink. But it's around age thirty that we gain clarity on our soul's purpose, on who we can be."

"You know, you're really annoying me. You're always lurking around, eating or drinking, and it's creeping me out. If you don't tell me who you are, I'm going to call the police," Naina said, more forcefully than she'd intended. She regretted it immediately, hoping she hadn't offended Holy Man. Yes, she wanted to find out who he was, but she didn't want to push him away.

Holy Man let out a loud laugh. "There's no reason for that, dear."

Naina was relieved he brought levity to the moment. Softly, she said, "Then tell me who you are."

"I'm someone sent to watch over you, provide you with a helping hand. You're not as alone as you think you are, Naina. There are bigger actions at work. The universe has your back."

"Do you have a name? Or a home? How do you always know where I am?"

"Why don't you think of me as a friend? Friends share a bond, and you and I are connected, Naina. We share a deep bond."

"We do?"

"What does your heart say? Do you trust me?"

Naina took a moment to consider this. "Yes, strangely, I do. You seem to be a wise man of some type."

"A Holy Man?" He winked at her.

Naina stopped walking, feeling the blood drain from her face. Could he possibly know she referred to him as Holy Man?

He stopped as well and turned around to face her. "I was sent to you, Naina, exclusively for you. That's all I can say. If you trust me in your heart, and you feel, in the deepest part of you, that I'm a safe person, then rely on that. Let that be enough."

Naina felt secure, more secure than ever before, even more so than she did with Raiya.

As if sensing the openness, Holy Man continued, "So, tell me about the angelite. Is it giving you a sense of calm and peace? Do you feel less alone? Have you been able to connect more with the divine?"

Before Holy Man, the box, the angelite, and Raiya, there had been an emptiness within her. Naina had woken up most mornings wishing for the end of the day, and had gone to bed wondering how she'd fill the next. Her routines kept her going. But she hadn't felt so desolate in the last twenty-one days. In fact, she had been happy. She had amassed several moments of joy, more joy than ever before.

"I have felt less alone," she offered.

"And?"

"Other than you, I'm not sure I have connected more with the divine. But I don't even know if you are divine …" She thought about the "hey". The memory brought shivers and she broke out in goosebumps. She hadn't heard another one, and she also didn't know if the voice was from the divine or if it was from something else.

"Be patient, Naina. Allow yourself to unfold, live in the moment, focus on you and what you want out of life. You'll figure out what you need soon enough. I can't wait to see what you come up with."

Chapter Fifteen

The next morning, Naina was not the first to arrive in the office. It was the first time it had happened. The moment she saw Alice, she knew something was wrong. Instead of setting things up, Naina walked into Alice's office. Alice looked directly at her, as if she had been waiting for her.

"Good morning," Alice said. Her tone was terse, and there wasn't even the hint of a smile. Alice usually smiled, and she had confessed it was sometimes only to encourage Naina to do the same, a demonstration it was possible to smile.

"Good morning?" Naina said, although she got the feeling Alice wasn't having a good morning.

"Have a seat."

Naina sat across from her boss. A shiver ran through her body and her hands became clammy.

"Naina, I'm sorry to say I've decided to let you go."

Naina wasn't sure she'd heard correctly, but based on Alice's expression, she didn't need to confirm it. Yes, she had just been fired. She sat quietly for a few moments. Hadn't she seen this coming? Why was she feeling so miserable then? In a small voice, she asked, "Why? I thought I was doing better."

"Yes, you were. But Naina, I need more, and I no longer think you can give me what I'm looking for. I've known you for a while, and I can see you don't have it in you. You're too meek and lack luster, and I need someone more personable and dynamic at the desk."

Naina blinked her big brown eyes at Alice, feeling numb. "Okay."

"I've terminated you and you'll receive pay for two weeks as a direct deposit, as usual. There is no reason for you to stay today. You can clear your desk and head out."

"Okay."

"I would prefer you do it before the others arrive."

"Okay." It took Naina a moment to realize Alice meant she needed to leave now. Her mind in a complete blank, Naina walked back to the reception desk and grabbed her purse. She stared at the space she had occupied for seven years and picked up nothing else.

Alice followed her. "You've got nothing to take with you?"

"No." Nothing in that space was hers.

"Are you sure?" Alice sounded incredulous.

Naina nodded slowly.

"Okay then … Best of luck, Naina."

"Thanks," Naina answered quietly. Her chin gave a slight tremble.

During the 678-step walk home, the trembling in her chin grew more persistent. She let out a quiet sob. Naina regretted what she had wished for the night before. She wanted to take back the feeling she wanted change. She didn't want change. At least not that quick. What would she do now? What would become of her?

The heat of the morning was oppressive and Naina stopped briefly, fearing she would vomit her Special K and milk. She was covered in sweat but was unsure if it was cold sweat from the nausea accosting her, from the hot and muggy morning, or from a combination of both.

❦

Naina sat down at her dining room table for what seemed like hours. Her stomach grumbling was the only indication it was time for her mid-morning snack, which usually consisted of coffee and digestives. But, she'd had them at the office, and she wasn't there anymore. She would never be there again, she realized. She should have had the presence of mind to take them when Alice had given her the chance. Except, she also realized, the digestives didn't belong to her. Alice supplied them.

She was in the habit of buying them for herself, but not regularly. She rushed to the pantry and was flooded with relief when she found a red packet of digestives. They were stale, but they would do. She needed to keep her rituals. She wasn't sure if she could handle any more instability and couldn't bear the thought of having something else as a snack.

She wished away the nausea and forced herself to eat. She sipped her coffee slowly and took small, tentative bites out of the biscuits. No matter how hard she tried to keep to normalcy, there was no denying there was nothing normal about that day.

She thought about going to see Raiya and telling him about getting fired, but reconsidered. She wasn't ready to talk about it yet and she was too scared to face the facts. She didn't want him to ask her about her future. She needed to figure it out herself, first. She had considered asking for his opinion, but that was when she had a job, a sense of safety. As she ate more of her snack, she grew impatient.

Just then it came again.

"Hey."

This time she was wide awake. She sat still for a few minutes, and gingerly got up from her chair. There was not a single item out of place, not in the living room, not in the kitchen, not in her bedroom, and not in her bathroom. She owned such few items that it was easy to tell with a quick glance around. She opened the main door and found no one on either side of the hallway.

Naina was suddenly spurred into ordering a Lyft. There was only one place for her to go.

Naina threw out the rest of the coffee and swallowed the bite of the digestive biscuit she had in her mouth, barely chewing, as if she was late for an important meeting. She wasn't. It was only one bite, but she gagged, nearly bringing up all she had consumed. She didn't bother with the rest of the biscuits and threw them out as well.

She couldn't wait to stand under the shelter of Angel Oak. Maybe it would give her the answers she was looking for. Armed with her crystal in her pocket, Naina got in the Lyft.

As she rode in the car, she hoped her tree would provide guidance. It was an odd thought, given she didn't believe the tree would speak to her. Still, she hoped the tree would at least bring her reprieve.

Chapter Sixteen

Naina had discovered a love for nature after a visit to Angel Oak soon after she had moved to Charleston. The tree entranced her and had become a special refuge for Naina. She first encountered it the one time her father and stepmother had visited. They had arranged a car through the hotel.

The tree was believed to be up to 500 years old, one of the oldest living oak trees in the country. It stood sixty-five feet tall and shaded 17,000 square feet of ground. The largest branch was 187 feet long. The tree was named after the estate in which it grew – Angel Estate. The ghosts of former slaves were believed to guard the tree like angels, and Naina always peered around the branches hoping to catch sight of one.

She had felt connected to the tree from the moment she had laid eyes on it, as if it provided the comfort and compassion her parents weren't able to. Ever since that first visit, Naina had gone to Angel Oak when she needed solace. That Tuesday was one such day.

Now that Naina was at Angel Oak, she traced the tentacular

branches that reached out like an octopus, some digging into the earth before breaking the surface once again. Naina felt empty and worthless and as she weaved in and out of the branches, she let her tears fall. No one wanted her. Even her mother hadn't wanted her badly enough to live on.

Naina placed her hands on the thickest part of the trunk. The thick roots curled up around it, and Naina had often thought the tree looked as if someone had sculpted it with Play-Doh. Just then, Naina sensed an aura around it, a golden light surrounded the tree, and in the sunlight it seemed as if glitter sparkled within it. The branches spread out in tendril-like cords that extended from the tree out into the ether around it.

As her breathing slowed, a wave of calm spread throughout her. She was overcome with an incredible sense of relief, and she hugged the tree, succumbing to its comfort. She begged it to explain the voice, her sadness, and all the abandonment. She didn't get a response but finally released the torrent of tears that had been building up for a while.

She hadn't realized how afraid she had felt since hearing the "hey". She was unaccustomed to the feeling, having always been secure in her routines. Despite living alone, and despite the loneliness she had only begun to shake off as of late, until recently, she had not been so desolate. When she had heard that voice, it was as if she had been slapped to face the reality of her utter despair.

Her knees buckled, and she knelt by the tree, her left arm still holding on to the trunk, her right arm lowering down to her lap. She let out a few hiccups as she watched a line of ants cross a root and then a butterfly rest momentarily on her calf. Strangely, they gave her a sense of comfort.

Without intending to, she dozed off. She drifted out of her

body, as if a shadow version of herself were floating above her. She saw herself laying on top of the thick roots of the tree, and it appeared to her as if the earthy thickness had enveloped her in a dark brown blanket.

She was instantly transported into a world where she was everything she wanted to be. She was able to communicate with the squirrels in the forest, the ferns in the ground, and the moss in the broken tree trunks. They didn't speak out loud, but somehow she understood what they were saying. Even she didn't have to speak for them to understand her. She was dressed in a fairy-like costume, with pink leggings and a pink and sparkly body suit that complemented her brown skin. Her silky long hair was converted into dark brown curls wrapped up into a neat bun.

In this world, she lived in a large house, and her mother was still alive. Her parents were still married, still together, and they occupied the bottom floor. She was surrounded by people who loved, supported, and respected her as much as she loved, supported, and respected them. She laughed and giggled at everything, as if happiness didn't have an end. She was the best version of herself she could ever be.

When Naina woke, she didn't know how long she had slept. She was cocooned against the tree. As she brought herself to a sitting position, a twig cracked in the distance. The previous reverie dissolved instantly, and her entire body tensed in a swift motion. She brought her knees up to her chest and hugged them tightly, hoping she would remain hidden by the girth of the trunk.

A few more twigs cracked, and it seemed steps were coming closer to her. She came back fully, physically back in her body. The hairs on her arms perked up into the air around her and her skin filled with goosebumps. She closed her eyes shut and dug her face into herself.

"Hello, there," came a male voice.

She didn't look up and held her breath.

"Don't be afraid. I won't hurt you."

She still didn't answer. His voice sounded familiar, but she couldn't place it.

"Are you alright?" he asked.

She nodded without looking up.

"Please don't be afraid. I am sorry if I startled you. I didn't mean to, dear." His tone was sweet and gentle. He sounded genuinely apologetic. "I'll wait for you in the clearing. As I said last night, ask your heart for guidance and you'll see I'm no threat. You have nothing to fear. Take your time."

She listened for his steps moving away from her. After a few moments of not hearing other sounds, she began to move. Her body was so stiff that she had to stretch it, just to get the blood flowing again. She debated whether or not to meet the man in the clearing. Really, she had no choice. She had to head that way. It was the only way out.

She didn't know what it meant to ask her heart, and debated on what to do. She held still and got no response. Her chest showed nothing. She put her hand on her heart and only felt its hurried beats. She took a few deep breaths to calm herself down.

After a brief moment, she closed her eyes. She brought into her mind an image of her heart, and asked her heart, as the man had suggested, and realized she felt no fear. She took a deep breath and with resolve, she followed the man's footsteps.

When she reached the clearing, Holy Man greeted her with a smile. "I'm sorry I scared you. I wanted to make sure you were okay. For someone to have fallen asleep hugging a tree, they had to have gone through something big."

"I'm sorry I couldn't place your voice. I thought you were a stranger." Naina was surprised she hadn't recognized Holy Man. She was so fearful she had assumed it was someone else.

However, in that moment, Holy Man did look like someone else. He didn't look as young as he usually did. Instead, he looked like he might be someone's grandfather. He had a benevolent and kind air to him, like he could easily strap on a white beard and red suit and be a Santa at a nearby mall. He had graying hair but no beard. Had his hair always been gray? She couldn't remember. His hazel eyes emitted warmth, the same warmth she'd seen all along. That, at least, hadn't changed. He was dressed in his perennial white and in his sockless brown loafers, but this time, he had a red walking stick in his left hand and a corn dog in his right. It wasn't the type of stick an older person would carry but rather the type a hiker might use. Naina noticed little mountain peaks etched throughout the stick. She sensed it carried some meaning to him, like perhaps he was a naturalist and felt a particular link to the earth. The thought comforted her.

Words poured out of her without control. "I heard a 'hey' in the middle of the night and again today. The voice was loud and clear. I feel as if something, not an actual living human being, wants to get my attention. I don't know what it's trying to tell me. I can't figure out if it's a warning. I thought it could have been my mother, but she died when I was a child. Then, I thought the tree was speaking to me and now that I'm here, I realize it's a foolish thought. I just don't know what to make of it all."

Naina was surprised she spoke the truth so effortlessly. She normally considered every word before voicing it. She was strangely at ease and had a sensation she had known Holy Man her whole life. She wasn't shy, but she didn't like speaking to people before getting to know them well. It made her feel stranger still that she opened herself up to him then. But then again, she trusted him in the deepest way. It made her realize, she hadn't developed the same level of trust with Raiya – at least, not yet.

"I take it this hasn't happened before? Hearing the voices, I mean?" he asked.

She was surprised to see not even a hint of judgment on his expression. "Never."

He tilted his head "What do you think it could be?"

"I don't know." She gave him a pleading look.

He looked back at her carefully. The warmth in his eyes extended to the rest of his being. She saw it, the warmth. It was a translucent airy substance that surrounded him, as if the energy around him had turned into an amoeba. It developed tentacles and a glittering gentle breeze emanated from him towards her. After a few seconds, the translucent tentacles reached her, enveloping her in their warmth.

Naina stood with her eyes closed and allowed herself to be embraced by the substance.

"You know the answer. Trust yourself. You hold the knowing within," he said.

When she opened her eyes, the warm substance had dissipated. Had she really seen it? Holy Man looked to her as he always had, his youth returned. Had she imagined it all? She willed Holy Man or the tree or Raiya or someone to give her answers, or direction, or something. What would she do next?

She had learned the world could change in an instant. Her mother could be dead by the time she came back from school. Her father could bring in a strange woman on a Saturday morning as she ate her cereal. Or her father could ask her to pack her clothes on the pretense of a holiday trip, only to hand her off to a boarding school.

Still, she wasn't ready for this. Despite owning so little that she could potentially get ready to leave at a moment's notice, there was nothing more unnatural to Naina than to deal with change. She wished she'd had time to secure what she'd do next before Alice had terminated her employment.

She rested her forehead on a nearby branch – many branches twisted their way into the clearing – the pulsing of the sap running through the tree reverberated against her hands, giving her the odd sensation of feeling the heartbeat of the earth. For the first time since getting the crystal, the angelite in her pocket pulsated in synchrony to the tree.

"Naina, who can you be?" Holy Man was leaning against the tree next to her, still eating the corn dog.

"Me."

"And, do you know who you are?"

"Naina …"

"Yes, but who is Naina?"

She thought about it for a few moments. She didn't know what to say.

"What is it that you truly enjoy?"

She was unsure of what he meant.

"What would make your heart burst into a billion blazing sparkles?" he asked.

Chapter Seventeen

Back in her apartment, Naina wondered if it all had been a dream. Had she really seen the air change? And fallen asleep at Angel Oak? That had been a first. And what about the strange dream? Were there other versions of herself that she could be? How was she supposed to know about the "hey"? More importantly, what would make her heart burst into a billion blazing sparkles? She had no idea.

She couldn't remember the last time she had felt much of anything. She realized, then, that she didn't let herself feel emotions. She'd had them, she'd just hidden them. With time, they had been buried deeper and deeper. She appeared aloof, stoic, unfeeling, but she wasn't. She felt it all. Sad. Defeated. Forlorn. Lost. Forgotten. Desolate. It was more than she could handle. She had never felt so much in her life.

She cried when she read books and the characters experienced loss or pain. She bawled watching Shailene Woodley act out a dying teenager in *The Fault in Our Stars*. She cried at the suffering of others, as she did watching newborn babies coo. She cried at hope and possibility.

She needed to learn to cry for herself. How would she do that? Even when a slight twinge of sadness appeared, she came up with scenarios in her head, impossible made-up situations. She drew inspiration from the many romance novels she'd read. She imagined she had been left at the altar or she had been jilted by the love of her life – he had fallen in love with someone else and she was heartbroken. Those scenarios would make her cry. Her real life, however, brought no apparent emotion. She had never cried for herself.

She didn't know why that question from Holy Man had brought up all of this. She still didn't know what would make her heart burst into a billion blazing sparkles. Those visions under Angel Oak had awoken something in her. They made her consider there might be hope and possibility for her.

She wanted to feel alive. She wanted to feel all the feelings, like she imagined all those people who annoyed her did. She wanted to feel like those people who cried at everything; like those who seemed to get giddy at watching a sunset; those who slammed their hands on the table after having a difficult conversation with their boss; or those who clapped when a plane landed.

She had been muted. Even when events went her way, like the day she had gotten the job offer from the real estate office.

"That's so exciting! Aren't you happy?" Elie had asked.

She knew Elie was right, but she hadn't realized she was supposed to feel elated until Elie had uttered the words.

The starkness of Naina's apartment killed the magic she had felt at Angel Oak. She was struck by the lack of personality – in her and in her space.

She envied people who could be themselves. As much as she wanted to be like James Bond and Jack Reacher, she also envied them. As much as she disliked Alice, she also envied her. She had it in her to be herself, to have a family, and to have a business. She could do it all, it seemed, and still look so presentable doing it. Naina had to struggle to have it all. She barely kept it together as it was, and she looked presentable by being overly simplistic. If she had to think too much about what to wear and how to present herself, she grew overwhelmed.

Naina wanted to feel her life wasn't over, things were still possible, her life was still possible, there was still time for her. It wasn't late – for anything. Most of all, Naina wanted to feel joy. To do that, she had to figure out how to be rid of the sadness. And of the ominous feeling she'd been carrying for days.

ॐ

Armed with this resolution in mind, she headed over to Raiya's apartment. It was earlier than usual for their afternoon chai. It was 4:32pm, only an hour sooner than he would have expected her. That should be okay, she reasoned. Raiya had never hesitated to knock on her door when he wanted. She'd been meaning to speak to him for days, and it was time for her to get over her hesitation. It was time for her to build trust with Raiya, as she had with Holy Man. And Raiya was someone who clearly didn't hold back when it came to feeling all the feelings. She was sure he would be of help.

Right before she was about to knock on his apartment door, Raiya's voice was audible. It sounded like he was on the phone. She placed her ear to the door to hear if he was on a serious call or if he could do with the interruption.

He laughed and then said, "Yeah, I'm still hanging out with the weirdo."

Naina froze in place. Others had called her a weirdo before, but surely Raiya wouldn't. He had to be talking about someone else.

And then he said, "Yeah, she lives just next door, can you imagine? I guess I'll have to put up with her quirks."

Naina felt the blood leave her face and she got even more still.

"Nah, she's not that bad. She's so shy. I've got to do all the talking. I guest it's what makes her tolerable. It's like talking to a therapist." Raiya laughed down the phone.

The sound made her stomach twist.

"The bonus is that I've gotten to know Charleston. This is an amazing culinary city and I don't want to miss out. So I take her along."

Naina's heart sank, her hands were cold and clammy.

"No, I haven't met anyone else yet. The guys at the start-up are the country club type. They're okay to work with but I wouldn't hang with them. It makes a big difference that I work from home, if you catch my drift. If they didn't pay me as well, I wouldn't be living here."

Naina heard a mug being put down on the counter.

"Yeah, I know I need to make better friends. In the meantime, I can put up with Naina."

And then, just like that, tears fell down her face. This time, she was definitely crying for herself.

Chapter Eighteen

Naina wasn't able to make the ten steps back to her apartment before collapsing to the ground. The world had been ripped away from underneath her and she'd lost her footing. She struggled to get up, clawing at the wall trying to grip at something, but the light green wallpaper was plastered so tightly, not a stitch gave way to offer her something to grab onto. She tried to find support around her, but nothing was available, the dark gray carpet had very little fuzz on it.

She lay down and struggled to breathe. Her heart beat faster than ever, the pounding blood reverberated in her ears. Hot and cold sensations passed through her simultaneously and soon, she was drenched in perspiration. Her face was wet but she couldn't tell whether it was from tears or sweat. It seemed like ages since she had cried, yet she couldn't determine what she was feeling.

Suddenly, she was overcome by fear. The thought of ending her life had occurred to her often; it would be much easier if she could release her struggle, let go, cease to be. But in that moment, the thought of dying terrified her. She didn't want to die. She wanted to live.

She tried to call out for help, have someone dial 911, but no sound came out from her. She seemed to be making gasping noises but nothing strong enough to draw anyone's attention. Her vision started to spin and she felt nauseous.

To her relief, one of her neighbors came down the corridor from the elevators. She had a small chihuahua trotting along on a leash. Small dogs irritated Naina because she thought the loud yelps they were capable of producing didn't justify their small frames. But in that moment, she was grateful. Maybe the chihuahua would see her and make enough noise for someone to notice her.

Ironically, the neighbor ran towards Naina before the dog did.

"Oh my goodness. Are you okay?" the neighbor exclaimed.

Naina grasped at her neck, unable to make a sound. Her chest rising and dropping rapidly against the floor seemed to make more of an impact than anything Naina uttered.

The neighbor crouched next to Naina, placing her hands on Naina's belly. When Naina opened her eyes even more, the neighbor comforted her by saying, "I'm a NICU nurse. I can help you."

She waited for Naina to give consent through her eyes. She held one of Naina's hands in her own.

"My name is Fiona and I live in 204. I'm going to ask you some questions. If you can't speak or nod, clench my hand to indicate yes, and don't clench it to indicate no. Got it?"

Naina clenched Fiona's hand.

"Great, you got it. Does it hurt anywhere?"

Naina didn't clench Fiona's hand.

"I take that as a no. Are you having chest pain?"

Again, Naina didn't clench Fiona's hand.

"Did something happen just now that upset you?"

Naina clenched her hand.

"Ah. Got it. Do you think you may be having a panic attack?" Fiona asked.

Naina clenched Fiona's hand.

"Have you had a panic attack before?"

Naina clenched Fiona's hand.

"I can help you through this. It helps that you are already lying down. I'm going to place one hand on your belly and I want you to try to breathe to it. As I press down lightly, I want you to try to raise my hand via your belly using your breath. I'll show you." Fiona placed a hand on her own belly and demonstrated a belly breath. "Do you think you can do that?"

Naina clenched Fiona's hand.

"Wonderful. Give it a try now."

Naina attempted to calm her breathing, and Fiona continued assisting her until it seemed like Naina's chest was no longer pounding the floor. After she'd calmed down enough, Fiona went into her apartment to get Naina a glass of water. It was then Naina noticed that the chihuahua had remained seated next to her, with both front paws on her thigh. Naina had never felt so comforted.

When Fiona came back with the water, she helped Naina sit up and sat with her as Naina took small deliberate sips. The chihuahua crawled onto Naina's lap.

"Mimi is a caring dog. She responds deeply to people's emotions. She's a wonderful consoler."

Naina nodded and placed a tentative hand on Mimi's back.

"Are you feeling better?" Fiona asked.

"Yes."

"Well enough to tell me your name?"

"I'm Naina. In 205."

"Hi Naina, it's nice to meet you. I've seen you around the building. I'm sorry I haven't had a chance to say hello before."

"It's nice to meet you too. I've heard Mimi often."

"Ooh. I hope she's not too loud?"

"The walls here are pretty thick so I only hear her when you walk in the hallways. Or when I pass by your apartment and Mimi rasps at the door."

"Yes, she doesn't like it when I leave her home alone."

Naina nodded and took another sip of water.

"Can I offer you something else, Naina?"

"You've already done so much for me, I couldn't possibly accept more."

Fiona took a tissue from her pocket and a small amber colored bottle. "This is clary sage essential oil. I'm going to put a couple of drops on this tissue, and I want you to take a deep inhale with it."

"What will that do?"

"Essential oils are a great support system for so many conditions, and I know that clary sage and lavender work wonders in calming the mind and relieving stress. I ran out of lavender, so I brought you clary sage."

Naina did as Fiona indicated and felt drawn to the flowery smell. She felt refreshed and clear.

"Do you think you're well enough to stand up? I can walk you over to your apartment."

"I'm better, thank you."

Fiona helped Naina get up. "Would you like me to stay with you a while?"

"I'm fine. I'd like to be alone."

"That's fine. Just know you can knock on my door if anything comes up."

Fiona walked Naina to apartment 205. "Let me leave you my number. You can call me if you need anything, anything at all. I mean it."

Naina and Fiona exchanged numbers, and when Naina settled down on her love seat, she realized small dogs no longer irritated her. Mimi was a tender dog and for a moment she fantasized about owning a dog, but when she thought about how much more work it would be for her to keep the house clean, she let go of the idea.

She also realized she hadn't come up with a story for Fiona. Until then. Naina was struck with the idea that Fiona wasn't married, but something told Naina she'd had a bad breakup, perhaps even a divorce. Naina wasn't certain, but she got the idea Fiona might have moved to Charleston on purpose and that purpose had been to get as far away as possible from a situation. Fiona might be someone who was kind and gentle, someone reliable, at least for now, and for the moment, that was enough.

Chapter Nineteen

The first time Naina'd had a panic attack was while she had been living with the boarder, Raquel, while she attended Candor Boarding School. By then, she had been living in Charleston for two years. It was the middle of the summer when the excessive heat and humidity had sent most native Charlestonians out of the city or out on to the water. Her classmates were at home with their families and would only be back to start junior year.

She was the only student living with Raquel, and that particular summer Naina felt especially alone.

She didn't interact much with Raquel and hardly saw her during the day. Raquel prepared meals in advance and left them in labeled containers in the refrigerator, and it was up to Naina to heat up her food, and often was the only person sitting at the dining table eating. Raquel was barely around, and she didn't in any way want to pretend to be a guardian for Naina. In fact, she went out of her way to ensure that she didn't know much about her.

"I'm not your parent. I'm not your friend. I'm not your confidant.

You don't need to tell me about your life, and I don't need to tell you about mine. I'll make sure you have a clean, comfortable, and safe place to live in. You are not allowed visitors, unless by my express permission. No parties, no gatherings, no shenanigans of any sort. I'll prepare all your meals and that's it. You mess up, even once, and you're out," she had explained when Naina first moved in.

Naina had followed the instructions to a tee, never wanting to give Raquel a reason to kick her out. It hadn't been hard to do because she hadn't been close to any of the girls or teachers at Candor. But at least when school was in session, she'd had people to talk to. When school was out, she didn't have anyone. Even when she encountered Raquel in the house, which wasn't often, they merely exchanged greetings.

Naina spent the summers on her own. To keep herself entertained, she read and watched TV – she had one in her room. She also went on long walks all over downtown. It was during that time that she had gotten to know Charleston well and connected with the city, feeling it was hers.

She had walked on every single street in downtown and had been proudest of discovering all the hidden alleys and passageways that weren't open to cars, as was Longitude Lane, which ran parallel to Tradd Street, and was believed to be as old as the city. Some were filled with foliage and provided the perfect reprieve from the summer heat, like Stoll's Alley between East Bay and Church Streets. Others, like Lodge Alley, between East Bay and State Street, were made out of bricks or cobblestones and had a quaint and cozy feel to them. There were a few remaining cobblestone streets in Charleston, including Chalmers Street and Adger's Wharf, which made the alleys appear even more whimsical. Soon, these alleys became some of her favorite spots around the city.

Can You Be

Historically, many of these alleys had been created as discrete walkways for people who didn't own horses and only moved around the city on foot, such as the enslaved and merchants, while the larger, visible streets were for carriages. Naina's favorite alley was Philadelphia Alley, which ran between Queen and Cumberland Streets, because it was rumored to be haunted by the ghost of Dr. Joseph Brown Ladd, who had been killed in a duel.

Naina had loved exploring the city, but all that walking hadn't given her people to talk to. She had walked alone, and back then her father hadn't provided her much of a stipend as he expected her to eat all her meals at Raquel's. So, she didn't have the means to sit in coffee shops or enter stores, and was unlikely to go places where she had a chance to interact with others.

Such was her solitude that on one muggy July afternoon, Naina had an awful realization she hadn't uttered a single word to anyone in almost fourteen days. When she had gotten back to her room that day, she thought of calling her father. But every time she had called him in the past, especially to complain in some way, like not having spoken to another person in so long, had resulted in a change. The fear of the change the call would potentially result in had flooded her with nausea. Soon, her body had been covered with sweat, despite the air conditioning being on at full and the ceiling fan running at maximum speed. Her chest had begun to palpitate, and before long, she couldn't breathe.

That day was the only time she had asked Raquel for help. Raquel, on seeing Naina's distress, had driven Naina to the emergency room. It was there that the doctors told her she'd had a panic attack.

When they helped her calm down, the doctor recommended she find ways to relax, "Like going out for walks," he had said.

Naina hadn't explained she already did that. Instead of stopping her walks, she had taken to walking more often, and instead of feeling down for not having people to talk to, she peered out on Charleston Bay and searched for egrets and dolphins, imagining herself having conversations with them. She walked around White Point Garden and Waterfront Park and made it a point to spot red robins and ground squirrels. She walked among the trees, making sure to touch each.

She had made a habit of it, and somehow, that made her feel better. She longed to visit Angel Oak but it wasn't until she got to college that she got extra cash from her father to be able to take a taxi from time to time to sit under the shelter of the great tree.

Chapter Twenty

It had been over an hour since Fiona had left her apartment, and Naina had not moved from her loveseat. Without realizing it, she had turned on Netflix to *Mindhunter*. She hadn't followed anything about the recent murders on the show and knew she would need to rewatch it. She turned off the TV and pondered what she would have instead of chai at Raiya's. She didn't have the ingredients to make chai, although she was sure that if she had them, she could have replicated what she had seen Raiya do so many times now.

Instead, she repeated her morning snack of coffee and digestives. As she did, she realized she hadn't eaten anything since she'd had coffee and digestives that morning. In the excitement of what she'd experienced at Angel Oak, she had completely forgotten to eat. That had not happened to her before. She was usually quite religious about her meals. Eating at least three full meals a day was important to health.

As she sat down at her dining table, she remembered Raiya had called her shy. Naina was quiet but not shy. Shy meant she was afraid to speak up or she had something to say but didn't say it for fear of something – rejection, judgment, criticism, something. Naina had no desire to express her thoughts. She was happy hoarding them in her head. Alice had made her feel inadequate, as if being shy were something to be ashamed of, even though she wasn't shy.

And now, Raiya had once again used the word shy as a derogatory term. She wasn't shy, she was quiet. She thought carefully about her words before speaking them. Alice had described her as an introvert within the first year of working at the real estate office.

When that had happened, Naina had gone to the library to research this further and found a link to Myers Briggs, discovering, through the definition she found, that she was indeed an introvert. She pondered questions and had to process them in her mind. It was her choice whether or not to speak up. Being an introvert didn't have anything to do with being shy. She wasn't afraid of speaking up. Being an introvert had everything to do with having to think before speaking. She always considered her words carefully.

Alice, and now Raiya, may have under-appreciated her and even demeaned her. But ever since the day Naina had discovered she was an introvert, which had been six years ago, she had worn her introversion as a superpower. She considered it an advantage that she thought before she spoke because it meant she didn't say things "in the heat of the moment". What she said wasn't rash. It was logical. It was meticulous. It made sense.

How would she act toward Raiya after overhearing his conversation? Naina stood up from the dining table and imagined Raiya was sitting in the chair across from the one she'd just left. She sat back down for a moment, thinking it would be better to envision him sitting in front of her, but her jitters got the best of her. She had to stand up for this. She paced from one end of the four-foot table to the other, considering what she would say to Raiya.

There was no way to avoid Raiya. She already wondered why he hadn't reached out to her yet, given that the time for their shared afternoon chai had come and gone. Surely he would notice she hadn't stopped by. Or would he?

She shook her head, dismissing the thought. Instead, she considered what to say as a comeback to Raiya. She grabbed the angelite, holding it tightly in her palm, making a tight fist around it. She stood up and stared at the empty spot Raiya had left on her sofa, and said, "I'm not shy. I'm an introvert, you idiot."

She didn't like the sound of that. She didn't want to lower herself to the same level he had reached. She didn't want to call him names.

"That wasn't a kind thing to say about me," she said, shaking her finger.

That made her feel like she was her father, and she didn't like that either. She considered what her mother had done when Naina had been naughty as a young girl. A memory came to her. She didn't remember her punishment. To scold her, her mother had made Naina grab her own ears while doing squats. Raiya had once shared his parents had made him do the same. It might have been an Indian thing. She couldn't ask Raiya to hold on to his ears and squat. Could she? Would that be penance enough for the words he'd said against her?

She paced around and stood in place for a moment before looking at the empty sofa again and saying with a solemn voice, "I thought you were my friend. Friends don't treat each other with disrespect."

She liked the sound of that. But then, it was clear he didn't consider her to be his friend. Was it even worth it for her to state the obvious?

She sighed loudly, realizing the futility of her exercise. How was it possible for so much to happen in one day: getting fired, hearing the "hey" again, having a supernatural experience at Angel Oak, Holy Man asking her about her heart bursting, discovering her friendship with Raiya had been a sham, having a panic attack, Fiona and Mimi helping her, and now this useless play-acting she'd never done before?

It was as if she'd lived an entire lifetime of experiences in one day. Was that how it felt like to have a full life? She hoped not, she hoped it wasn't as terrible and empty as she felt then. But at least, now, she understood why she'd had an ominous feeling. An odd type of relief came over her and she looked around for something to cover Raiya's spot on the sofa.

Just then, it came again. "Hey."

Naina stopped dead in her tracks. She had continued to pace. It was the third time now she'd heard it. Holy Man had said she would know the source. She closed her eyes and got very quiet. "Mama, is that you?"

Chapter Twenty-One

Naina knew it wouldn't be long before she would be forced to face Raiya. Their schedules had been too entrenched for her to escape him that easily. After getting done with the role-play, she noticed several missed calls from Raiya, as well as many text messages asking her where she was.

She was too preoccupied with the third "hey" to pay any attention to them or even worry about them. Instead, she went to bed but hardly slept. She spent most of the night wondering how to figure out if the "hey" was her mother. She googled all types of mediums but decided against getting in touch with any of them. Holy Man had told her she'd know who it was. But he hadn't explained how. She would ask him the next time she saw him.

The next morning, Naina was buried underneath her bed covers when came a knock on the door. She knew it was Raiya doing his usual morning visit. He knocked twice before walking away. Another text message came from him then, asking if she was okay.

She stayed in bed for much of the day, something she had never done before. It was an odd feeling. Not moving, not showering, and not following her routine. It was oddly refreshing, even though she spent much of her time staring into space. She got up to eat her meals and then got back into bed.

By 3:00pm, her own body odor was intolerable, and she finally had a shower. Afterwards, she prepared her coffee and digestives and sat down on the loveseat to watch TV when there was a knock on the door.

"I know you are in there, Naina. I know you haven't left your apartment all day … I have been listening and I know you haven't opened your door." It was Raiya.

Naina didn't respond.

"You may not want to talk but I want to see you. Please open the door."

Again, she didn't respond.

"Please. I just want to make sure you're okay."

She still didn't respond. She knew all too well he didn't care about her.

"I will not move away until you open the door. The only way for me to leave is for you to let me see your face so I can make sure you are okay."

Naina sighed loudly and, surprising herself, got up from the sofa. She grabbed the angelite and opened the door to Raiya. "I am sure you don't give two shits about me. Stop pretending. I overheard your phone conversation. I know you think I'm a weirdo. You said it to me at dinner when we went out the first time, but then, I didn't think you were making fun of me. In your conversation, I know you meant to make fun of me. You confessed you merely tolerate me. Now that you have seen my face, and that I am clearly not okay – because of you – leave me alone." She slammed the door on Raiya's face.

⚡

Naina had to wait only two minutes before there was a knock on the door again.

"Naina, I am sorry. Please open the door. Please let me explain."

She did not answer. She grasped the angelite tighter in her hand.

"Please. I beg you. I want to explain."

"Go away, Raiya. I don't want any of your fake excuses."

"Please open the door, Naina. Let's talk."

Naina did open the door then. "Why, so you can give me more of your feeble excuses? I thought we were friends. I thought we had a genuine bond."

"We do, I swear we do."

"How can you swear? You just belittled me in front of your friend."

"I had no idea you were listening."

"What difference does that make? Would you not have called me a weirdo then? I'm glad because now I know how you truly feel about me."

"I don't feel that way, Naina. I don't know why I said that."

"It was hurtful. You hurt me. That's not what friends do."

"You're right. That isn't what friends do. I'm sorry. Please can I come in so we can talk?"

"I can't talk to you right now, Raiya. I am too hurt to deal with you right now. And you need to think about why you would say those things. If you're truly my friend and truly sorry, then that's what you need to do."

With that, Naina closed the door again. She walked back to her loveseat and sat down, staring out the window. She held the angelite in both hands and brought it up to her heart. She closed her eyes and sat in silence. A few minutes passed before Raiya's door closed. The coffee she'd prepared had gone cold, but she didn't have the energy to heat it up or to make a new one.

֎

Naina did not know how to deal with pain. She had never learned how to do it. Or grief. Holy Man's question reverberated within. She went for a walk on that Wednesday evening in late August and ran into him at White Point Garden. He stood at a gazebo in the center of the park, eating a sausage and egg sandwich. "What's bugging you, Naina? I can see you're distressed."

"What about the 'hey'? You told me I would know who it was and I don't have a clue."

"Do you not?"

"No."

"I believe you do."

Naina gave him a sideways glance.

"What does your heart tell you?"

Naina took a deep breath and spoke softly. "It's my mother."

Holy Man smiled and took another bite of his egg sandwich. "What else is bothering you?"

"What about the magic at Angel Oak?"

"What magic?" he said, his mouth full. "What else?"

Naina sighed. "I thought Raiya was my friend but he turned against me."

"What is this really about? What truly hurts you about his behavior?"

Naina didn't respond.

"What is your biggest pain about this?"

"Hurt. Betrayal. Punishment. Rejection."

"And what is that really about for you?"

She didn't respond again. She didn't know how.

"Think about it as you head back home. If you get to the bottom of what you're truly feeling it will make it more likely for you to see how to resolve the issue with Raiya."

Naina and Holy Man walked back toward her apartment in silence. She realized she had no idea what was at the bottom of her emotions, what was beyond the words that kept coming up for her. Hurt. Betrayal. Rejection. Punishment.

When they reached the front door, they parted ways with Holy Man saying, "Write a letter to yourself about how you feel. See what comes up."

And so she did. She sat at her desk, angelite in front of her, and began to write. She rambled on for a while, writing incoherencies, until suddenly, her writing started to bring her clarity, her writing connected her to her true feelings. To write a letter to herself about how she felt, she had to admit she had feelings, she felt pain, and she had been hurt. She had to accept she had been carrying this pain for years and no matter how much she tried to suppress it, it had grown larger and larger, so much so she was no longer able to contain it.

She had to admit time was running out and when she woke up in the middle of the night, she worried she was missing out. She worried because of her age. She worried she had no partner. She worried she was so close to the age her mother had been when she'd dropped off a bridge.

All signs pointed to being lost, especially because she couldn't envision a partner or a possible one. Even Raiya, who had felt like the brother she'd never had, was now lost to her. That's what hurt the most. When she had just started to feel hope, to feel like she belonged, he had pulled the rug from underneath her and left her to free fall.

Should she be more patient? Should she try to mend the situation with him? Was there a way to mend it? Or did she need to move on?

She connected with her heart, as she had done at Angel Oak, and knew she had to find a way to fix things with Raiya. She just didn't know how. Would he call her? Would she call him? She struggled with acknowledging her feelings, yet her body called out to her.

She was afraid to be hurt, to continue to be hurt. She would be disappointed, by whatever Raiya said, whatever he offered as an explanation. She knew he wouldn't respond like she wanted him to, but she also knew she had to take a chance. There was no point in trying to avoid this further.

The possibilities closed around her, like she was running out of options, like she was never going to get the family she yearned for. And that hurt. She felt defeated. She had lost at life, and at times wondered how so much loss was experienced at such a young age. Was it possible for her to still find a way to win? The magic she had experienced at Angel Oak must have been a figment of her imagination. Or was it? So many things she had thought were improbable, had actually come to be.

Just then, there was a knock on the door, and Naina nearly fell off the sofa from the shock. Her heart raced as she walked to the door and when she expected to see Raiya on the other side of the frame, it turned out to be Fiona and Mimi.

"I wanted to check in on you and see how you're doing. Are you feeling better after the panic attack?"

"I am in some ways but in others I'm totally lost. Would you like to come in?" Naina surprised herself with the openness she felt towards Fiona. She poured some water for Mimi in a bowl and prepared coffee and digestives for Fiona and herself. As she did, she shared she had been fired from the real estate office, but she didn't mention Raiya.

"Were you happy at your job?" Fiona asked.

"Not really."

"That's the impression I got from the way you talked about it. It seems a change may be good for you. Maybe you didn't want it quite this way, but it seems to me as if life has forced you into a change. Wouldn't you rather be working somewhere where you feel happy?"

"Yes, for sure. Someone asked me what I would do that would make me blissfully happy, and I cannot come up with an answer. I don't know what kind of job I want to have. I don't know what I want to be."

"Maybe you do have an answer, but for some reason you are resisting this change, and that is why the answer isn't coming to the surface. Is that possible?"

"Yes ..."

"Sometimes, when we're feeling stressed and anxious, it's really difficult to find clarity. Are you willing to try an exercise with me? It is called EFT, for Emotional Freedom Technique. It's also known as tapping and it's a simple yet powerful exercise proven to reduce stress and cortisol levels in the body. All it takes is a few minutes a day, repeating a statement, and tapping different areas on your body. I use it myself to help me feel more calm and peaceful."

Naina closed her eyes. There was nothing more appealing than to feel calm and peaceful.

"Are you willing to try it with me now, Naina?"

Naina nodded eagerly.

"You can do this with your eyes open. I don't want to pry but think about why you're resisting change. You don't need to give me details, just tell me simply, what is preventing you from moving forward?"

Naina opened her eyes but avoided making eye contact with Fiona. "I'm afraid."

"We'll work with that fear, but instead of focusing on that, what is the opposite of the fear you feel? In other words, how do you want to feel?"

"Safe. Stable."

"Great, we can work with that. As we go through this exercise you'll repeat to yourself, 'I am safe.' Follow along with me, Naina, and repeat what I'm doing. We will use the index and middle finger and tap five times on nine points in the body. Let's begin by tapping the outside of the palm on the side of the hand, right below the pinky. As you tap, say to yourself, 'I am safe.' Then tap your eyebrows, again repeating, 'I am safe.' Now move to your temple on the side of the eye. Follow the eye socket bone and tap below your eyes. Move to underneath the nose, right on the dip that's between the nose and the top of our lips. Next on to your chin. Now go to your collar bone. Then underneath the arm, around where your bra strap is. End with tapping the top of your head."

After they were done, a tingling sensation spread from the top of Naina's head down to the rest of her body. She felt lighter and took in a deep breath, feeling it was easier on her chest.

"Did that help?"

"Yes, definitely." Naina gave Fiona a quick closed mouth smile.

"This should also help you with your panic attacks."

Can You Be

Fiona shared that before becoming a nurse she worked in an accounting firm and hated her job. She realized she wanted to work with people, and of all types of people, babies brought her the most joy, perhaps because they were the most vulnerable and least likely to stand up for themselves, much like Mimi and other animals. Once she realized that, she started night school and continued working during the day, and after three long years, as soon as she finished nursing school, she quit her job and started working at the NICU. She hadn't regretted it one bit. What helped her get through this was to constantly ask herself, what one small step could she take to get her closer to her goals?

After Fiona left, Naina finally admitted she didn't know what her goals were. She knew what she wanted, but she had no goals. She resolved to figure out what they were. She didn't know how she would determine them, but she vowed she would.

Chapter Twenty-Two

The next day, a hurricane reached Charleston. The storm started that afternoon of late August and continued into the night. Naina was duly prepared with food, water, flashlights, candles, and all she needed to survive through the night.

Even so, Naina wished she had Raiya to huddle together with, and she wished she could have passed the storm in his apartment. His windows were shielded from the direct onslaught of wind and rain, and he had more streaming options than Naina. Raiya sent her a text asking if she wanted to come over but Naina didn't respond.

She also wished she had the courage to walk to Fiona's apartment and ask her to spend the night in each other's company. That would have allowed Naina to hold Mimi in her lap. She was certain their presence would provide some comfort, but the fear Fiona would dismiss her in some way was greater than Naina's need for company.

As the winds howled and the relentless rain pounded the windows, she turned off all the electronic equipment. Keeping electronics powered off gave her peace of mind, although having something to stream would have helped her pass the time. She didn't pick up *The Iliad* or *The Bhagavad Gita*, afraid they would lead to yet another "hey". She wished then she had brought books from the library. In the future, she would. All she would need was to wipe the books down with an antibacterial wipe, and perhaps even read the book while wearing gloves.

Since she didn't have anything to distract her, she covered herself in blankets, aware they wouldn't protect her if her windows shattered and the storm swept through her apartment, but they would at least cause her less harm. There was something about having something heavy on her body that allowed her to feel a certain amount of comfort. The only true solace was her angelite, which she kept in her hand at all times.

Thankfully, the storm wasn't as bad as Naina anticipated. It was a category three and it didn't make landfall in the city as predicted. The eerie calm came sometime in the night and the hurricane passed through the next morning. Several people lost power. There was flooding in some areas, but it wasn't as bad as Naina had feared. The power went out for a couple of hours in the morning, and the winds weren't raging as she had thought they would, so she allowed herself to spend the day settled with a bowl of popcorn and a marathon session of Jack Reacher. Naina kept her angelite securely in her pant pocket the whole time, and kept her blankets draped securely around her.

She thought she might hear another "hey" but it didn't come. Perhaps it had been muffled by the wind or rain. Or maybe it had been blown away by it?

The next day, after it was certain the power was back for good, and her phone battery was fully charged, she called her father and told him she'd been fired.

"I'll cover your expenses until you find a new job," he replied.

Naina was relieved, and got ready to walk around Charleston, to assess the damage of the storm.

Before she left, her father called back. "Naina, I have been covering your expenses for too long now. I should have listened to your stepmother long ago and cut you off. You'll be thirty in a couple of months. It's high time you fend for yourself. I know this won't be easy for you, so I'll wire $50,000 and that will be it, Naina. I'll give you no more for the rest of your life. But that should be enough to keep you on your feet for a while, until you figure out your next endeavor."

"Since when is it known for parents to pay their children's expenses at our age?" her stepmother spoke loudly in the background. "We're retired. If she were a dutiful daughter, she would be sending us money. She's a spoiled girl."

"What will I do?" Naina squeaked.

"Get a better job," her father said.

"Okay." There was nothing else to say. Naina hung up. Tears swelled up in her large brown eyes. It was time she learned how to be an adult and fend for herself.

She went out for a walk, as planned, feeling numb. Somehow, the conversation with her father felt like it had been forthcoming. What had taken him this long?

The city had suffered from flooding, but otherwise, it looked clean. Sadly, it seemed that unlike the storm, her life had undergone a change beyond repair. There was no way to put it back together. She had no job, no Raiya, and no support from her father. But soon, she would have a lot of money, and she would need to find a way to restore her life. Maybe she could find some of those goals Fiona had told her about.

Can You Be

She came upon a father teaching his daughter to ride a bike, and suddenly she was nostalgic for something she would never have. She was struck with a longing to be elsewhere. Was she feeling *fernweh*? It was German for having a longing for far-off places. Naina had taken German in college and still retained certain words. It couldn't be fernweh, however, because she wanted to be in a place where she was loved for who she was, but she didn't long to be in a different place. She simply longed to be loved for being herself. Or was it *sehnsucht*, then? It was German for crossed emotions about aspects in one's life that may never come or are left undone. That seemed more fitting. She yearned to have fond childhood memories with her father, and she knew she would never have them.

She had stopped in the middle of the sidewalk – there was hardly anyone out – and her breathing shortened. She took a few deep breaths and kneeled down, eventually sitting on the sidewalk. She thought of tapping and did a round of EFT. She tapped the points Fiona had shown her and was impressed she recalled them. She remembered to use an affirmation. She thought for a moment, and said, "I will find my goals."

She repeated the affirmation and did another round of tapping. It helped her feel calmer, but wasn't enough. She considered her feelings again, and readapted the EFT saying, "I am safe. I will get back on my feet."

That finally helped her feel settled, and holding on to a sense of calm, she walked back home.

❦

Naina often imagined what it would be like to hang. Her mother had jumped off a bridge and the thought of jumping off of the Ravenel Bridge seemed too public. It also didn't appear to be high enough.

Naina wondered if she could hang herself. Would the ceiling fan hold her weight? Even if it did, she would have to take some form of liquid courage. She couldn't do it on her own. Perhaps a sip of whisky would give her what she needed to climb upon a step stool and do the deed. Would the step stool be tall enough for her to reach the noose? And where would she find the rope? She would have to buy it from a hardware store. She had seen many tied to boats when she had walked through Shem Creek, which meant she could probably find the type of rope used to tie boats. They seemed strong and secure enough.

She was sure there was a YouTube video that showed her how to loop the rope around the fan to make a noose. Assuming she was able to do that securely and managed to get the rope around her neck, would she have it in her to do the final deed? Could she kick the stool away from underneath her?

She didn't know. What she did know, was she had no whisky and thus no courage to speak of. How had her mother gotten her act together to jump? Had she felt as forlorn as Naina did just then? Even if she had, how had she found the wherewithal to end her life? And why had Naina not been reason enough for her to stick around?

"Hey!" The statement was loud and clear.

Instead of reacting, Naina sat catatonic on her loveseat, the soft murmur of the evening news playing in the background. She struggled to get up. She wasn't exhausted. She was bored. She tried to envision climbing Mt. Everest or doing some other magnificent deed, Reacher or Bond style. But she couldn't picture it. Not then, at least. She didn't have it in her to end her life or to be bothered about what came next. It would all be too much effort. Too much effort to figure out how to die and too much effort to figure out how to live.

Can You Be

She knew Bond and Reacher didn't really exist. But she wanted nothing more than to have someone like them in her life. James Bond was handsome and appealing. He was so worldly and so smart and escaped any scenario. Jack Reacher was similar although perhaps he wasn't as handsome. Still, the two of them were heroes and she wished she was a hero. It wasn't that she wanted to be an athlete or anything similar. She didn't want to run on the roofs of buildings or battle bad guys. She didn't have the need to be agile, but she wanted to not need anything or anyone. To feel she was enough on her own. To make sense of her life on her own. To have nothing she was attached to. To just be.

She couldn't imagine leaving her hot and stormy paradise of Charleston. Especially not then. She grabbed her angelite and covered herself in a blanket. Even snuggled under the safety of the covers, her toxic thoughts became unbearable.

Chapter Twenty-Three

When Naina woke, she regretted she was still alive but got up anyway. She had no plans for the day and after her milk and Special K she got a notification from her bank. As promised, Naina had received the wire transfer from her father. She knew it was the last gift she would receive from him, she had taken for granted he would contribute, financially, to her life. She knew it was his way of compensating for not being present for her. But she also knew, if he hadn't been there for her in the ways she truly needed, there was no point in continuing to expect to live off of him. She needed to fend for herself, and make the best of this final $50,000.

Maybe she could do all the things she never thought she'd be able to do. Like travel. She had flown by herself to San Francisco with no issues. Surely, she could do that again. Or could she? Maybe she could leave the country. She thought of all the places she'd seen James Bond and Jack Reacher visit on screen, and racked her brain to think of suitable destinations.

Perhaps she didn't have it in her to do it on her own, but she'd heard Alice and the other people at the office saying they had done tours and cruises, and it seemed everything was arranged for them. She could do that, couldn't she? If everything was organized for her, she could definitely leave the country.

Naina had convinced herself she hadn't left the United States. That wasn't true. Her parents had taken her to India when she was a child, but she had no memory of it. As far as she was concerned, she would be traveling abroad for the first time.

She felt called to see something different, to do something for herself, to broaden her horizons and actually take that trip that had always seemed like part of the lives of others and not her own. She had always lived in a way that made it easy for her to pack and go, and she was finally going to jet off somewhere, except she was planning on coming back. But did she really have it in her to travel? Did she really have the resources to do that?

Her anxiety rose as she thought about the impending travel she hadn't yet planned. She did tapping to calm her nerves and clear her head. She did a couple rounds of EFT, and repeated the affirmation, "I am safe," in the first round and then "I have all I need to figure out my life," in the second round. She inhaled clary sage and her heartbeat slowed.

She opened her laptop and studied her finances. Naina's bank account showed the $800 from her previous balance, plus the $1200 from her last paycheck, and now the money from her father. She did a rough budget of how she would use the money over the next few months:

Rent for one year = $24,000

Utilities, food, insurance, and other expenses for one year = $9,600

Trip = $5,000

Savings = $13,400

Her heart beat faster as she thought of the prospect of having a savings account for the first time in her life. That meant she would have a security blanket, or at least that's how it felt. The remaining $13,400 would be plenty for her to figure out what she would do next. She might even be able to enroll in some courses. She had no idea what she would study, but she was going to give herself until the end of her trip to make concrete plans.

She took a deep breath and did another two rounds of EFT, assuring herself she was safe and had the resources needed to embark on the next stage of her life.

ॐ

Where would she travel to? She had no idea, but knew a walk would help. She headed toward Waterfront Park and after staring at the iconic Ravenel Bridge, the one she now had certainty she couldn't jump off, she still had no answers. The sun blasted overhead, with no cloud visible in the vast blue sky. There was certainly no evidence of the recent hurricane.

She stopped at Bakehouse to cool off and ordered an iced latte. As she slid into one of the booths at the cafe, feeling the most confused in a long time, Holy Man slid into the seat in front of her holding two brownies, each on a separate plate.

"Hello, there," he said and passed one of the plates to her.

"Will you ever tell me your name?" she asked. When had he walked in? There had been no one in line behind her, and they were at the only occupied booth.

"Don't you already have a term for me?" He winked.

Naina smiled. Somehow, this time, she wasn't surprised he knew. "I'm trying to decide where to travel to."

Can You Be

"What's holding you back?"

Naina took a bite of the brownie. The chocolate melted in her mouth. It was a true indulgence.

"The most fearsome aspect of fear is the fear itself. You have to move through it. Accept you're afraid, accept you're nervous about the decision you're facing, but don't have that be a reason to hold you back. Imagine how you would feel if you kept on with the life you've been living. You wouldn't want that would you?"

Naina spoke softly, "No, I wouldn't."

"Don't hold yourself back. We can be our own worst enemy. You're the only one who can live your life. What have you envisioned for yourself?"

Naina envisioned a life in which someone would wrap their arms around her when she needed comforting. Someone would hold her hand when she was feeling uncertain. Someone would make her a chicken noodle soup when it was cold out and would then eat the mushroom cream soup she had learned to make. Someone would set the table while she cut up the salad. Someone would look up how accurate *The Crown* was and discuss if Claire Foy, Olivia Colman, or Imelda Staunton made a better Queen Elizabeth II. Someone would tell her whether it was worth it to read Nicholas Sparks's *The Notebook*. It had been such a heartfelt movie, and they would tell her whether the book was better or worse. Someone would help her look at a world map and determine where to travel to. Someone would review the pros and cons with her about the decisions she was making.

She had never made a pros and cons list because she hadn't needed to. All the key decisions in her life seemed to have been made for her, and the few she had made for herself, like working at the real estate office or which classes she would take at the College of Charleston, she had decided without thought. She had never had to consider her options.

Could she really put together a pros and cons list? Would she be able to do it for this trip? She imagined it would be a fun exercise, but first, she had to decide where to go. There had to be options to draw out her pros and cons.

Holy Man handed her a catalog of tour organizers. They had been eating their brownies in silence and Naina had been so immersed in her thoughts she had forgotten he was there. He was looking at her with interest, making Naina feel there had been no need for her to share what was on her mind. It was as if he already knew what she was thinking. He left her with the brochure and walked out of Bakehouse, leaving Naina reading through descriptions of all the potential destinations. There were over thirty options but one tour kept calling to her. It would take her from Sweden, down the Baltic states, and back up to Finland.

The description said the Baltics were "mini nations that often went underappreciated," and in the tour they would learn about the countries' proud nationalistic approach that had helped them maintain their sovereignty as others historically vied to control them.

It sounded magical to her and like the perfect combination of well-known countries – Sweden and Finland were easily identifiable on the map – and lesser known ones – she had to look up where Estonia, Latvia, and Lithuania were located. She was so absorbed in reading the description of this trip that, until that moment, she hadn't noticed the discount. Typically, solo travelers had to pay a premium, but that month the fee would be waived. There were only four days left in August, which meant Naina had little time to make her decision.

Can You Be

She started making a pros and cons list but got distracted with other thoughts. Who would she be with on the trip? Would she like them? Would they like her? Could she change herself to make sure they liked her? Did she even need to? Would they be people she met again or did she only have to tolerate them for the ten days they would be together? Did she even have it in her to be anyone other than herself? Could she just be?

When she reviewed the list, she had written only one item on each pros and cons column, and it was the same: I don't know what I'll be facing. Naina gave up on the idea of the pros and cons list.

As soon as she got back to her apartment, she contacted the tour company and searched for flights. They offered her additional savings if she booked immediately. She checked her budget to make sure everything was within her means. As soon as she determined it was, she paid for a spot on the tour. She then bought her flights into Stockholm and out of Helsinki. She would go in a month's time, thirty-three days to be exact.

Naina didn't know whether to succumb to the nerves she was feeling or allow her heart to swell with excitement. She went to her closet to determine what to pack. She folded all of her belongings and realized they easily fit in her suitcase. She didn't pack, otherwise she would be left with nothing to wear. Still, it gave her peace of mind to know she had all she needed for the trip.

Now that she was certain how much the trip was going to cost, she adjusted her budget:

Rent for one year = $24,000

Utilities, food, insurance, and other expenses for one year = $9,600

Flight = $900

Baltic Tour = $3,333

Miscellaneous trip expenses = $767

Savings = $13,400

She still had $13,400 to figure out her future, which seemed like more than enough money. She would still allow herself to wait until the end of the trip to consider her options.

Chapter Twenty-Four

Ten days later Naina sat at City Lights Coffee and Holy Man, dressed in the same white linen suit, slid into the chair opposite her. He carried a coffee cup while munching on a Key Lime bar. Once again, Naina wondered when he had arrived. She seemed to constantly miss his entrances and exits. She'd been sitting facing the doorway and had not noticed anyone walk in. She was busy brainstorming career options. She really wanted to figure out what she could be.

Even though she would wait until after the trip to take any action, she hoped to at least decide on her next step. She was mired with confusion and needed at least a semblance of certainty. She wanted to take one thing at a time as Fiona had suggested, but was desperate to know what direction she was headed, even if it wasn't what she'd hoped.

"Let me see your crystal," he said.

As always, she carried the angelite with her. She took it out and put it in his hands. After booking the trip to Europe, Naina spent more and more time in coffee shops. With no job to go to, she didn't want to spend all day in her apartment. She went for walks and invariably ended up in coffee shops. She read through local job postings, imagining herself in any of the roles but not feeling connected to any.

Holy Man let the angelite spin in his palm, closed his eyes, and held it still in both hands. His lips moved as if reciting an incantation. He opened his eyes, his expression solemn, a sharp contrast to his usual jovial and lighthearted way.

"You know what you love, Naina. It's something you dedicate much of your time to." He touched his index finger to the tip of her nose.

It brought Naina goosebumps. Until then, she had forgotten her mother used to do that to her.

"I've booked my trip. I'm all set to go in less than a month."

"Yes, I know that's settled. This is about something bigger."

Naina drew a blank.

Holy Man gave her back the crystal. He finished off the Key Lime bar and coffee and wiped his mouth. Before leaving, Holy Man said, "Repeat this to yourself, Naina. 'I can. I will. I am.'"

Naina didn't understand, but didn't ask him to clarify. She went back to reading the classifieds in the Sunday paper. It seemed archaic to look for a job that way, but she figured it would help her decide what she loved to do. It was then she noticed the sign for help wanted at the coffee shop. She asked the lady behind the counter who explained they were looking for a barista. No experience necessary. She would be taught the day-to-day tasks. What was better, she would be paid the same hourly wage she'd received at the real estate agency.

Naina visualized herself working behind the counter. Maybe

she would even learn how to have a personable attitude. Spending so much time with Raiya made her feel it was possible.

Just then, two college-aged women walked into the coffeeshop, and settled in the table next to hers. "I would give anything to have someone show me how to take care of my skin. Just a couple of natural products, and that's it. So much of what is out there is pure hype."

Naina knew the answer. Had she been bolder – like Raiya – she would have turned to the women and answered their questions. She had a natural skin care regime. Her skin was as smooth as fresh-woven brown silk.

Something sparked within Naina in that moment. What if, she wondered. What if she taught others how to take care of their skin in a natural way? Her simplicity and frugality had led her to discover that true skincare didn't require expensive creams. What if this was her thing?

She brushed the thought aside. She couldn't bring herself to speak to those women.

ॐ

A week later, for that's what it took for Naina to gather all the supplies, she set up a makeshift treatment table in her bedroom. She had shared with Fiona her idea about teaching others how to use natural skincare, and Fiona had offered her face for Naina to practice on.

"I think facials are the best way to teach others about natural skincare. Otherwise you'd have to become a sales representative for a natural skincare line or something. I can't imagine you doing that," Fiona had said.

"I can't see myself doing that either. Sales isn't for me," Naina had confirmed.

"But if you were to become an esthetician, you could."

"What do you mean?"

"My esthetician taught me my skincare routine. The first time I had a facial with her, she explained everything she did and recommended all the products I use now. She didn't have to do much selling because the effects spoke for themselves. It didn't feel like she was hard selling, but more like she was educating me. I go to her at least once a month."

"That seems more like something I could do. If I could develop the skills, of course."

And so they had agreed to schedule a trial facial for that Friday evening in mid-September. Naina hadn't been able to imagine what it would be like to give another person a facial, having never had one herself and this session with Fiona would give Naina the chance to consider being an esthetician.

Naina had researched online all she could about doing facials. Her own routine wasn't enough. She needed to ensure the face was properly cleansed. This seemed the most crucial part of the facial and typically involved using a cleanser, as well as exfoliation and extractions. She didn't feel capable to do extractions on Fiona but could at least use a cleanser and exfoliator.

Naina didn't have a treatment table and learned that even a portable one cost around $500, which wasn't in her budget. She had put together a makeshift one at the end of her bed, and sat on a stool while working on Fiona's face.

Naina's hands shook, unable to dispel her nerves throughout the facial, and what was supposed to take twenty minutes, took nearly an hour.

The mattress wasn't a stable surface. The product bottles got knocked over several times, and Naina had to move them to the floor, but then leaned down regularly to get what she needed. Her lower back was sore from the effort. After going through an entire box of facial tissues attempting to remove product off of Fiona's face, parts of the tissues broke off, with remnants still visible on Fiona's face and on Naina's hands.

"Naina, don't take this the wrong way, but the massage was the worst part. The cleanser and exfoliation were acceptable, minus the residue left on my face."

"Residue?"

"Yes, I still have a bunch of product on my skin. I felt the exfoliation beads throughout the facial and it wasn't nice." Fiona wiped her face and removed some of the shreds of tissue still attached.

Naina's head grew hot, even though the AC and fan were on. "I'm so sorry, Fiona."

"The massage didn't feel relaxing. Your hands are cold and clammy, although I know it's because you're nervous. So, I understand. But I also felt your nails—"

"Oh no. Did I scratch you?"

"No, no. I'm fine. You didn't scratch me at all. But feeling your nails wasn't pleasant."

They remained silent for a few moments. Naina's face and body grew warmer and she sweated profusely.

"You just need more practice." Fiona tried to sound enthusiastic.

Naina knew it was a lost cause. Even though it was her first attempt, there was no way she could become an esthetician. Training seemed beyond her reach.

At least it was only fourteen days before she went on her trip. Time was passing quickly. Not only would she distract herself with preparing for the trip, but she would stop trying so hard to resolve things right away. She hoped being away would give her the clarity she needed. Maybe she would get inspired while being abroad and figure out what she would do with her life, what she could be.

Chapter Twenty-Five

In the first days of October, when she landed in Stockholm, it was past two in the morning in Charleston, and yet Naina felt more awake than ever in her life. It was eight in the morning in Sweden, and the taste of possibility was in the air. The crispness helped, and she took the cleanest and purest breath she had ever inhaled.

She dropped things off at the hotel and, just for good measure, she did a couple of rounds of EFT to make sure she was calm before being picked up by a large overcrowded bus. The Stockholm portion of the trip was handled by a third-party.

Even though it was two weeks after the start of fall, she needed a winter coat, but didn't care. For the first time in precisely two months she felt free, as if the burden had been lifted, as if she was certain that no terrible occurrence could behold her.

Still, she had her angelite on her, and wore a face mask. Naina continuously wiped down surfaces, and sanitized and then moisturized her hands, to ensure she remained as germ-free as possible.

Her and the more than thirty other people on the bus learned Spotify, H&M, IKEA, Ericsson, and Volvo were some of the global companies that had originated in Sweden. As she listened to the information the tour guide shared, she considered, if she too could be a tour guide.

They visited the City Hall, which held the annual banquet for the Nobel prizes. They went to Stockholm's well-preserved medieval city center called Gamla Stan. They walked through the winding streets, taking in the shops, restaurants, and galleries. There, they visited the Royal Palace and the Stockholm Cathedral. The buildings and streets were far more grand than anything she had seen in Charleston or in San Francisco, as if history truly permeated in every step of the city. History emanated from Charleston and San Francisco, but not quite in the same way. There had been some type of settlement in Stockholm since the Stone Age, and the city had been founded in 1252. This type of trajectory simply did not exist in the cities in the United States.

They went to the Vasa Museum, which held the best-preserved seventeenth-century boat, and although it had sunk and was restored after spending hundreds of years under water, 98% of the ship was original.

In the evening, they were given time on their own and Naina ordered *ärtsoppa*, a Swedish yellow-pea soup made with chicken. It was served with pancakes topped with fruit syrup and whipped cream.

Naina certainly knew enough about Charleston to be a tour guide, but she didn't know if she'd be comfortable dealing with such a large group of people on a daily basis. The job would be repetitive, having to blurt out the same information every day. Naina had cherished her routines – still did – but perhaps she needed to break away from them. No, she wouldn't be a tour guide.

As she made her way back to the hotel, she felt given the chance, she could make a life for herself in Stockholm. Naina loved that in Charleston she had the proximity to the ocean and rivers. All of Sweden was close to a source of water too; and whether it be ocean, lake, or river, some type of water was usually within reach. The country was sparsely populated and a majority was covered in forest. There was a high chance she'd find trees as inspirational and magical as Angel Oak.

If Naina'd had the chance to grow up in Sweden, her life would have turned out quite differently. Perhaps she would have been more likely to find a satisfactory job that paid well and made her feel she had access to the type of life she wanted, without having to depend on her father for money. Sweden had one of the most egalitarian societies in which the income gap between the working and upper classes was one of the smallest in the world, and men and women were treated relatively equally.

Both parents were eligible for parental leave up to eight months. Naina didn't know if either of her parents had taken time off to care for her when she was born and although she would never know, she vowed if she ever had a child, she would take as much time as possible to ensure her child was well taken care of.

The more she learned about the country, the more she felt she would fit in given the chance to grow up there. The only deterrent was the weather. The highest temperature that day had reached 54°F, but she learned temperatures in the winter averaged around 25°F and daylight was limited to six hours, which was truly depressing.

Between the jet lag, tiredness, and all that circled her head, Naina slept soundly for twelve hours before catching a flight to Tallinn, Estonia in the morning.

Chapter Twenty-Six

When Naina landed in Tallinn, she was surprised she got through the airport and into the taxi in less than twenty minutes. Erroneously, she had considered the country would be more disorganized, yet everything was processed seamlessly.

She arrived at the hotel in ten minutes but her room wasn't ready. She walked around the old town and had a cardamom roll with a Fentiman's Victorian lemonade for lunch at Maiasmokk Kohvik, the oldest coffee shop in Tallinn, which had been there since 1864.

It wasn't a traditional lunch, but she had been too nervous to enter a restaurant on her own. This one had a long line of tourists and she overheard them ordering in English. She made a quick decision and got in line. She stuck her hand in her purse, hoping her angelite would bring her comfort and realized she'd left it in a different bag than the one she had brought. She debated on whether or not to do tapping in such a public place and chose against it. Before she knew it, it was her turn to order. She pointed to the first pastry she saw and ordered a lemonade and a coffee that was much too strong. She was delighted that the pastry was delicious. There was something about the sweet doughy bread that reminded her of Indian food. Perhaps it was the cardamom, but Naina wasn't sure. It made her yearn for a home she'd never have.

❧

Naina took a brief nap before meeting the rest of the group and a cold sweat enveloped her when she faced the other six tourists along with the tour guide and driver. This time, she made sure she brought her angelite with her, and held it in her palm. The sense of familiarity calmed her, but she regretted not doing tapping in her room before meeting everyone. She hadn't expected the tour to have so few people.

There were two other women and the rest were men. Their snug group of eight meant Naina couldn't lose herself in the group. She had expected it would be a large group, like in Stockholm, where she could remain anonymous. Now, she would be forced to interact with everyone and, to her dismay, the first activity was to introduce each other. The Stockholm tour hadn't included any introductions, save for the tour guide, and she didn't remember his name. He had merely been the voice over the headset she'd been asked to carry.

First to introduce himself was the guide, Priidik. He was six-feet tall, stocky, with solid muscles, as if he worked out for a major part of the day. He was Estonian but had traveled extensively throughout the region. His hair was golden blonde, which surprised Naina, as she had expected him to look more Russian, yet he appeared more Scandinavian. He noticed Naina looking at him. "You're probably surprised to see a blonde Estonian ... that's one of the comments

I get asked about most by newcomers to the area, and you'll be surprised to hear Estonia has the highest number of blondes per capita of any country in the world. We are more closely associated to Finland than any of our Baltic neighbors. Even Estonian as a language is Finnic, whereas Latvian and Lithuanian are Baltic."

Naina's face grew hot and she looked away, but not for long. Priidik had the deepest blue eyes Naina had ever seen. Despite her embarrassment at being caught looking, she couldn't stop staring at his eyes. Others in the group were also staring at him. Since he was the tour guide, it was inevitable to look at him and it dawned on Naina she could stare at him without concern. She was now completely certain she couldn't be a tour guide. She wouldn't be able to tolerate so many eyes on her at once.

She allowed herself to look at Priidik freely, as he shared he was fluent in Latvian and could get by with a little Lithuanian. Naina chided herself for not knowing the three countries had different languages. She had assumed that because they had been previous Soviet territories, most people spoke Russian.

"Do you speak Russian?" one of the ladies asked, seemingly having similar thoughts to Naina.

"Very little. Only a small percentage of the population in the countries we'll be visiting speak Russian as a native language, with the exception of one of the cities on our tour, and that is Narva, where over 90% of the population speaks Russian. In other places we'll be visiting, Russian-speakers are a minority. In Estonia, 24% are Russian-speaking; in Latvia 37% are Russian-speaking; and in Lithuania, only 8% are Russian-speaking."

Naina was curious about the other participants. A man stood next to Priidik who looked as though he was related to him. There were the two ladies in their mid-fifties who Naina assumed were friends. Naina guessed they might have wanted to go on a trip together for a long time and had finally found the opportunity. Two men stood close to each other, as if they were a couple. Naina assumed they had been together for so long they no longer knew where the one ended and the other began. Finally, there was a man on his own. He exuded bitterness, as if life hadn't treated him kindly and he wanted to ensure everyone knew about it.

Before Naina got a chance to get carried away making up stories about her fellow tour goers, the introductions continued. Next were the two ladies, Gemma and Caroline. They were from Glasgow and spoke in an accent Naina found hard to follow. They both worked but she couldn't understand in what. Her guess of them had been right. They were life-long friends and one was a recent widow and the other had never married.

"We've been wanting to travel through Eastern Europe since we graduated uni, but life got in the way and we weren't able to make it work until now," Gemma said.

"I had to lose my husband to find time to travel, it seems," Caroline piped in. Gemma put her arm on Caroline's arm and squeezed tightly. Caroline looked back at Gemma gratefully.

"In Estonia, we don't consider ourselves to be Eastern European," Priidik clarified.

"What's considered Eastern Europe, then?" one of the men asked. It turned out he was Xavier, the other single traveler in addition to Naina. He was sixty-five and had just retired after a life-long career in the mining industry. He had gifted this trip to himself. He was from Perth, Australia and his hair was completely white.

"I am not sure what Eastern Europe is anymore," Priidik confessed. "I understand the perception came from being part of the Soviet Union, when this area was considered part of the eastern bloc or the former communist Europe, but since that's been dissolved, we are really northern Europe."

"Try explaining that to an American. I'm not sure they'll buy it." He introduced himself as Lou.

Lou and Pat were a retired gay couple from San Diego, California. They'd had a medical practice together and were avid travelers. They had visited at least one new country every year while they had their practice, and often managed two or three a year. Since retiring, they upped their count to at least three new countries per year. This trip would fill their quota for the current year.

"When we're done with this tour, we'll have visited eighty-three countries together. With our age of seventy-three, that's quite a feat," Lou said.

Pat looked right at Naina, who was clearly the youngest of the group, save Priidik, who also appeared to be in his mid-thirties, and said, "But don't you concern yourself. We're still fit as fiddles and won't be slowing you down … except maybe when it comes to stairs." Pat winked.

Naina attempted a tight smile, and nodded her head in case it wasn't obvious she was smiling. So far there wasn't anyone who had a profession she was interested in finding more about. She had no interest in medicine or mining. Her only chance was to get clarity on what the ladies did. Maybe they could provide some insight.

There was dead silence as everyone looked at her. Naina worried her inability to smile had already upset them.

"What about you?" Priidik asked, looking at her.

"Me?" Naina squeaked. She cleared her throat.

"Yes, tell us your name and a bit about yourself, like where you're from and why you're on this trip?"

Naina cleared her throat again. "My name is Naina." She said it slowly so everyone would understand. Several in the group repeated it out loud, and she nodded slowly, pleased she hadn't needed to correct anyone.

"Where are you from?" Priidik asked again.

"Charleston, South Carolina in the United States."

The group nodded back. All eyes were still on her and Naina cleared her throat again. She played with her angelite in her hand, averting everyone's gaze.

Priidik cleared his throat. "Why did you decide to come on this trip, Naina?"

"Oh ... yes ... right. Sorry." Naina's face flushed hot as everyone seemed to look back at her sympathetically. She kept her hand on her angelite and took a deep breath. "I got fired from my job at a real estate firm. I was the receptionist. I wanted to treat myself before deciding what to do next. This is my first trip abroad."

"I'm sorry to hear, darling. I'm sure you'll figure it out soon," Gemma said.

"I'll give you some tips if you want to stay in real estate," Caroline chimed in.

Naina knew there was no way she was staying in real estate, but nodded politely. Now, she only needed to know what Gemma did.

"Do you mean this is your first time outside of America?" Xavier asked.

After several moments of silence, the group exchanged looks with each other. Naina stared at the floor, still playing with the angelite in her palm and deeply grateful she hadn't left it behind. "That I remember."

Xavier guffawed.

Naina's face got warm, and she held on tightly to her angelite.

Priidik pointed to the man standing next to him, the one who looked like he was his father, and said, "Right then, let me introduce you to Artur, our driver. He is a native of Tallinn but doesn't speak much English. He's an excellent driver and will be taking care of us during our entire trip. He requested that all of you bring out your bags each morning and deposit them in the back of the van. He will organize them himself in the car, and he will take the bags out of the car."

Artur was six-foot two-inches, stocky built with ash blonde hair. He looked to be in his fifties and, once again, appeared as if he was related to Priidik.

"Are you two related?" Gemma asked, once again as if reading Naina's mind.

Naina was more impressed with the ease in which Gemma asked questions than at Artur's size, although Naina hadn't seen muscles that big on anyone before. He looked capable to easily juggle several suitcases on his own, and Naina wondered if handling bags was one of the ways he kept so fit. Still, there was a softness about him. He was as big as a bear and as gentle as a teddy. He had been smiling and nodding while Priidik spoke.

"Welcome," Artur said, his smile so big it reminded Naina of Holy Man. All that was missing was the sparkle in his teeth. And there was a wisdom about Artur, like he'd lived multiple lives and had knowledge to share.

"We may look alike, but we're not related," Priidik said.

There was something about Priidik that made Naina feel the same about him, like he too had a lot of wisdom to impart. But instead of sharing sage advice, Priidik gave them an overview of what they were going to see over the next eleven days, and took them to walk the old town.

"Estonians are, in fact, directly related to the Finnish but have had a different outcome to their history. The Finnish consider Estonia as its unfortunate cousin, and have many times provided aid to us. Even when Estonia was occupied by the Soviets, Finland used the cover of 'cultural cooperation' to provide financial and other types of aid to Estonia. The affinity between the two countries remains to this day, and it was estimated that nearly 80% of Finns have visited Estonia."

"You're very good with your percentages," Pat commented.

"I know my history well," Priidik replied.

Naina related. She too knew concrete facts about Charleston.

As they walked through the old town, remnants of this history were visible, from Lutheran style churches to Russian Orthodox ones.

"How do the Estonians feel about the Russian invasion into Ukraine?" Xavier asked.

"They feel quite strongly about it. All the Baltic countries do. They all regained independence from the Soviets between 1990 and 1991, and feel proud of this. They vehemently condemn Russia encroaching over Ukraine," Priidik explained.

"Even the Russian speaking ones?" Xavier followed up.

"The ability to speak Russian has to do with cultural roots, not country alliances, so yes, even Russian speakers do not generally support Russia invading Ukraine. There are exceptions, of course."

"I find that hard to believe," Xavier scoffed.

The group continued to walk in silence. Naina hoped this wasn't a sign for how the rest of the trip would be.

❧

The streets around Tallinn felt to Naina like walking through a medieval town. Quaint houses and cobbled streets were found throughout the old town, and not just in select areas as in Charleston. Tallinn was clearly older, and Naina felt as if she had been transported in time, which made sense when Priidik told them the city became self-governing in 1248, although it was founded two hundred years before, which made it much older than Stockholm. There had been a settlement in the area for nearly five-thousand years.

"The only medieval experience in the US is Excalibur in Las Vegas," Lou pointed out, clearly trying to dissipate the tension in the air.

Naina realized she wasn't the only one doing mental comparisons.

"And it comes with drinks, dinner, and 'The Tournament of Kings.' If you want to make it more cultural, you can go for dessert and a nightcap at Luxor with the Egyptian pharaohs. It may even be King Tut, as I recall," Pat added. Everyone in the group, except for Naina erupted in laughter, the air finally gaining some ease. Naina had never been to Las Vegas and had no idea what they were referring to.

"Tallinn is one of the best preserved capital cities in Europe," Priidik explained. He shared that it had been intact since the thirteenth century and, because of it, was a UNESCO World Heritage Site.

Yes, everything she was likely to encounter would be far older than Charleston. But Tallinn felt more approachable than Stockholm had. The air was equally crisp and clean, like there wasn't a single pollutant in proximity. The old town was small and manageable, giving Naina the sense she could easily find her way around and regretted she wasn't staying long enough to accomplish that. She would have loved to learn more about the countless ghosts that surely inhabited the city.

Just then, Naina was captivated with the pink-orange hues that came over the town as the sun set. She marveled at them on St. Olav's Church Tower. She couldn't imagine what it would be like to have eighteen hours of sunlight in the summer or eighteen hours of dark in the winter, as was common this far north. Even in October, they averaged slightly more than nine hours of daylight, with the sun rising after 7:30am and setting around 6:30pm.

Priidik took them to a local bar where drinks were served from leather skins, as if to recreate medieval times. After the brief reprieve, they continued their walk through the cobblestone streets. They ended the evening at an authentic Estonian food restaurant. They started with shots of Vana Tallinn, a legendary liquor of Estonia, the recipe for which remained a mystery.

"Estonian for cheers is terviseks. It means, to your health," Priidik said.

Naina took a sip of the Vana Tallinn and let the liquid burn as it made its way to her stomach. She realized she hadn't eaten anything since the cardamom roll.

"What is cheers in the other languages?" Gemma asked.

"In Latvian it is priekā and it means, in pleasure or in joy. And in Lithuanian it has the same meaning as in Estonian, to your health and is Įsveikatą."

"There is no way I'll remember those," Caroline said laughing.

"The Estonian one is simpler," Lou piped in. "I thought of topsy turvy, and it's like saying turvy-sex."

The entire group broke out into laughter, including Naina, but she wondered how they all engaged in conversation so easily. If she hadn't been at the introductions, she would have sworn they'd known each other previously. They spoke with ease and confidence, and Naina wondered if she would fit in or stand out because she wasn't talking much. All she mustered were a few nods here and there and an occasional snug smile as the chatter continued throughout the meal.

She didn't know why it happened then, but at that moment, it dawned on her she would never again have to make the 678-step walk to the office, and suddenly, she felt free.

Chapter Twenty-Seven

They started that October morning with a buffet breakfast at the hotel. Naina was determined to try new foods and do her best to release the structure she'd created at home. She had read about foods eaten in Sweden, the Baltic countries, and Finland, and already knew it was unlikely that she'd find Special K, 2% milk, digestives, or any of the foods she typically prepared for herself at home. Still, facing the buffet table made her heart beat faster. At the hotel in Sweden, she had stuck to muesli, yoghurt, and berries, but here, she was determined to stretch her limits.

Angelite in her pocket, Naina arrived at the breakfast room right at seven when it opened, so it was less likely she would have to sit with one of her travel companions, and so she had plenty of time to decide what to eat. After all, they didn't have to leave until nine.

Naina was relieved she was the first to arrive and despite passing the first hurdle, she took a few deep breaths before picking up a plate and facing the buffet. She served herself one of each item and at the end of the line her plate looked like a skeletal version of the buffet display. It consisted of a spoon of salad, a cucumber, a cherry tomato, pickled herring, a meat ball, a sausage, muesli, a spoon of yoghurt, one slice of toast, one egg, and one roasted potato. She placed the plate at a table and poured a glass of orange juice as well as a glass of water. She served herself a flat white coffee from an automated machine and sat at the table, doing two rounds of EFTs before tasting everything. She repeated the affirmation, "I am safe to try new things." She took a deep breath. And then a few more. And finally, she began tasting the food.

She took tiny bites and chewed slowly making sure she wouldn't have to spit out any food she didn't like. Naina liked the taste of it all albeit, being certain she wouldn't usually have salad or fish for breakfast. Even the pickled herring was tolerable.

By the time she finished her plate, Gemma and Caroline arrived for breakfast and asked to sit with her. Naina nodded, relieved they hadn't seen her plate. She watched them carefully as they oohed and aaahed and commented about all of the breakfast items. The ladies had opted for only the warm food.

"Did you try the fish, Naina?" Caroline asked.

"I did."

"How was it?"

"Not bad."

Gemma laughed. "Did you have to spit it out?"

"No, I ate it all."

"You did better than my students would, I'm sure," Gemma added.

"Students?" Naina asked.

"Yes. You must have missed it yesterday. I shared with everyone that I'm a primary school teacher."

"And I work in real estate. Same as you used to," Caroline piped in.

"Sorry ... I didn't miss it. I know you both mentioned what you did but I couldn't understand what you said. I have a hard time with the accent," Naina admitted sheepishly, although she was relieved to finally know the women's professions. No, she definitely wasn't going back to real estate, but was teaching an option for her?

"Oh darling, don't you worry yourself. We'll try to tone it down, won't we?" Gemma said reassuringly.

Caroline nodded, "We sure will, doll."

The ladies asked Naina questions about where she worked and the circumstances under which she got fired. Naina was surprised at how comfortable she felt speaking with them. The sympathetic look in their eyes was reassuring.

"You're safe with us, hen. I dare say you're safe even with the rest of the guys. They all look like they're good folk," Gemma assured, as if reading her mind. "We're all friends here, so don't worry about what you say. We won't judge you, for sure." Gemma motioned between her and Caroline, who nodded and smiled reassuringly.

※

Following breakfast Artur drove them to Väike-Õismäe, a Soviet-era neighborhood designed in the late 1960s. The name meant, "lesser blossom hill." Artur parked the van and the group walked around the neighborhood as Priidik explained it was designed such that the buildings formed concentric circles around an artificial lake, which was surrounded by tracks, paths, green areas, shops, schools, and many other facilities. The taller buildings were located toward the inner part of the circle and the shorter ones toward the inside. It was meant to be conducive to creating a community feeling so there was interaction among the families and residents; it was meant to be an urban utopia.

Naina couldn't see how it would have been considered a utopia. The buildings looked bleak and inconsequential.

"Were they meant to be this dull?" Gemma asked.

Once again it was as if Gemma was reading her mind.

"Construction was purposefully not extravagant to give it a standard or plain feel, so everyone was in a comparable situation. In the end, the full planning for the community didn't come to fruition and the extensive facilities weren't built. From the original seventy-five grocery stores that were planned, only three of them opened. This resulted in residents having to stand in long lines just to get their food and other staples. It was far from the intended utopia, and now stands as an eccentric area to visit towards the outskirts of Tallinn," Priidik answered.

Naina much preferred the old town. It had more character and charisma than this neighborhood, but she kept her thoughts to herself. The weather was similar to Stockholm, but still, Naina was grateful when they all returned to the van. The neighborhood gave her a chill she hadn't felt earlier.

They stopped at a Circle K for coffee and a snack, giving Naina hope she might be able to keep up with her mid-morning coffee and biscuits throughout the trip. Sure, she was determined not to consume digestives or a similar type of biscuit. She would try something new.

She was thrilled the coffee was available through automatic machines and everything was translated into English. There were a few baked goods, which included *pirukas*. They were interestingly filled pastry pockets and, in case Naina didn't like the taste, she bought herself a KitKat. At least she would have a backup.

Can You Be

Naina approached Priidik outside the van as she sipped on a flat white and took a bite of the piruka. The pasty ended up being savory and was filled with ham and vegetables. She liked it, but she was also happy she had gotten the KitKat because she had been after something sweet. "Will we be stopping for snacks every day?"

Priidik smiled at her reassuringly. "We will definitely stop for regular breaks, yes. And if you ever feel the need to stop, please don't hesitate to speak up."

"I will, thank you."

"You know what you should try that originated in Estonia?"

Nania's mouth was full and shook her head.

"Marzipan. It's been made in Tallinn for six hundred years."

"I didn't realize it came from here. I thought it was from the Middle East."

Next was a tour of Rummu Quarry Prison, where an energetic Latvian who spoke clear English took them enthusiastically throughout the abandoned facility. Naina had never visited a prison, having only seen them in shows, but *Orange is the New Black*, *The Night Of*, and *Prison Break* didn't prepare her for this.

Even though it wasn't in use, a cold sensation lifted the hairs on the back of Naina's neck when she saw the entrance. The driveway had openings in the concrete floor where guards used to check the undercarriage of arriving vehicles. By the time they visited the maximum-security cells which had a lingering smell of urine and excrement, she'd had enough. She'd always imagined her life was restricted, but the confinement she felt walking through the buildings was beyond her comprehension. Even the main prison guards' comparatively luxurious accommodation, which were larger than her apartment in Charleston, felt tight, damp, and enclosed. The rain didn't help and as they walked from one building to another, the dampness soaked through her being.

Naina searched for her angelite and, in dismay, realized once again, she didn't have it. She turned out all the pockets in her coat and pants, and everything in her bag, laying it out on the wet grass. Her pulse quickened and closing her eyes, she did a quick round of tapping, repeating, "I will find the angelite."

When she finished, she remembered she had removed the angelite from her pocket before brushing her teeth after breakfast, and had likely left the angelite in the bathroom.

Xavier stood over her. "Lose something?"

Naina glanced at him as she collected her items back into her bag. "I thought I had but turns out I didn't."

"You could help her pick up her things, couldn't you?" Caroline commented as she approached them.

"It's okay, I've gathered everything," Naina said.

Xavier walked away from them.

"Are you okay, doll?" Caroline asked.

"Yes … I thought I'd lost something but now I think I left it at the hotel."

"Is it that crystal ball you carry around? I've seen you with it."

Naina wondered how Caroline knew. "Yes. That's right."

"It must be a special crystal. I'm sure you'll find it, doll."

Lunch was at an American styled diner and as everyone bit into their burgers, Priidik asked, "Was that everyone's first time visiting a prison?"

Gemma and Caroline had been to several, mostly in Scotland, Northern Ireland, and Ireland. Xavier had visited Alcatraz, and Leo and Pat had gone to all the ones Gemma, Caroline, and Xavier visited, and many more throughout their trips in Croatia,

Romania, and Bulgaria. They were looking forward to the other prisons planned for the trip. It turned out Naina was the only one who had visited a prison for the first time.

"How was it for you?" Leo asked her.

"Daunting …"

"Because of the size?"

"Because of the horrible conditions. I can't understand how humans can survive under those circumstances."

Pat nodded. "Prisons aren't meant to be humane. They are meant to house people who have committed heinous crimes, remove them from society, and punish them. They don't go there to go on holiday. I think the thought of prison is what hopefully deters people from breaking the law."

Naina understood that, but she still found them inhumane. She hadn't been locked away, but she had felt as if she had during the years she had lived at boarding schools. She wasn't able to leave, even during the holidays because her father and stepmother didn't want her. She understood what it felt like to be stuck somewhere and never wanted to feel that way again.

On the way back to Tallinn, Naina asked Priidik about crystal shops.

"Tallinn used to be a good place to buy crystals in Soviet times. I think most of what you can find now is from Czech Republic or Germany."

Naina didn't express her disappointment and sat quietly in the van for the remainder of the ride back to Tallinn city.

That afternoon, they walked to Linnahall, an abandoned complex designed for the 1980 Summer Olympics hosted in the Soviet Union. At the time, Estonia had been occupied by the Soviets, and the structure had been designed to be a multi-purpose venue that was originally called the V.I. Lenin Palace of Culture and Sports.

The crumbling empty buildings had been used to house an amphitheater, ice hall, seaport, and heliport but weren't well maintained and were decorated with graffiti.

The rain had dissipated but clouds still hung low in the sky.

"The movie *Tennet* was filmed here," Priidik stated, rather proudly.

Naina hadn't watched the movie and didn't have a frame of reference, but it seemed that others in the group had and became engaged in a conversation without Naina. Several times, Naina thought she spotted Holy Man, but when she looked closer she realized it wasn't him. Could he travel? She didn't think so, but wasn't sure.

They walked on from there, along the coast, and on to Patarei Prison. Naina refused to go inside, already too disturbed by the morning visit, and opted instead to have a drink at one of the local bars outside the prison, a place where youths chose to party. She felt more confident ordering on her own and preferred to look out onto the Baltic Sea than to learn about another place where people had been held captive. She was grateful no one in the group questioned her decision, and Priidik had been accommodating enough to suggest she sit this one out.

They ended the evening by walking through the fisherman's neighborhood called Kalamaja, which was close to the water and had many traditional looking homes and buildings. They walked toward industrial and old warehouse areas that had been modernized and ended up in a restaurant called F-Hoone. The group shared a plate of meat dumplings covered in creamy mushroom sauce with roasted onions on top. As a main dish, Naina ordered the salmon fillet with ricotta gnocchi. Everything tasted fresh and like an explosion of flavors in her mouth. How was something seemingly so simple, also so tasty? Would she be able to prepare food like this, one day?

Before heading to the hotel, Priidik took her aside. "Are you feeling okay? I noticed you were affected by the prisons. What is it that concerns you?"

"I'm sorry, I didn't know I would be affected. I hadn't been to a prison before and I didn't know what the experience was going to be like. I have a hard time imagining people having to live under those conditions. It bothered me more than I expected." She left out how bothered she felt without her angelite.

Priidik looked at her with concern. "But are you okay now?"

"Yes." Naina took a deep breath, realizing she'd been taking a lot of those. "Yes," she said again, more convincingly.

"We still have three more prisons to visit on this trip, one in Latvia and two in Lithuania. You can opt out of those as well. Don't push yourself to do something you don't want to do. We can take it as it comes."

This trip was pushing her in more ways than she had expected, and Naina nodded in response. She was grateful that instead of showing contempt towards her, he was compassionate. "Thank you. I'll see how I feel when the time comes."

Chapter Twenty-Eight

Naina hardly slept at night, tossing and turning throughout, flitting in and out of dreams. Her throat was parched for much of the night and she drank more water than usual, which meant she also kept on getting up to pee. But really, she couldn't shut her mind off, imagining herself in prison. She had spent much of her life believing she was limited, but seeing Rummu Quarry Prison made her realize she didn't know what it meant to be truly limited.

When she got out of bed, the damp and mold still infested her nose and she tried her best to rub the smell out. Naina did several rounds of EFT. She wondered if not having the angelite with her had affected her? Or was it really just about the prisons? Or was it both?

She would make sure from then on to keep the angelite secure in the outside pocket of her shoulder bag. She would try her best not to take it out. Maybe she didn't need to hold the crystal but merely keep it close to her. That would be the safest approach since, from that point onward, they would be staying in a different hotel every night. Losing her crystal would be disastrous.

At breakfast, she once again served a little of everything on the buffet, but this time, she served more of what she had enjoyed the previous morning, which included two slices of brown bread, three meatballs, and two servings of pickled herring. She dared enough to make an open sandwich out of them with slices of cheese, as she had seen in Sweden, and delighted in each mouthful.

They checked out of the hotel and as promised to Artur, everyone left their bags outside the van before boarding, allowing him to organize the luggage as he pleased. The van sat twelve so the seven of them had ample space to spread out. Priidik sat in the front right and Naina sat in the single seat on the same row. Leo and Pat sat behind them, Gemma and Caroline in the row behind that, and Xavier took the back seat.

"These aren't assigned seats. Anyone can choose to sit where they like or even move around as we travel. I would request though, that you always leave these two seats up front for me so I can make sure to speak to all of you and also communicate with Artur."

Naina was comfortable where she was. She had a window seat and she could look out of the front windshield. There was no way she was going to move around.

As if sensing her intentions, Priidik added, "But if any of you become attached to your seat, that is okay too."

They visited the Maarjamäe Memorial Complex, which overlooked Tallinn Bay, located towards the outskirts of the city. The obelisk was immediately visible. Priidik told them it was built in honor of the Bolsheviks who had died during the 1918 Russian Civil War.

It was controversial because these same Bolsheviks had fought against the Estonians at the time. When the Soviets invaded the country, new monuments started to appear in the 1950s as pro-Soviet expressions. The ones at Maarjamäe were no longer maintained and had thus fallen into disrepair. Instead, a counter-monument was set up in 2018 to commemorate the nearly 75,000 Estonians killed during the Soviet rule.

Naina didn't realize so many had suffered under the Soviets. The day before, she had thought the worst part of the Soviet presence in Tallinn had been the drab looking buildings from Väike-Õismäe.

Naina spent the ride to the village of Tuhala in contemplative silence. She had known communism was restrictive, but visiting the memorial complex was the first time she learned it had been this deadly. Naina had understood the purpose of communism was to ensure that all people in the society were in equal standing and thus had equal opportunities. It was meant to be more inclusive and supportive of the community. People were meant to work together and support one another and everyone was to have equal access to all resources, including education and jobs.

Naina had learned that in reality, those in the highest echelons of government had lived in luxury while the rest of the population had not. Opportunities were limited, and people were often forced to work in jobs they didn't want or that offered no advancement. Government was harsh on opposition and on dissenters, and they tried their best to quell it. Instead of true education, they often resorted to propaganda to control the narrative and information available to its people.

She had known all this prior to the trip. But until that day, Naina hadn't realized people had been killed under communist rule, and that shook something in her. Restriction could lead to death.

When they arrived at the Witch's Well, however, her interest perked up. The Witch's Well was a natural geyser connected to an underground river that overflowed during heavy rains, but locals liked to blame witches for their flooding woes rather than nature.

Priidik explained, "Witches are celebrated in Estonia. On the 30th of April, in Tartu, there are the Walpurgis celebrations, also known as *Volbriöö*. It's a pagan tradition that takes place before the beginning of spring where people dress up as witches and light bonfires to cast off evil spirits. They do this in the early morning hours while it is still dark and before the dawn settles and the sun rises. These days, to be honest, it's more of an excuse to party than an actual tradition, but I am sure this is one of the few places where witches are sought after and not shunned."

When they were back on the van, Gemma asked, "What other similar superstitions are there?"

Priidik replied, "The sauna has a special place in Estonian life—"

"Like in Finland," Lou pointed out.

"Yes exactly. Some consider them to be sacred. It was thought that health problems could be healed in the sauna, especially for those who worked hard, as the sauna could provide ease and relaxation."

"Isn't it illegal for someone to walk or cycle in the dark without wearing a reflector?" Xavier asked.

At the same time, Gemma followed up with another question. "What other quirky beliefs are there?"

Priidik answered them both. "Yes, Xavier. And Gemma, it is considered bad luck to lie down naked in the forest before April 23, which is St. George's Day."

Several in the van burst out laughing, except for Naina. Why would anyone want to lie down naked in the forest at any time of the year, Naina thought, but didn't say.

"One should also not utter the name of an animal while in the forest, unless one wants to summon that animal to make an appearance. As such, people would not utter the name of a wolf when strolling through the forest, unless they intended for the wolf to cross their path," Priidik added.

"Do they do anything? The animals, I mean, after they appear?" Lou asked.

"Essentially, you are giving the animal permission to hunt you."

"A role reversal!" Pat exclaimed.

"Tell us more," Caroline said.

"Storks are readily found in the region. They are everywhere and they are a sign of good luck, and of faithfulness in a partner."

Naina hadn't noticed the storks, but made a point to look out for them. Sure enough, she spotted one in a field right away.

"What happens to all the babies then? Maybe the storks live in the Baltics but deliver the babies elsewhere, that's why the population is in decline," Xavier noted.

Priidik continued as if he hadn't been interrupted, "Honey and bees bore great significance. Sharing honey and sharing beehives were symbols of loyalty, decency, hard work, and fertility. A dying grandparent was sure to pass down beehives to their children, and it is believed the importance of honey stemmed from the Middle Ages when honey was used as currency."

Naina cleared her throat. She finally found the opportunity to voice a question she'd been mulling over. She didn't feel as awkward asking questions one-on-one, but it was daunting to ask questions everyone in the tour group would hear. Was this a sign teaching wasn't for her? She didn't have it in her to speak to large groups. "What about trees? Are there as many trees here as in Sweden?"

"In the Baltics, in general, forests are special. After all, a great portion of Lithuania and about half of Latvia and Estonia are covered by forests. Forests are also special places for Estonians. One can't think negative thoughts or express negative words in forests, as it is believed to call in bad energies."

"Are there any special qualities to forests or trees?" Asking a question to the group wasn't as daunting as Naina'd expected. And maybe she could get some clarity on the magic she had seen at Angel Oak.

Priidik smiled at her. "That's an astute question, Naina. Forests hold a lot of healing elements. There is a reverence for trees and in the spring many people drink birch sap because it is believed to be a rich healing tonic with plenty of vitamins. Wild garlic tonic is consumed to boost health. It is important never to deplete the forest of birch or garlic, and to ensure to leave some for others, including the spirits of the forest. Rowan trees are believed to bring happiness and people often hang a branch from a rowan tree to ward off evil spirits, or they plant a rowan tree close to their house to bring in good luck. Oak trees are particularly sacred and they too have healing qualities, believing to cure headaches and depression. This particular belief though, is from Lithuania."

"Is nature worshipped?" Pat asked.

"You can say that. Nature worship or fear of nature are common elements in Baltic culture, and the weather lends a mystical element."

Coincidentally, a light mist settled over the fields. The fog seemed an open invitation for creating myths and monsters and in these tales, trees could be magical and shadows could be fathomed into witches.

The parts of the country not surrounded by trees and forests were surrounded by water. Priidik had earlier explained how the three countries had coasts on the Baltic Sea, and numerous lakes, rivers, and marshes spotted throughout. To Naina, the water that didn't come from the ground, seemed to come from above. Rain seemed to be constant, and when it wasn't, the land was covered in mist and fog.

"Enough of this mumbo jumbo," Xavier stated, disdain so obvious in his tone that it effectively killed the conversation.

Naina decided she preferred ghosts to witches, but she kept her thoughts to herself.

Chapter Twenty-Nine

To Naina's delight, they stopped at another Circle K for a coffee and a snack before heading to Sillamäe. She loved Circle Ks because of the automated coffee machines with explanations in English for all of the coffee options, including lattes, cappuccinos, and flat whites, the latter of which had become her go-to selection.

Naina had learned a flat white had a higher ratio of coffee to milk compared to a latte. The taste of the coffee, although stronger than what she was used to in the United States, was more intense, rich, sharp, and flavorful. In a latte, she tasted the steamed milk, but in a flat white, she didn't. It had quickly become her beverage of choice.

The gas stations with Circle Ks were scattered all along the roadside, and the shops offered all types of snacks, from hot dogs and sandwiches to various packaged snacks. While she always stuck to a flat white and a pastry, that day, she finally tried marzipan. It felt too grainy for her and she decided to stick to her pastries in the future. She noticed that Xavier was eating a Balbiino Onu ESKIMO caramel ice cream bar.

"Isn't it too cold for ice cream?" she asked, surprising herself at first and later feeling proud she was making conversation with someone and asking questions before they asked her.

"I don't mind. It doesn't make me feel cold. I hardly ever eat ice cream, but while I travel I allow myself to cheat. We've also walked so much that we can afford it."

"Have we?" Naina asked.

"We did 11,435 steps on Sunday and 29,345 steps on Monday. Today, we've already reached 2,000 steps," Lou added.

"You have a FitBit?" Gemma asked.

"No, you can track it on the iPhone Health app," Lou replied, showing everyone his app on the phone.

"I didn't know it was possible to track steps on a phone," Naina commented, again surprising herself by speaking a thought out loud. Maybe she too could become good at conversations with a group of people. It wasn't as scary as she had imagined.

Afterwards, they stopped at a restaurant called Meretare for lunch. It was by the Baltic Sea on the Narva-Jõesuu Beach and had views unlike anything Naina had ever seen before. There wasn't a single table with an obstructed view. It didn't matter where they sat, they had an open view to the beach and sea. Any restaurant she'd eaten at in Charleston or in San Francisco, didn't offer direct access to the beach nor for every single table to have such a wide view of the ocean.

When the group stepped onto the terrace to consider sitting outdoors, Naina had to do a double take. At first, it seemed Holy Man sat on a table by himself, but when she looked again, it was an older couple. She checked that the angelite was safe in the outer pocket of her shoulder bag and placed her palm on top of the bulge. She wouldn't take it out unless it was vitally necessary. She had no Holy Man, but she had her crystal.

Can You Be

It was 48ºF but the wind was so strong, it felt like it was nearly freezing, and the group sat indoors. After ordering Caesar salad with tiger prawns, Naina wrapped herself tighter in her coat and asked to go for a walk on the dark hard sand. Xavier also went for a walk, heading straight for the water. He wanted to touch the Baltic Sea, he said, although he wasn't going to swim. Naina wasn't so inclined although she wanted to go further than the Scottish ladies who remained on the ramp close to the restaurant.

As Naina walked on the sand on that first week of October, she was reminded of her beloved Sullivan's Island beach, whose sand was similarly colored, although the beach in Narva was much wider. The breeze was so intense it threatened to blow her away. Naina might as well have been in a hurricane, but then realized it wasn't quite as bad. Still, she had to continuously wipe her eyes and blow her nose from the onslaught of cold air.

Xavier stood in the water with his pants cropped up, and seeing him gave Naina the courage to walk closer to the water and touch the sea. She didn't take her shoes off but reached down with her hand and touched the frigid water. It was only fall in Estonia but already chillier than the coldest of winters in Charleston.

In the evening they drove to Narva, checking in to the hotel. As Priidik gave out the room keys, he handed the key to room 314 to Xavier, saying, "You are in the Pi room."

"The Pi room?" Xavier asked.

"Yes, you have room 314."

"Yes, I have room 314."

"It's the Pi room," Naina said. "Like the number Pi?"

"I don't get it," Xavier said.

"That's okay, Xavier. You go off to your room. Naina gets it." Priidik winked at her.

Naina's face flushed with warmth, certain she was blushing.

After settling in, the group walked around the border city. Naina wasn't sure if it was the proximity to Russia, but to her it felt as if they were in Russia, and not in Estonia. Priidik had told them before, but reminded them that the majority of people in Narva – he estimated that it was over 95% – were native Russian speakers. There were forts on either side of the Narva River, one in Estonia and the other in Russia. The Estonian one was Narva Castle, built by the Danes in the thirteenth century. The Russian one was Ivangorod Fortress, built by a Muscovite prince in the fifteenth century.

The buildings were imposing and although they oozed history, Naina felt as if they would soon be needed for defense.

"Makes you feel like the Russians could just swoop you up, doesn't it?" Pat said, as if picking up on Naina's sentiment.

"I don't want to go anywhere near there," Gemma commented.

"There are a lot of business opportunities in Russia," Xavier chimed in.

"I'd stay as far away from those, if I were ever to advise anyone," Lou said. "I feel as if there are people looking at us from that fortress across the river, you know? Like they would have all sorts of cameras following our every step."

"Sounds a bit paranoid, doesn't it?" Caroline said.

"I'm sure the Russians have plenty on their plate than to follow a bunch of tourists around," Priidik quipped.

"But do they know this tour has three Americans?" Lou asked.

"Three?" Xavier asked.

"Naina, Pat, and myself," Lou replied.

Xavier gave Naina a sideways glance. "Naina speaks so seldomly, I forget she's even here."

"That's not nice," Gemma said. She turned to Naina and placed her hand on her arm. "Don't you worry, hen. We know you're here and you're an integral part of our group. Ignore Xavier."

When they stood on the bridge by the border, Naina's phone chimed welcoming her to Russia. She knew this was the closest she'd ever get to the country. She wasn't sure whether or not to feel worried, but clearly, she wasn't the only one. She wondered how much of it had to do with being American, as it seemed the most concerned were Lou and Pat. She hadn't felt particularly threatened, except of course, by Xavier's animosity, but she didn't have to cross the border to experience that. To her, Narva felt much safer than he did.

They walked up to a Lenin monument, one of the last left standing in the European Union, around the Narva fort, and back down again. They had dinner at the river waterfront, spitting distance from the Russian border. Priidik explained how many in the city felt more affinity to Russia than Estonia. They watched Russian TV and prior to the invasion of Ukraine, regularly crossed the border into Ivangorod. Before the invasion, they were also more likely to visit St Petersburg than to head toward Tallinn, given the Russian city was closer than the Estonian capital. He didn't know if people still made the same choice.

After dinner, they went out for drinks. Priidik stood next to her and she nestled a beer in her hands. She rarely drank beers but during this trip she'd acquired a taste for them. A Le Coq, it was called, a local Estonian beer and according to Priidik, brewed by the oldest and largest drink makers in the country. The rest of the group chatted heartily, but Naina kept to herself and her beer, hiding behind the group chatter.

A lady approached the table and invited them to a concert. The group debated whether or not to attend. Naina had already decided she wouldn't go. She was sure the noise would be intolerable and wanted to spend the least amount of time with Xavier as possible. She had reached her limit in conversation as well as in new experiences. All she wanted was her bed.

Just then Priidik leaned down, "Are you going?"

She said no.

"I'll walk back with you," he offered.

Her heart did a little flip.

As the group separated, the older tour attendants headed into the night, and the younger ones retreated back to the hotel. Priidik and Naina began their walk back. What would they possibly speak of? Hadn't they shared enough information already? She didn't have to ponder for long.

Chapter Thirty

On the walk back to the hotel Priidik dominated the conversation. He explained how the Baltics had been subject to various invasions as so many of the surrounding nations had tried to control them. With a few exceptions at key times in history, the Baltic states weren't known for being violent. They put up a brave face to their invaders and never gave in. They weren't aggressively demonstrative of their resistance, yet resist they did.

"The first major invaders into Estonia were the Danes in the thirteenth century, as part of the Northern Crusades. There have also been invasions by Swedes."

"Were they all considered Vikings or by then would they have been separate countries?" Naina asked.

"Although they were all known as Vikings, we consider them as Scandinavians. Viking is more a way of life, and they had separate settlements that distinguished them as Danes and Swedes. After all, they spoke different languages."

Priidik continued to explain that Russians, Swedes, and others made several attempts to take over the country. Germans also invaded, but eventually lost state power – although not land or nobility – ironically, with help from the Russians. Sweden then attempted to take over the country. During one of the many conquests the Russians tried, this one by Ivan the Terrible, the Russians established themselves in Narva, and thus, their presence in the city began. Later, the Swedes helped expel the Russians and Estonia was ruled by the Swedes for a good number of years. Russian tsar Peter the Great conquered the Baltic countries and Sweden ceded to Russia.

"Do you want to continue hearing more?" Priidik asked, checking in with Naina.

"Yes, please. I love learning history. I'm surprised these countries were subject to so many invasions."

"Some of it has to do with geography. Estonia and Latvia are easily accessible by sea. Lithuania is well nourished by rivers, and thus also accessible. The countries are en route between some big civilizations, so they were easy targets."

Priidik told Naina Estonia became a country with great effort. Estonian peasants went through some reforms in the late 1800s that left them feeling empowered, and this helped increase their appeal for national consciousness. The start of the Russian revolution in 1905 motivated Estonians to do the same for themselves, and what started as a small movement, grew across the country. Struggles ensued over the years, although most were quieted down. The independence efforts finally gained traction in 1917, alongside the Russian Revolution in the same year. Estonia gained its independence in 1918.

Ironically, they had to regain independence from the Soviets in the 1990s. The world wars saw Germany take control over much of the region, and the Soviets helped liberate the area from the Nazis. In 1940, Estonia was incorporated into the USSR. Germans occupied again in 1941, but by 1944 the Soviets were back here in Narva. By late 1944, the Soviets were well established in Tallinn.

In the years of the Soviet occupation, thousands of Estonians were killed and many were deported or placed into camps. An estimated 80,000 Estonians were subject to mass forced migrations and by 1990, the ethnic Estonian population had decreased from 90% to 60%. During the deportations, farms decreased, which caused a lot of discontent and helped to fuel the eventual re-independence in 1991. That movement to restore independence wasn't rooted in violence but rather in national identity, strength of character, and indelible tradition.

"And Estonia has done well?" Naina asked.

Priidik nodded. "We may be a small country, but we have a strong economy. It has been in the Euro zone since 2011, Estonia is part of the World Trade Organization, and since 2004 it has been part of the European Union and North Atlantic Treaty Organization. We conduct our elections electronically, which is extremely efficient – although paper ballots are available."

"Then why did Xavier make that comment about the storks? About the decline of the population?"

"There are two possible reasons. In Estonia, the ethnic population in 1939 was almost equal to that in 1993, and that was due to the executions, deaths, deportations, and people escaping or getting exiled from the Soviet regime. Of course that's not the case any longer. Currently, there are limited opportunities in the Estonian countryside, which results in several challenges, including how to keep youth in the country and how to keep up farms. They are still in decline since now they are left to the elderly to maintain."

It was clear Priidik was passionate about his country, and it was not surprising, as this was his home. Naina felt equally passionate for Charleston, especially after rediscovering it with Raiya. She had lived there since she was fifteen years old when she arrived at Candor. She liked Charleston, she enjoyed her life there, but she wondered if there were other places she could live. Stockholm had seemed like a good choice, save the weather. So far it seemed like Estonia was similar. If she did stay in Charleston, would she ever speak so passionately about the city and encourage people to visit there? She hadn't done it in the past, and it dawned on her that it must have been one of the reasons Alice decided to fire her. If she couldn't speak passionately about the city she lived in, how could she encourage someone to buy a house there?

Naina loved Charleston and everything about it. She loved its history, the ghosts, the colored houses, and the cobblestoned streets. What had held her back then? Why wasn't she attached to the city she so loved? Maybe it's because she hadn't expected to spend so much of her life there. She had moved to Candor expecting to eventually be moved out by her father. She hadn't imagined she would go to college at all, and when she got admitted into the College of Charleston it was a welcome surprise, as was getting her job at the real estate office. She hadn't expected to get fired, but she also hadn't expected to last as long as she had there.

"I am boring you, aren't I?" Priidik asked.

"You are definitely not."

"You tend to be so quiet."

"I know … I'm sorry … As I said, I love history. I know all about Charleston history and not much about this area, so this is fascinating to me. I was just thinking."

"Care to share your thoughts?"

Can You Be

Priidik was looking directly at her. His eyes expressed interest, not the contempt or annoyance she had often seen in Alice's face at the office when Naina went for long periods of time without speaking. It seemed Priidik genuinely wanted to know. She was surprised the angelite in her shoulder bag was pulsating, as it had done at Angel Oak. They were walking through a park just then, and she wondered if her crystal might be resonating with the trees.

"I'm in awe of the attachment you feel to your country. You're clearly passionate about it, and I understand. This is your home. Not only are you so knowledgeable, but it's clear you want others to know about it and understand the beauty and uniqueness of Estonia."

Priidik's expression lit up. "That is true. I want everyone to experience the beauty of Estonia and the wonder of the Baltics. We don't have a high tourism industry and I want to change that. These countries have so much to offer. We are prepared to run our tours for larger groups, but we normally don't get more than twelve people."

"I prefer the smaller group," Naina said, surprising even herself. She had thought she would have preferred the anonymity of the larger groups. "I mean, this is only the second tour I've been a part of. I was on the add-on in Sweden and there were many people. I was just a nameless face. But here, you pay attention, and you cater to me. Like making me feel it was okay to step out of the prisons. I don't think that would have happened in a larger tour. There wouldn't have been this level of individual attention. I like that."

"What made you choose the Baltics? Most people would go to one of the better-known destinations for their first trip to Europe. Like Paris or London, I would assume. Why come here?"

"I've always felt I was less advantageous, which seems ridiculous now that I say it, because after having visited the prison, I don't feel that way."

"You haven't committed any crimes, have you?" Priidik asked, clearly joking.

Naina let out a short giggle. "No, I haven't...It's hard to explain but I've always felt as if I was imprisoned."

"It's not usual for people to compare their lives to prisons."

"I guess not … I've just grown up in limiting situations. Boarding schools I couldn't leave, jobs I didn't like, but I didn't do anything to get out of the conditions I felt I was tied to, and being here has made me realize I am not as limited as I thought I was."

"Not as much as you would have been had you been in prison."

"Yes …" A translucent airy substance in the form of tendrils extended out from her toward Priidik, similar to the one she had seen at Angel Oak. Could she be experiencing the magic of the place? Was this something all trees had in common? She searched for Holy Man. He stood behind a tree munching on something indistinguishable. He smiled and winked. The airy substance enveloped the entire park, like a fog, except there was no visible fog. It was a cold and dry night in the first week of October.

"So why the Baltics?" Priidik asked again.

Naina tried her best not to be distracted by Holy Man or the tendrils extending between her and Priidik. "In those limiting situations, I've felt small. Like people don't notice me. Like I'm not worth paying attention to. And so I wanted to travel somewhere people don't normally choose … places that are off the beaten tracks. So no, I purposefully didn't want to go to Paris or London or anywhere like that. I did add Stockholm and Helsinki at both ends of the trip, but I wanted to make sure I saw something people normally didn't."

"That's interesting … I feel honored this is where you have chosen to go on your first trip outside of the United States. I hope we live up to your expectations and hopefully your trip will be so enjoyable that when you leave here you will share your experience. Maybe you can help place these countries on the list of places to visit." Priidik smiled with a sense of pride and enthusiasm Naina had rarely seen before.

Naina smiled back, surprising herself for feeling comfortable holding her smile. It was as she had felt when she started her friendship with Raiya, except that Priidik had a more genuine expression in his eyes. She chided herself for not noticing the lack of authenticity in Raiya's eyes sooner. That must be why people say you live and you learn. She had to learn what it meant to not be authentic, to recognize it when it was right in front of her. There was something different about Priidik. He had a soft quality to him.

"I'll try my best," she said. The tension and worry from the beginning of the walk had eased. She was surely and slowly coming out of her shell.

Chapter Thirty-One

The next morning, they drove to Lake Peipus. On the way there, they stopped briefly along the Narva River, a stone's throw away from Russia on the other side of the riverbanks. Naina contemplated throwing rocks to the other side, but considered otherwise. She didn't have a strong arm, and a few rocks weren't going to cause much damage. Plus the people on the other side of the river weren't the ones who were invading Ukraine.

The day wasn't particularly cold but it was raining, and Naina was eager to get dry. There was a tank that served as a memorial to those who had perished in World War II. Naina took a couple of photographs and ran back into the van's shelter.

They had lunch at Kolkja, a fish and onion restaurant run by the Orthodox Russian community near Mustvee. The women who worked in the restaurant wore traditional dresses and spoke in Russian. It made Naina feel she was actually in Russia, which wasn't much of a stretch, given that the only thing separating Russia and Estonia was the lake.

Can You Be

Priidik explained they were ethnic Russians who had settled in the area back when they were fleeing persecution from Russian Rulers – Ivan the Terrible and later Peter the Great. These groups of Russians were called Old Believers because they were Russian Orthodox who didn't want to abide by the changes brought by the tsars of the seventeenth century.

As they sat around lunch, Priidik explained their next stop would be the city of Tartu, famous for its university.

Priidik asked the group what schooling was like in everyone's country. Everyone took turns sharing their experience and how that had led them to their profession. When one person finished, the next person was ready to share. A couple of times, two people started talking at the same time, and eventually one of the two had to concede and allow the other person to speak first.

The only person who wasn't eager was Naina. Her face and neck grew hot as she listened to everyone's responses. She felt more comfortable sharing with the group, but still avoided being put on the spot. She also wanted to find what connections people had between their schooling and eventual profession. Perhaps there was something for her to learn.

She wanted to feel part of the group – for the others to recognize her as part of the group – but she didn't want to divulge too much. When it came to her turn, she touched the angelite in her shoulder bag and took a deep breath. With her eyes glued to her plate, she spoke softly, "I didn't have much direction. I didn't know what I wanted to study or what to do for a career. I wasn't even sure I'd go to college. I applied to the College of Charleston because it was where I lived and I didn't want to move to another city. I had already moved a few times as a child. At one time I had thought of becoming a lawyer because my mother was a lawyer." Most in the group had sympathy in their eyes.

"And why didn't you?" Xavier asked, his expression cold.

"I don't know."

"Huh. I never understand youth. You have all the opportunities presented to you and you don't use them. Wouldn't being a lawyer have been better for you than being a receptionist?" Xavier said.

"That is hardly the right approach, Xavier," Gemma said. "Everyone has their reasons for making the choices they do, and they don't have to be logical or satisfactory to you."

"I was asking for people to share their experiences without judgement," Priidik added. "I think it's important for people to share without us expressing criticism."

Caroline said, "Please continue, Naina. Tell us what you studied in school."

"I completed a degree in Integrated Studies," she said.

"That sounds like typical American nonsense," Xavier said. He spoke in a raised voice and was visibly frustrated.

Naina was unsure of what to say. All but one in the group looked at her with tenderness.

"Integrated studies sounds a bit like liberal arts, wouldn't you say, Naina?" Lou asked.

"Yes, I guess so."

"And what in the world is liberal arts?" Xavier asked, throwing his hands up in the air.

"Liberal arts degrees allow students to study a variety of subjects so they don't have to specialize in a particular subject matter," Lou said. "Is that similar to what you studied, Naina?"

"Yes, yes it is." Naina's eyes went back to her plate.

"As I said, typical American nonsense," said Xavier.

"Xavier, you had your chance to share your conversation. I ask you to treat Naina with respect and allow her to share. I am asking you kindly," said Priidik.

The sternness in his voice made Xavier look away. He crossed his hands in front of him.

"Don't worry, Naina, please continue telling us about your background," Priidik said.

Naina didn't know what else to say. Xavier continued to look away.

"Don't mind him, hen. We all know he's got a chip on his shoulder that he needs to work out. And what made you want to work at the real estate office?" Gemma asked.

"I honestly don't know. There was a sign for a job opening and I walked in to ask for employment."

"And they hired you, just like that?" Gemma said, smiling.

"Isn't it remarkable when things work out?" Caroline added.

"How is it then that you can afford a trip like this? You must have been saving up for a while," added Xavier, his eyes squarely on her.

"My father gave me some money," Naina admitted. Her voice now really soft.

"How does a thirty-year-old feel entitled to live a lifestyle she cannot afford?" Xavier asked.

"That is enough from you, Xavier," Priidik said, his voice calm, yet firm.

With a loud humph, Xavier threw his napkin on the table and walked off.

Priidik turned to Naina. "I am really sorry you have to go through that. Please don't pay attention to Xavier. The rest of us are not judging you, and we don't agree with his approach."

"He's right though," Naina said. She had been living a life she couldn't afford. If her father hadn't helped her out, she wouldn't have been able to go on the trip, she wouldn't have been able to pay for her rent, and she wouldn't be able to live the way she did. Even Naina couldn't explain the choices she had made and as everyone else shared their experiences where their education was clearly tied to their employment and it seemed like the decisions they made for their lives were intentional, Naina didn't have words to explain why hers weren't. It had made no sense for her to study liberal arts. It had been the easy choice. And even Naina had to admit that finding a receptionist job had been easy. It wasn't what a typical college student did after graduating, but it had worked out for her.

She had to recognize, though, that it had worked out for her because her father had supported her financially. He may not have been there in person, but he had supported her in the only way he knew how.

۞

When the group left the restaurant, Xavier was standing by the van. He didn't look at anyone and the moment Artur opened the van door, he was the first one in.

The drive to Tartu was a quiet one. Priidik shared information about Tartu, explaining it was a university town. He said he had asked the question about education because he was going to tell them about the education system in Estonia, but he would do so another time and allow everyone to rest after the heavy lunch they'd had. He gave Naina a look filled with compassion, and Naina quickly wiped away the tears collecting in her eyes. When they arrived in Tartu, it was still raining and the dampness had seeped into Naina's bones. When they checked in to the hotel, she was relieved to hear Priidik say they would take some time to rest before

180

going for an afternoon walk. Hopefully by then the rain would have subsided.

The rooms were four feet wide and ten feet long, with a twin bed placed against the wall, and hooks on the wall that were meant to function as a closet. Naina placed her bag on the floor, right next to the bed, but the remaining space was so narrow she needed to step over the bag to reach the bathroom. The room was so constricted it was hard to think.

At least there was a balcony, and Naina walked out for fresh air. Holy Man leaned on the van, chewing on some type of pastry, smiling at her as if he were impervious to the rain. Despite her better instincts, Naina ran back into the room, into the hallway, and out to the parking lot. By the time she got outside, Holy Man was no longer leaning on the van. Was she having visions? She was sure of it. There was no way Holy Man could have traveled.

She headed back to her room, feeling the most defeated she had felt in a long time. What had happened to the "hey"? She hadn't heard one of them since the hurricane. Maybe it couldn't travel either. She sat on her bed and took the angelite out of her shoulder bag, cupping the orb in her hands. Tears flowed down her face, wetting her top. She cried until her tears dried out.

It occurred to Naina that she had indeed been truly fortunate and that her father had really been of great assistance to her. She hadn't realized it before, but had she had to survive from the salary she'd earned as a receptionist, she would have likely ended up living in a tiny place, similar to the room she was in. This, however, would be a good experience for her, in case she wasn't able to get a decent job after her father's money ran out and she had to move out of her apartment. It was as if the universe was giving her a taste of what she would have deserved.

After everyone had rested and the rain had stopped, the group walked around Tartu, through the city and to a set of bridges. Priidik explained that the first bridge was the Devil's Bridge and a bringer of bad luck. The second bridge was the Angel's Bridge, and a bringer of good luck. Apparently, walking underneath both bridges ensured the luck was cancelled out.

They proceeded to an old gunpowder vault called Püssirohu Kelder, where they all stopped for beers. Most of the conversation occurred between Gemma, Caroline, Lou, Pat, and Priidik. Xavier was quiet and, unsurprisingly, so was Naina. Gemma and Caroline sat next to Naina and told her to not pay any attention to Xavier.

"Don't worry. I'm used to not being the most popular person in the group," said Naina.

"You're plenty popular, hen. He's the one who's not popular," Gemma said as Caroline nodded.

Naina was grateful for the efforts they made to make her feel like a part of the group.

For dinner, they continued walking through the city and reached a place close to the hotel called Kolm Tilli. However, before entering the restaurant, Xavier excused himself.

Priidik had a few words with him outside the restaurant and when he came back in, he didn't mention Xavier and no one asked about him.

The dinner conversation, to Naina's relief, centered on the future. She enjoyed listening as others discussed the likely scarcity in the future and the effects of climate change. Naina surprised herself by saying, "I heard much of the US will be covered in water. The coasts will flood, California will have a large earthquake and disappear, and the East Coast will be swallowed up by storms."

Gemma placed a reassuring hand on Naina's. "It makes sense.

With the glaciers melting, much of the Earth will be under water."

Naina half smiled. "I see it already in Charleston. We get so many hurricanes much of the beach is eroding."

"It's funny that all these millionaires seek houses by the ocean and will soon be without homes."

It was then Naina realized that the awkwardness from the lunchtime had washed away. She was relieved she wasn't the one cast out. Xavier had cast himself out. Naina would have been that person except the one thing she would never do was deliberately hurt another. She had been hurt so many times she swore to herself never to do it to another person. She may have hurt others inadvertently, but at least she never did so purposefully. She couldn't control hurting another without knowing, although she would try her best not to ever do it. She knew for sure she wouldn't deliberately hurt anyone.

Chapter Thirty-Two

Xavier joined them for breakfast but then again, he had little choice as they all had to check out of the hotel, get into the van with their bags, and drive into the old town. Thankfully at least, on that early October morning, it wasn't raining. It was cloudy but dry.

After everyone had placed their orders for breakfast, Priidik broke the tension. "Education in Estonia is very important. It is accessible to all, regardless of income, and there are equal opportunities for all children regardless of economic status, so all kids, rich or poor, have the same classes, extracurricular activities, and even lunch, school transport, and textbooks are free for everyone. The literacy rate is in the top two in the world where 99% of all adults know how to read and write.

"Tartu is well-known as a university town. University of Tartu is the country's most famous and oldest university. There are many foreign students who come to study here and so although most classes are taught in Estonian, there are a large number of courses taught in English, especially those related to IT and computers."

"I can't believe people come from abroad to study here," Xavier noted.

"It means they really admire the education provided," said Priidik.

Naina couldn't imagine leaving the United States to attend school. Somehow, it seemed incredible people would feel so strongly about their education they would move to another country to pursue it. No matter how much she had moved within the country, she couldn't picture living elsewhere, and much less to pursue studies. It was clear people felt a deep passion for their future in a way she hadn't felt before. Was there something she could have felt as passionate about that she would move to pursue it? Could there be such a thing to inspire her to that degree?

She kept on coming back to skin and natural products. Did she have it in her to study esthetics? Maybe there was a way for her to get good at giving facials, learn from what she had done wrong during the trial facial with Fiona, and do so without leaving Charleston. She'd have to look into it.

After breakfast, the group had a free day to walk around Tartu, and as they all separated, Naina walked on her own, more at ease than she had been the first day in Tallinn. Tartu had quaint light-colored buildings set on stone-covered streets.

Despite being nearly thirty, Naina was finally becoming a true grown-up, able to fend for herself, walking comfortably in a foreign city on her own. Granted, Tartu, particularly in the old town, was quite small – even smaller than Tallinn and much smaller than Charleston. It was so easy to get around it would have been hard to get lost. Still, she was proud of herself.

She strolled through an open market in the middle of the old town. There were foods and souvenirs, and all types of crafts and handmade jewelry. Naina was drawn to a man selling linens. He explained Estonian linen was renowned, and she wasn't sure whether to believe him or not, but Priidik wasn't around to ask. The look in the man's eye gave her the feeling he was being sincere. Perhaps he did this job to help his family, like maybe his wife was at home making the linen, and he sold it for her. "Where do you get the linen?"

"My sisters make these by hand. I just sell them on their behalf."

So it was his sisters, not his wife. Close. Naina loved the softness of the fabric, and so she bought her first-ever souvenir for herself, a hand-made linen tablecloth and a smaller decorative placemat for a table that Naina didn't yet own but knew she would eventually purchase.

As she walked back to meet the rest of the group, she was determined to find a job that involved helping others, that allowed others to feel better about themselves. The notion of skincare seemed to keep calling to her.

※

Artur drove the group into Latvia. They visited the Līgatne Soviet Secret Bunker, a 213,000 square-foot underground fallout shelter. A guide pretended to be an old Soviet comrade and spoke to them as if they were still in Soviet times. Naina was fascinated by how the subterranean shelter was created below a hotel. No one would have known it was there unless they descended the few flights of unremarkable staircase. There was a thick metallic door that ensured the space remained completely sealed off. Its construction was completed in 1982, giving the feel the group had stepped back in time. Everything still looked like it was in the 1980s.

It was still in its original condition, and it was fully equipped with sleeping areas, control centers, offices, and various other facilities. The shelter was created so that up to 250 of the Soviet elite would have a place to hide out if there was a nuclear attack and remain there for three months.

Priidik had arranged for the group to eat in the bunker's canteen and receive a meal similar to what the people would have eaten in the shelter. They were served in small trays and told that if they had been in the 1980s, they would have had to eat in shifts as the canteen accommodated no more than thirty or so people at a time.

Naina ate her dinner quickly and asked to walk around the beautiful wooded areas that surrounded the building. She was growing claustrophobic and knew she had to get out before the panic set in. As soon as she got out, she took several deep breaths and calmed herself down with the EFTs. It wasn't long before the rest of the group joined her.

"It's quite intense being down there," said Gemma, looking at Naina with tenderness and compassion in her eyes.

"I bet there has been no air circulation in there for the last forty years. It was difficult to breath underground, wasn't it doll?" Caroline added.

"Yes, it was. The air was stale," Naina said. Her apartment in Charleston was above ground, but the fallout shelter was better decorated and equipped. There was staleness in the air, but the shelter had been made for life. In her apartment, there was fresh air but she had made it so stark, it stunk of death. She definitely needed to change things around. Or move out. She felt more suffocated thinking about her apartment.

"You need to get thicker skin, girl, if you want to do well in the world. Get over your sensitivity or something," Xavier commented.

"She wasn't the only one feeling that way," Lou said.

Pat added, "I couldn't wait to get out of there, myself. I followed Naina out. She isn't weak. That place is something else. Gives you the chills to know what existed there with no one on the outside even suspecting its existence."

Naina was appreciative that everyone stood up for her when it came to Xavier and his comments. She knew eventually, she'd have to gain the courage to stand up for herself.

Chapter Thirty-Three

Naina now looked forward to breakfast and the opportunity to discover new foods. The Latvian options consisted of oatmeal porridge served with jam, and barley porridge served with bacon bits and butter. They also offered rye bread with butter and herring or salted raw salmon. She tried it all in small portions, as she'd done in Tallinn, and she made sure to sample a bite of everything.

Artur drove them an hour to Salaspils Memorial Park, and it appeared as if they were in the middle of nowhere as there was nothing nearby, not even a gas station. Naina wanted to use the restroom and hoped there was one there.

They got out of the van and walked on a wide path surrounded by pine and birch trees. A constant breeze swept through whispering in her ears as if the leaves were trying to communicate with her. Sparks of tendrils extended from the canopy down towards the forest floor, as if a fog had been settling into the park. But there was no actual fog. That day, in early October, was the warmest it had been so far in the trip. The sun was shining bright and it was 61ºF.

Around her was the same airy substance she had seen at Angel Oak and then in Narva.

Priidik told them there had been a hard labor camp on the site. "The park is a reflection of part of the country's difficult history."

It was eerie walking through a place with such a past. There was no evidence of the existence of these camps. It just looked like a regular forested area. A large concrete building stood in front of them. There was no mention of the camp that had once been there other than a line displayed on the concrete building that read, "Aiz šiem vārtiem vaid zeme."

Priidik said it was from a poem written by a former prisoner and it translated to, "Beyond these gates the land groans."

The concrete structure was a type of museum. It showed how the memorial park had been envisioned, designed, and eventually constructed. On the other side of the concrete building were a series of large statues and monuments that honored the Latvians and other Soviet citizens who had perished there, but strangely to Naina, there were only references to outside things. If Priidik hadn't explained this had once been a labor camp, Naina was sure she wouldn't have known. Priidik told them this was where Camp Kurtenhof had been housed and had held around 23,000 people. Kurtenhof was the German name for Salaspils. The camp had been built by the same Jewish prisoners who had been forced to live there. These prisoners were brought in from different places in the country as well as Germany, Austria, and the then Czechoslovakia. Many of them died during the construction as they had little shelter from the winter. The camp eventually housed political prisoners, dissidents, and convicts of the Nazis. It served as a transit camp as prisoners were transported from one region to another.

As Naina walked around the park, she was haunted by the large concrete structures. Some of them were so imposing, it was hard to capture a good image of them. They were so large Naina felt like a dwarf next to them. They were spread over a large area, and it took a few minutes to walk from one sculpture to the next. What she had thought would be a quick visit to a concrete building and nine statues, turned out to be nearly a two-hour affair.

The structures were meant to represent the prisoners who had once been at the camp. There was a man lying down trying to push himself up. There was a woman standing in front of her children, trying to protect them. Some were kneeling, yet defiant. One prisoner helping another one stand, and others in single-handed fist salutes. It was haunting and depressing, conveying the resistance held in the spirit of the people who didn't break even in the most heinous of circumstances. The structures had equally haunting names, such as Solidarity, The Oath, The Unbroken, and The Humiliated.

The voices of the trees chimed up then. Naina watched intently, wondering if they knew about the atrocities that had taken place there. After a few moments, she understood they did. The tendrils still settled as a fog among the trees, but she knew she was the only one who could see them.

She understood then that the airy substance was the voices of the spirits in the area. Angel Oak was haunted, the forests in Narva must have been as well, and these had to be. There was magic in the air but also a haunting, the type that elevated trapped souls.

The breeze unsettling the leaves spoke to her. The trees were conveying to her that the place had held on to its grief, and the grief was made worse by the lack of visitors. There was no one else there, and Priidik shared anytime he had visited in the past, there were few others around. Perhaps if the park had more visitors there would have been more people to shoulder the burden. Naina wondered if the trees in Latvia were similar to those in Estonia and they brought healing to people. She hoped they did, and she really wanted to believe they brought some type of solace to the people who had been imprisoned at the camp.

There had been no restrooms at the park, and Naina couldn't help but think there would be more visitors if the park offered more facilities. With it being a remote area, people would expect to see at least a toilet, if nothing else.

⚛

In a somber mood, they drove to Riga. Naina had a fidgety ride to the hotel. At every bump in the road, Naina was afraid her bladder would burst and the pee would leak onto the cushioned seat.

To distract herself, Naina asked, "Priidik, can you tell us ghost stories? Are there good ghost stories about the area?"

"There's a few in all the countries. Since we'll be visiting the Great Cemetery in Riga this afternoon, I'll tell you one from it. There was a dispute between a non-believing man and a religious woman, and she cursed him, saying he'd never get into heaven. He said that if that was the case, he would cling on to her so she also wouldn't get into heaven. It is said the ghosts of both haunt the cemetery."

When they arrived at the hotel in Riga, it turned out she wasn't the only one who felt the same. Everyone made a mad dash to the toilets the moment they got off the van.

The rooms weren't ready, so they stored their bags and took a tram to visit German mausoleums. Naina didn't take public transportation in Charleston and realized how much easier her life would be if she had access to it to get around the city, or if she had a car. She wouldn't invest in a car just yet, but it was something to consider for the future.

Can You Be

Tallinn and Vilnius, according to Priidik, were easily walkable cities. Yet Riga required public transportation to get around some areas. It was a truly big city, even by international standards. When they got off the tram at the Great Cemetery, though, the mausoleums were right there.

Naina enjoyed walking through a cemetery, having often done so in Charleston with the many to choose from around St. Philips Cathedral and St. Michael's Church. This one was more wooded and the grass overgrown, and it was clear people didn't care for the dead here in the same way they did in Charleston. The airy substance she had now grown accustomed to was present in this cemetery as well, except it wasn't as visible, even to Naina. She wondered if it had something to do with the proximity of the city.

It was sunny still, as it had been in Salaspils, and the rays formed spotlights around different parts of the cemetery. There were only a select few mausoleums with flowers as a clear indication someone still cared about the dead, but many of the other mausoleums were in disrepair, a few even boarded up where access was no longer granted because they were a hazard to the public, the structures visibly cracking from abandonment.

They took a tram back to the hotel, and then Priidik arranged to have a local guide take the group through Riga on a walking tour outside the old town. The first stop was Riga Central Market, which had over three thousand market stands arranged throughout five Zeppelin hangars. They had been built when it seemed Zeppelins would be the mode of transport in the future. The Hindenburg disaster in 1937, where the LZ 129 Hindenburg caught fire, killing 36 people, led Zeppelins to become obsolete. At that point, the hangars had been converted into a market, which at one point was the largest market bazaar in Europe – some places still claimed this title.

They then proceeded through other areas of Riga. What struck Naina the most was the city's architecture. According to the tour guide, Riga had more than eight hundred buildings with an Art Nouveau design.

The tour guide shared these buildings had contributed to the regal appeal of the city, which was once known as the Paris of the Baltics. "In most of the Baltics, the architecture can be split between the dreamy and mythical looking buildings made during the German and Scandinavian times, and the dreary industrial buildings from the Soviet times. Here, in Riga, there is an added benefit of finding buildings with Art Nouveau architecture."

Naina was fascinated by the fantastical creatures, which included dragons, animals, mermaids, plants, flowers, human forms, and an assortment of odd shapes.

They had dinner at a seafood restaurant and Naina realized she was finally comfortable speaking with the group. They were halfway through the trip and she had been watching the others, learning it was easy to incorporate small talk. She tried her best to ignore the sweat and damp clothing odors that emanated from Xavier. He was her least favorite, for obvious reasons. The others were easy to get along with.

"What are your thoughts on the future, Naina?" Lou asked, as if on cue.

"That's a big question."

"You haven't made any grand efforts to secure savings, I'd assume, being a receptionist," Xavier said.

"I have not."

"Don't you give much thought to your future?" Xavier added.

"I do think about the future, but perhaps not as much as I

should. I've been more concerned about making it day-to-day."

"And that's enough for you? Don't you want more?"

"I guess I do, but then again, I didn't care about having a good job, and that's why I settled for being a receptionist at a real estate company. Some may consider it a low paying job, especially for someone who graduated from college, but I didn't feel challenged to do more." Naina's face grew hot, as if all her blood rushed to her head. She no longer felt comfortable.

Xavier, though, seemed to not want to stop the questions. "So you gave up?'

Naina wondered why he seemed so intently focused on her. She took a deep breath. "It's not that I gave up, but I didn't think I would be able to live out this lifetime." Naina's confession hung in the air.

"Because of things like climate change, right? You young ones seem to be so concerned with all the catastrophes affecting the world," Lou reasoned, clearing the air.

Naina took that as her cue to end the conversation, and Priidik to ask for the bill.

On the way back to the hotel, Naina walked next to Gemma. The others discussed Depeche Mode songs Naina knew nothing about.

"Have I appeared to be too shy and reticent?" Naina used the words Alice had used to describe her.

"Yes, I would say so, hen," Gemma replied.

"Is there something I can do about it?" Naina confessed she wished she knew how to be more conversational. "I just don't know what it takes."

"It's simple, dear. Don't overthink. Share opinions about what we're experiencing or what we're eating. You don't have to share personal information, if you don't want to, but you can discuss topics."

"I've tried, and I think I did today, but I'm afraid I was too combative. Perhaps I argued too much with Xavier?" Naina was not only afraid she had expressed dissenting opinions, but also, that she had shared more than she should.

"No, you did great, hen. Really great. You expressed your opinion, followed it with fact, and handled him with tact. You were direct in your communication and he may not agree with you but you expressed yourself clearly. That is what it means to have conversations with others. Don't be afraid. Be who you are."

Naina was silent, taking it all in. Maybe she was being too hard on herself and she was handling the conversation better than she thought she was.

As if reading her mind, Gemma said, "To me you seem to have handled it well. It isn't about being wrong or being right or saying something worthwhile or educational, although that certainly does work, but it is more about contributing to the conversation to keep the group engaged. And don't use Xavier as a gauge. He's got a stick up his ass."

When they got back to the hotel, she realized she hadn't checked in with her angelite throughout the exchange that evening. Maybe she was evolving, shedding her old skin. Could the time spent among the trees have had an effect on her? Had they passed on some of their magic?

Small talk consisted of simple elements, like the weather or what book she was reading or movie she had watched. She could also express her thoughts and opinions in a way that contributed to the conversation. All of this didn't take as much effort as she had once thought. It was merely a matter of divulging some – not

Can You Be

all – of what was already in her head.

Chapter Thirty-Four

The next day, Artur drove them to the Irbene Radio Telescope, a Cold War relic hidden in the forests north of Ventspils. It used to be run by Soviets and was seemingly used to spy on Americans but no one would confirm. The group was able to walk the grounds and the buildings, many of which were now in ruins. They climbed onto the parabolic disk and walked on it as if it were a climb on the moon. They also got into the nearby building which was collapsing and through a long tunnel into another nearby telescope area.

It felt, once again, as if Naina had stepped back in time. But this one didn't feel oppressive. It felt expansive. The forest around her wasn't trapped in a filmy fog like it had been in Salaspils. Did this have something to do with the spirits? She couldn't shake that thought. There didn't seem to be an air of suffering in this space as there had been in the others.

As Artur drove them to Liepāja, the group sat in silence. It was amazing to Naina that so much of the Soviet operation was underground or hidden. It seemed like so much effort to make it that way.

Had she also made an effort to remain hidden? How long had she kept herself small and unseen? If she was honest with herself, which she was intent on being, she had to admit she had stayed under the radar for much of her life. Like this area she was in, she would crumble into ruins if she kept herself closed-off, and she could no longer afford to be a vestige of the 1980s. She needed to allow herself to grow up and to be seen.

As part of the tour, she was forced to see the positive and negative experiences others had had. Life was about ups and downs, and it was becoming clearer to Naina this was universal. Everyone had pain and joy, suffering and bliss, love and hate. Maybe it wasn't so bad for her to confront her suffering. All around her, she saw the perseverance of life, despite all they had endured. People in the Baltics not only survived, they thrived.

As soon as Naina walked into the hotel in Liepāja, she was amazed by the glass displays filled with various forms of amber. The receptionist explained amber was made from fossilized tree resin. At one point, the Baltics had the largest deposits of amber in the world – the Baltic forest was believed to have created more than 100,000 tons of amber.

Naina wanted to buy a piece. It would complement her angelite and even act as a backup in case she lost or misplaced it. She would do her best not to lose it, but it would be nice to have something additional.

Amber was of organic origin, unlike most other crystals that came from rocks or minerals, and offered strong protection to anyone who carried it. In medieval times, some had used it as a protection against sorcery and witchcraft. It had high spiritual qualities and was meant to preserve the spirit. It protected from evil and was worn for good luck. It was used to reduce fear, illuminate the dark, bring clarity, magnify wisdom, and heal emotions. Amber seemed like exactly what Naina needed, especially after the receptionist mentioned it was used to soothe grief and manifest change.

And just like that, at the start of the second week of October, she now had two crystals to carry wherever she went.

After Naina placed the amber safely in her shoulder bag next to the angelite, the group went for a walk around the city and on the beach. Priidik said it would be a good place to catch the sunset and maybe an after-dinner drink. On their way there, they saw a double rainbow. A light drizzle fell from the partly cloudless sky as the sun made its way down the horizon.

"I wonder if we're getting double the luck," Gemma said.

"Why do you say that?" Naina asked.

"Rainbows are signs of luck. If we're seeing a double rainbow, maybe we are getting a double dose."

Naina hadn't seen rainbows in Charleston, but knew they had to be there. There was plenty of rain and sun to stir some up. Somehow, Naina had missed them. But she wasn't missing this one. This double rainbow spurred Naina to walk faster, as if her legs were being propelled by it. It appeared to be following her, and grew brighter every time she glanced up. The light drizzle dripped dew on her head and lay a wet foundation on her jacket. She walked past Jūrmalas Park and up the sand dunes only to be blasted by the pink, amber, and purple tones of the sun setting.

In any other sunset Naina had witnessed, the sky hadn't quite blossomed in the same way. Yes, the yellow, orange, and sometimes pink hues surrounded the sun and the sky around it, but the clouds extending beyond it were still white or gray and the sky was still blue. As the sun settled, the sky changed gradually, the brighter hues disappearing at the edge of the horizon.

But in Liepāja, there wasn't a spot that wasn't lit up in ombre shades of yellows, oranges, pinks, ambers, and purples. The colors soaked up the entirety of the sky. Naina twirled to make sure she captured everything around her and no matter how hard she looked, there wasn't a single colorless gap. Even the sand beneath her feet and the ocean spread ahead seemed to be absorbed in brightness.

Was every sunset in the Baltics an explosion of color? Was the end of every day as wondrously beautiful? Similar colors had exploded over St. Olav's Church Tower in Tallinn. It was as if the same beautiful colors permeated throughout the Baltics.

Holy Man seemed to appear then. Behind her, near the dunes, a man stood next to the boarded area, dressed in white. Despite the drizzle, the strong breeze, and the frigid air, he wasn't wearing a coat. Interestingly, he licked an ice cream cone. He didn't approach her, he merely waved and smiled. Naina waved and smiled back, relieved she had seen him again. It assured her she hadn't imagined the previous sightings. She hoped he would speak to her, but she didn't care for it to happen then. She was captivated by the sunset.

She liked the sea air better here. In Charleston, the humidity was often so high it pressed on her chest. The only drawback in Liepāja was the wind blowing in her face. She breathed but not deeply, the gusts sweeping away her inhalation before she could fully take it in. On the East Coast Ocean, she had no trouble breathing.

Half the sun was still visible and she ran down the soft dunes onto the harder, compacted sand still light in color and sprinted to touch the gentle waves of the Baltic Sea. She tasted its saltiness after lightly dipping her fingers in the ocean water and bringing them to her lips. Suddenly, she knew the world held possibility. The shackles around her were lifted and she didn't feel boxed in. She just needed to seize the moment and make it hers. Yes, there was a path for her.

੨⋆

Naina hadn't noticed when everyone had arrived. She had been so overcome by the sunset she hadn't realized the entire tour group was on the beach. Most of them stood closer to the sand dunes, and Naina was the only one near the crashing waves. It was the first time Naina had run ahead and not away from a group of people.

As if on cue, Priidik indicated for her to join them. They walked to a nearby beach bar that had an unobstructed view of the full stretch of sand in front of them. By the time they each ordered a drink and sat down in the outside terrace, the sun had all but disappeared. Eventually, most felt cold and moved inside.

Everyone was in a good mood, and Naina laughed unabashedly, unconcerned about possible wrinkles. She felt lighter.

They stood by the bar chatting. Priidik leaned down and whispered in her ear, "I'm so happy to see you enjoying yourself."

"Thank you," Naina said, uncertain of how to react.

He leaned down again, whispering, "I was afraid you were having a difficult time."

"I'm not. This has been a great trip. I'm seeing so much and learning so much. I couldn't have asked for anything more."

He leaned down so close, his lips touched her ear, sending an electric shock through her whole body. "You've just made my day."

When he straightened back up, he peered directly into her eyes, and she got the distinct feeling he could see inside her.

"If I get reactions like yours, I feel my purpose here is fulfilled," he said.

"If you keep on taking me to places like this, I will feel like my purpose in life is fulfilled."

"Are you flirting with me?" Priidik raised an eyebrow.

Naina surprised herself and smiled. She too raised an eyebrow. "I might be."

The two of them stood slightly apart from the rest of the group. It wasn't so far they were excluding themselves, but it was far enough for them to not be overheard.

"So you have been enjoying yourself then?" Priidik asked.

"Very much. This trip has been life changing. I feel like, already, I'm a different person. Like I came here as a small and fearful individual, and I'm slowly emerging out of my shell."

"You seemed so quiet and hesitant I thought you were nervous or aloof."

"I was nervous. I wasn't sure what to expect. I'm also not good in groups, and I didn't know what it would be like traveling with a small group of people for so many days." Naina was once again surprised she spoke to Priidik with such honesty.

"Are you a bit of a recluse?"

"Yes, I guess I am. I don't have many friends. But I've developed a friendship with most people here. I didn't think I could, and that's really enjoyable."

"I have seen you stepping into your own and it's been really nice to watch. You started as a caterpillar and slowly evolved into a gorgeous butterfly."

"You are calling me gorgeous?" She embraced a full faced, full wrinkled smile.

"Yes, yes I am."

"Who's flirting now?"

Priidik laughed and Naina soon joined him. They continued conversing with each other, separate from the group. Naina shared more of how the tour had changed her. Priidik told her he became a tour guide to show others the beauty and wonder of his country and its neighbors. He thought the Baltics had great potential and he wanted to make sure others were aware of it. Passion oozed out of Priidik.

"I've never felt that passionate about something."

"I think we all need passion. Otherwise, what is the point of living?"

Naina knew Priidik was right. She considered if skincare and esthetics brought her the same amount of passion as Priidik had, but was still unsure.

On the walk back to the hotel, the drizzle had stopped and the clouds had cleared. That October night wasn't very cold, even for Charleston standards. The full moon lit their path. Priidik and Naina kept each other's pace, ahead of the group. A couple of times, their hands touched as if Priidik were trying to hold her hand.

He did for a few moments, and Naina smiled at him. He smiled back, but looked back at the group and let go, yet smiled back at Naina once again.

Smiling wasn't something she liked to do but it was something she was learning to do. She had been deeply afraid of having wrinkles on her face and had stopped herself from smiling, although there were many things she couldn't prevent from making her smile. One was puppies. They were too cute and too adorable. Also, children playing and discovering new things. There was nothing better than to see young ones exploring the world. And now Priidik was on the list. Priidik definitely made her smile.

Can You Be

That night in early October, as Naina settled in bed, it was clear how quickly change could happen. In a matter of days, she had visited three countries, and she still had two more to go.

Yes, Naina had always been afraid of change. It was what she feared most, but upon reflection, she had faced nothing but change in her entire life, no matter how much she had resisted it. Even her routines had resulted in her getting fired and in her father permanently pulling away from her. What if Fiona was right and change was good? Maybe what she needed most was to stop resisting change and see it as a positive.

What if she was resilient? She had grown better and stronger because of all she had been through. She was resourceful, and an effective planner. She had demonstrated that during her travels. What she had accomplished took courage, and she was still on the journey.

Change was here, once again. The cells in her body were jittery, almost whispering to each other in glee and excitement because they knew it was a joyful celebration, as if it were the stroke of midnight on New Year's. Congratulations, cheers, hugs, and kisses had been exchanged and everyone was ecstatic because although they didn't know what was coming, they were sure it was going to be good.

For the first time in her life, Naina sensed that every act she took, every passing moment, was supportive of her and her efforts. Everything she was doing was aiding her towards what she had always wanted, towards the nurturing and supportive family she wanted, and towards the independence she had yearned for. Everything she was doing was bringing her abundance, joy, love, health, and prosperity.

She didn't know what lay ahead, but she was increasingly certain she could handle whatever came her way. And she knew it would be great. It sent shivers throughout her being, as if every cell in her body were twinkling with possibility.

Chapter Thirty-Five

Naina was too hungover to have breakfast, something she hadn't experienced since a random night in college when she had gone out with Caitlin after a school game. That morning, at the start of the second week of October, Naina woke with the room spinning and the thought of food made her nauseous. The euphoria from the night before had dissipated.

She took two Advil with black coffee she made from the kettle in her room. That was all she could stomach as they drove out to the Northern Forts.

"Aren't you worried about what might happen if the Russians succeed in their invasion of Ukraine?" Pat asked.

Naina was grateful to Pat for asking a question, for now she had a reason to look at Priidik without regret. She had avoided eye contact with him all morning, unsure of how to behave with him.

Priidik looked directly at Pat. "Russians have lived in the Baltics in small numbers for many centuries."

He went on to explain what he had already told Naina during

their walk together in Narva. He talked about how the Baltic countries first gained their independence in 1918. Naina didn't care she had heard all of this already. She listened enraptured, staring at the vibrancy in Priidik's eyes and listening to the enthusiasm in his voice.

Priidik still didn't look at Naina. "The Baltic states retained their sovereignty until World War II broke out and during that time the Soviet Union forced the Baltic countries to allow them to station their armies in these lands. The lands went back and forth between German and Soviet control. At the end of the war, and specifically between August of 1944 and May of 1945, the Soviets retook control of the Baltics."

Naina glanced back towards Pat. He had closed his eyes and wasn't the only one. Everyone in the group, save for Naina and Priidik – and Artur, of course – had dozed off. Priidik made eye contact with her for the first time that morning. It sent shivers throughout her body. She smiled.

He smiled back. "These set of nations are prepared. They have fought against the Russians time and time again, even if it hasn't been in an out-right war."

Priidik continued his discourse as if he was giving a speech. It didn't seem he was at all impacted by the morose state of the group. He hadn't appeared to blink. Maybe that's what he did when he was hungover. She couldn't stomach food and he couldn't stop talking. Naina was grateful they hadn't stopped for the usual morning coffee and snack because she wouldn't have been able to stomach it.

Priidik carried on, describing the consequences of Soviet presence in the Baltics. Cultural practices, self-expression, and religious practices were suppressed. The economy had also been stifled.

Can You Be

Songs had always been of grave importance in the culture of the Baltics and provided its people with a sense of national identity. The most impactful independence movement by the Balts was the Singing Revolution. The singular strike happened on August 23, 1989, when two million Balts, which at the time were two-fifths of the native population, formed a 370-mile human chain from Vilnius through Riga and on to Tallinn, demanding independence. It was known as the "Baltic Way". Soon after, national leadership grew and set-up efforts to regain their independence. Through a series of votes, events, referendums, signed treaties, and other such measures, the countries regained their statehood. Lithuania was once again independent on February 9, 1991, and Estonia and Latvia on March 3, 1991.

Priidik finally stopped his discourse and turned away from Naina. Meanwhile, Naina could have continued listening for much longer. She loved hearing about the struggle for independence. Maybe Naina needed to find a way to develop her own sense of identity, her own quiet strength, her own way to reclaim herself. She wished she could stage her own singular singing revolution, albeit without the singing. She wasn't good at that.

❦

The Northern Forts were abandoned concrete bunkers by the sea built by a Russian tsar. They originally encircled the whole of Liepāja and were part of a large fortress that functioned as a naval base. However, less than ten years after the buildings were constructed, they were considered unnecessary. Some parts were blown up, and the rest were abandoned. Several large broken structures were strewn on the beach.

Naina would have liked to explore the ruins with Priidik, but he had walked off with Xavier and the Scottish women and Naina had no desire to follow them. She was fine on her own, and she was captivated. Large cement ruins had settled on the soft sands and many imposing structures had fallen into the ocean. The sun shone brightly and the beauty of the day gave a cynical tinge to the ruins.

It looked like the set of *Planet of the Apes*, in particular the scene where Charlton Heston rides on a horse along the beach, and chances upon the remains of the Statue of Liberty, finally realizing he had been on Earth all along. Naina wanted to kneel on the sand in despair, as Heston had done, but there wasn't a palpable sense of despair arounds these buildings. The ruins looked sad but nothing sad had happened in them. Nothing happened in them at all. There definitely wasn't any type of airy substance emanating in and around the area, not even from the trees. The buildings had simply been made redundant. There was no real significance to them.

When they got back in the van, Priidik was still avoiding her. He didn't share any other speeches but chatted instead with Artur. It was Naina's turn to fall asleep. When she woke up, they had arrived at their next stop.

Chapter Thirty-Six

"**W**here are we?" Naina asked.

"I believe we're in Lithuania. Right, Priidik?" Pat asked.

"That is right. We are in a town called Plateliai," Priidik answered.

Naina was sorry to have missed the border crossing into Lithuania because she was napping. She had wanted to see what the transition was like between Latvia and Lithuania. It was the day after she had woken up with a hangover but she was still queasy and lethargic.

The restaurant served a lot of interesting food. Some in the group ordered beet soup and others ordered pork, lamb, and other dishes. Although Naina was feeling better, she was still not fully settled from having drunk so much. She ordered a coke to settle her stomach and some dumplings for lunch.

Afterwards, they visited Plokštinė Missile Base, another Soviet-era underground facility. This one had apparently been one of the first missile bases the Soviet Union had built underground and was made up of four silos and a series of tunnels. It was, of course, no longer operational and one of the silos had been converted into a Cold War museum.

Naina didn't wait to see whether or not Priidik would avoid her. Had he been purposefully ignoring her before? She wasn't interested in playing games, and sped through the museum, staying far ahead of the rest of the group. Although she was below ground and the air was heavy and damp, it wasn't as oppressive as it had been in the bunker. Still, she walked quickly through all of the exhibits, realizing she wasn't interested in the events of the Cold War. She may have imagined the connection with Priidik or misunderstood it. She didn't want to think about it and was instead looking forward to having a popsicle at the museum shop. She rushed until she got there.

She had been curious about trying a popsicle, having seen Xavier eat one daily. She didn't want to admit she wanted one, but since she hadn't eaten much that day, this would be the most opportune time. And she did. She ordered a Twister. It had two flavors twisted around each other, and the orange and lime combination was the most delightful taste of the day.

ॐ

On that rainy Monday afternoon between early and mid-October, Naina was in disbelief when they arrived at the Hill of Crosses. The clouds hung low and although the rain was just a pesky drizzle, it gave the entire region a surreal air. There were so many crosses it was impossible to count. There were thousands or even millions. They ranged from a couple inches to several feet in height, some with the most ornate of designs and others in the simplest of constructions, held together by rubber bands.

They were a mere seven-and-a-half miles north of Šiauliai, but they could have been in the middle of nowhere. The hill was isolated. Priidik said the city was founded in 1236, and the area where the Hill of Crosses now stood was believed to have been a hill fort, although the first of the crosses were thought to have appeared in the area around the time the city of Šiauliai was founded. It had been used by residents as a symbol for their desire to be independent against invaders.

Crosses continued to be placed there over the years. In 1831, during a Lithuanian and Polish uprising against the Russians, peasants placed crosses to remember their missing and dead. People continued to place crosses on the site and by 1940 there were about four hundred of them. When the Soviets occupied Lithuania, the Hill of Crosses stood as a sign of defiance and the number of crosses grew. The Soviets destroyed and removed them several times, but locals still found a way to continue to place crosses. In 2007, there were an estimated 100,000 crosses, but by that point there was an exceptional and overwhelming number of them.

Naina momentarily forgot to breathe. People's faith and perseverance in the face of oppression was remarkable. Crosses were placed in an organized yet chaotic fashion, covering almost every spot on the hill, some hung upon others. There was no way of knowing just how many crosses there were. It would have been impossible to count the number of crosses unless someone was employed to methodically keep count.

The ride to the hotel was quiet. Everyone seemed subdued. Naina's stomach had settled by then, but she didn't have a big appetite. She ate a quick snack and went back to her room. She needed to rest.

But Naina wasn't able to rest. She was in awe of this demonstration of the power of faith. She didn't have a sense of faith. She wasn't even sure she believed in anything. She reasoned there was a higher power, something that governed it all, something that kept the universe ticking, but she didn't know if she believed in God. She could, but she didn't need it to be so. Maybe it was enough to believe there were higher forces, like a team of people who collaborated to make sure everything functioned properly.

Ironically, she hailed from the Holy City, yet she hadn't been infused with any of its faith. Although, Charleston had allowed her to believe magic was possible. Angel Oak was the main culprit. But she wasn't sure if she believed in the holy. She had to, she guessed, otherwise why would she have named Holy Man as such? And wasn't there holiness in all of magic? Wasn't magic holy?

Perhaps that was where Holy Man came from. He was other-worldly. There was no denying it. He didn't move through time and space like the rest of humanity seemed to do. He appeared exactly when she needed him and he always looked exactly the same. She had the feeling he had been sent to her from the beyond. Was his mere existence a beckoning call for her to place her own cross on the hill? Did she have it in her to have that kind of faith?

Chapter Thirty-Seven

Naina finally had an appetite. She woke up with a strong emptiness in her stomach, as if she hadn't eaten in days. She was eager to get to the restaurant to have breakfast and for the first time in her life, possibly, she ate voraciously. The buffet breakfast was arranged on a couple of tables and had a selection of yogurts, breads, cold cuts, eggs, and cheeses. She had several servings.

After checking out of the hotel, they visited the Ninth Fort. Three large structures were clearly visible from the parking lot. Naina at first thought this was the reason they had visited the fort. After all, the three large monuments were erected in a place where a large portion of the Jewish population had been killed, and the structures were meant to be a memorial to the victims of Nazism.

But it wasn't. The fort was nearby but in a separate complex, and it had been constructed by the Russians to defend its western border. However, in 1941, when the Nazis invaded Lithuania, it was taken over and the Soviets had to leave.

Before World War II, there had been a large Jewish population in Lithuania; about a third of the population in Kaunas was Jewish. However, after the Nazi invasion, 40,000 Jews were held in a ghetto in Kaunas, and the Ninth Fort was used as a mass killing site. The Jews killed there were brought from all over Lithuania, and even from other countries, including Germany. Close to 50,000 Jews were murdered at the Ninth Fort.

Naina felt sick to her stomach and ran out of the fort into the bright and sunny day. Despite the sun, she shivered, as if it was twenty degrees below the 54°F it actually was. She'd learned about the holocaust of course, but she'd never seen evidence of it or seen the pain of those suffering or heard their stories or learned about the years of torment and torture they endured. It was hard for her to breathe, but she wasn't having a panic attack. Immense grief enveloped her so tightly she thought it would consume her whole.

As they made their way back to the parking lot, the monuments, rather than being impressive appeared as lackluster representations of the atrocities that had occurred at the site. She thought they had been made of steel, but Priidik clarified they were poured concrete on steel skeletons, which further disappointed her.

They drove to Kaunas and had lunch at a fast-food chicken place. It was a nice change to the home cooked meals they had been receiving. At many of the restaurants they had eaten thus far, the food was hearty and nourishing, as if a grandma had cooked. This was their first taste of fast food. Although Naina didn't usually eat fast food, somehow, the change was comforting.

After lunch, Artur dropped the group off in the Kaunas city center where they were allowed to explore on their own. Naina drifted aimlessly, unable to shake the grief. She settled in a park on a bench, staring up at the cover of trees. The clouds had come in, but it wasn't any cooler. She was grateful it wasn't raining. She was also grateful they had the evening on their own.

She had just spent the morning hearing so many harrowing stories of people who had been murdered and so many others who had survived and persevered despite their circumstances. They had been filled with the desire to live. How was it then people like her mother were pushed to end their lives? How was it possible some wanted nothing more than to live and others would do anything not to?

Naina didn't know how her father had reacted to her mother's death. She had been dropped off at a family friend's house. She stayed with them for a period of time but she couldn't recall how long. When she came back home, there was a stepmother already in place. A few weeks after, she was shipped off to boarding school.

She struggled to keep alive the details of her mother's face but no matter how hard she tried they remained a blur. The only photo she had of her mother was the one of her third birthday where she posed next to her father. Naina often stared at it for hours on end. But she had no other clear memories of her mother. The image in her memory was paralyzed in that one pose with the one expression. It hadn't occurred to Naina to look for any other photos of her mother. When her father had shipped her off, she didn't know she'd eventually yearn for one. She only had the photo she did because it had been placed inside a frame that had been packed with the belongings she took to school, but she couldn't remember packing it. Someone, perhaps her father, had packed it for her. She didn't always remember her father's face either but that didn't bother her. For her mother, though, she often lost sleep.

By the time Naina got back to the hotel, she was soaked to the bone. She hadn't realized it had been raining.

The day Naina lost her mother stood out in her memory in that it wasn't remarkable. She struggled to remember, but all that stood out was being pulled out of school by her father, being held in his arms – one of the last tender moments she'd have with him. She didn't know who, perhaps it had been her father, perhaps it had been the family friends she had stayed with those first few days, who had explained she wouldn't see her mother again.

She wished she remembered the details, and often pulled together pieces from other days.

Her mother likely woke her up like she did every morning, gently, touching her on the head and whispering, "Rise and shine, my dearest *beti*. Allow those beautiful eyes to meet the day."

She likely sat at Naina's bedside and caressed Naina's face until she woke. The first image to greet her was her mother's smiling face and twinkling eyes, but she didn't appreciate them then. She didn't know yet she wouldn't see them again. Instead, likely, she groaned. Naina didn't want to go to school, she never wanted to go to school.

Likely, Naina's mother kept her company until Naina was in the bathroom, brushing her teeth. Only then was it certain Naina was not going to fall asleep again.

No matter how hard she tried, Naina couldn't remember what she'd had for breakfast. Her mother always made her breakfast. It wasn't until after she'd died that Naina got into the habit of having milk and cereal. While her mother was alive, she always prepared something fresh. It was likely to be a *paratha* or omelet – Indian style with cumin, onion, and cilantro.

Naina wished she'd had more interest in cooking and had learned how to dry roast potatoes and peas to make *gughuri*. She wished she'd jumped out of bed every morning and hurried down to the kitchen to see her mother roast dry crispy *chivda* and peanuts to make a snack. Or paid attention when she made the milky, ginger chai her mother drank as Naina shoved her breakfast down her throat.

Naina wished she had savored every mouthful, that she knew that the morning of December, precisely one month after Naina's seventh birthday, would be the last time she would have a breakfast cooked by her mother. She wished she had known it would be the last day she would receive tenderness. She wished she'd known then she wouldn't feel it again, so that she could have captured the moment, remembered it in detail, and bottled it up to soothe her for the rest of her dark days.

Instead, Naina went to sleep not understanding what it meant to not see her mother again, not knowing there would never be another person to tuck her into bed, there wouldn't be another person to whisper in her ear, "Sweetest of dreams. May they all come true, my dearest *beti*."

Chapter Thirty-Eight

The next morning Naina had the simplest meal she'd had thus far on the trip. The continental breakfast was laden with sweets, an assortment of cakes and cookies. Naina settled for toast and coffee. After checking out, Priidik introduced them to a local guide who told them they would be visiting other forts around the city.

"Is it okay if I stay in the van?" Naina asked after taking Priidik aside.

He placed his hand on her shoulder and squeezed it lightly. "I can guarantee you won't see what we did at the Ninth Fort. What we'll see today are abandoned forts that were also built by the Russians and used by the Nazi's and Soviets, but they were only ever used as forts."

Naina was grateful for his reassurance, as she was glad that the other forts didn't have horrid stories as in Ninth Fort. But she wasn't glad Priidik had avoided her this long. "Hey, so why does it take for me to pull you aside for you to acknowledge me?"

Can You Be

Priidik let his head hang for a moment. "I'm sorry, Naina. I know I have been avoiding you, and it's not fair after the connection we've shared. I've been concerned about how it would come across to the others, if they thought I was favoring you, and in the process I've been pushing you away. I'll do better. Can you please give me some time?"

Naina nodded. She understood, to a degree. She understood Priidik needed to make sure everyone in the group felt included, and that responsibility didn't include romantic trysts. She'd give him some time, but not too long.

The mood in the other forts was lighter. These were abandoned structures many locals volunteered to maintain to preserve their heritage and drive tourism. The guide explained the forts may not have been the proudest part of their history, but they were still part of their story, and as such they wanted to celebrate and maintain them. Naina was relieved that, once again, she'd been exposed to the Baltic penchant for perseverance, for making the best of their limiting circumstances, for wanting to turn things around positively and ensure their luck wasn't temporary but rightfully theirs.

The guide took them to an area in Kaunas similar to the one they had seen outside Tallinn. On that sunny afternoon in October, they visited another Soviet era neighborhood full of concrete block buildings built to create a sense of community. The buildings still had a drab look to them but the local residents were working hard to revive the neighborhood, celebrate it, and build a true community around it. It was called the Šilainiai Project.

It was a contrast to the other lackluster looking neighborhood they had visited, only because it had been infused with life and a sense of pride. The residents hadn't created these structures out of their own will. Rather, they had been forced to live within them, but

221

they didn't want to maintain the dullness that hung around them. They wanted their home communities to be lively and delightful.

It was encouraging people enjoyed living in these neighborhoods. For the first time, she was grateful for the building in Charleston she lived in. She only knew two people, Fiona and Raiya, and although she wasn't speaking to Raiya and she barely knew Fiona, it awoke in her a need to stay in the building. For the first time in her life, she had a strong desire to remain living there. She would stay, and she would try her hardest to form a sense of community.

⅜

The sense of hope and peace Naina had experienced that morning in Kaunas dissipated when they walked through Grūtas Park.

When they had first arrived, Naina thought they were there to see exotic animals. Albino kangaroos and emus jumped freely behind their cages, bringing her a sense of levity.

As the group walked around, it didn't remain that way. The park was the home of a large collection of Soviet era statues and relics. When Lithuania regained independence in 1991, Soviet statues were removed, and a local businessman requested they be displayed at the park. His intention was also to recreate a gulag style Soviet camp, complete with paths, guard towers, and barbed fences, as if to ensure the cruelty of the Soviets was not forgotten.

All these statues represented people who were oppressors. Naina knew they had once represented a utopia, a promise for an ideal world the Soviets strived to create. But she couldn't connect with that idea. In her view, when the original statues had been erected, the people had been celebrated for their cruelty to the locals and their loyalty to an unjust and manipulative regime.

The trees at this park weren't magical or eerie, and it was odd the statues were surrounded by natural beauty, as if their brutality had been discarded. Naina walked quickly, in front of the others, with her hand placed over the angelite and amber crystals, and waited for them at the coffee shop within the park.

As they left Grūtas Park and headed to Druskininkai, Priidik sat next to Naina in the van. "These statues seem to have affected you quite a bit. Are you alright?"

"Yes, it was just a bit too much with everything else we have seen."

Priidik nodded, as if he too felt the same way. "There is an article I read about an American photographer, Matthew Moore, who photographed discarded Soviet sculptures and monuments. He visited places all over the old Soviet Union where the statues had originally stood, as well as the areas where they had been moved to. He said something in this article that really stayed with me. The areas where the statues had been removed from needed to have them removed as part of their healing process. And seeing the statues in their original form spoke of the propaganda they had stood for. He said 'statues and monuments almost always convey a false history – a history that was chosen based on our current political beliefs.' And that is all they are, Naina. They don't hold meaning unless we give them meaning."

His words sunk in, taking hold of her emotions in a way they no longer controlled her. "I guess you're right."

"I could have chosen to show you another park with statues, one that is quite different. We won't have time on this trip, but it would be worth visiting if you like, at some point in the future. It's called Orvidas Garden, and it's in Salantai. This park is full of religious statues that survived Soviet rule. The founder, Vilius Orvidas, was a Christian and an artist, and as a form of rebellion he created a sculpture garden that spoke to the resilience of his faith."

"I would love to see it," Naina said. Priidik reached for her hand.

When they got to the hotel in Druskininkai, the others in the group went for a walk into town to have dinner. Naina ate a quick dinner in the hotel and went for a walk on her own around a park across the street.

She couldn't make sense of all she had witnessed. With such a mix of varied history she didn't know how to put two and two together. There was cruelty and mass killings and oppression but there was also hope and belief and ancient history.

Naina felt a heightened connection to her ancestors. Despite or perhaps because she lived away from them and from her family, she felt them, as if they were a part of her. She didn't know much about them but she knew they had been keeping tabs on her. Seeing so much history awoke in her a curiosity to learn about her own family. Who were they and where did they come from? Would her father tell her more?

Naina even felt connected to the children she didn't yet have but knew were coming. She had an opportunity to build a future for the generations who would follow her. She didn't yet have a relationship, but she knew she would. She knew she would get married and have children, but she would be the mother for them – the parent for them – that her own parents hadn't been able to be for her. She would heal her shortcomings and be the person she was meant to be. She didn't know how she had suddenly awoken to this knowledge, but something told her she would.

Somehow, she knew healing herself would heal all those who had come before her and all those who would come after her. She was being presented with an opportunity to heal her ancestral and future lines.

Can You Be

"Open your heart," Holy Man said.

As she'd reached Nemunas River, he'd appeared eating the same Twister popsicle she had eaten at the missile base.

"How did you get here?" Naina asked.

"I have my ways." He smiled.

Naina didn't know what he meant. "How do I open my heart?"

"Opening your heart is about not judging yourself, not judging others, and holding love for yourself and for others. It is about opening up to joy. When you are critical and judgmental of yourself or of others, you hold on to resentment and bitterness. This keeps you closed and limited. It is how you have been for most of your life. But you now have a chance. You are exploring all the glorious wonders the Earth has to offer. Don't hold on to the limited view you have had of yourself, of your life, and of what is possible for you. You don't have to continue experiencing what you have before. You have a chance to break this cycle and heal yourself by remaining open. You have endured a lot and it can end.

"Open your heart with love, with compassion, and with forgiveness for those who have let you down. You have let yourself down, as well. Offer yourself the same love, compassion, and forgiveness. Allow yourself, with this trip, to start anew. Do it for yourself. Do it because no one else will do it for you and do it because you owe yourself the best life you can have."

It was as if Holy Man had read her mind, just before, while she had been discovering her connection to her ancestors. "But I am so afraid of being hurt. I have been hurt before. Who's to say I won't be hurt again?"

"Fear comes from our ego. Fear holds us back. You are facing the unknown on this trip in a way you have never done before because you do not know what you will see, the places you will

225

visit, the history you will encounter. But you aren't at the mercy of the winds. You are safe and guided. The universe is supporting you. I am supporting you. You are supporting yourself. You are not alone and you have nothing to fear. Just because others have hurt you in the past doesn't mean it will happen again. What you have lived through, what you have experienced, doesn't define you."

Tears streamed down Naina's face, allowing her to finally release so much of what she had been harboring within. "What do I do with the hurt I hold inside?"

For the first time, Holy Man had nothing to say. He threw away his popsicle and faced Naina. He held both of her hands in his and closed his eyes. A glittery glowing energy emanated from him. It wasn't fully lit, and she knew others weren't able to see it. But she could. The energy reached out from him and into her. And as it permeated her energy, her skin warmed. The warmth spread from the surface into her interior until her heart warmed, as if there was a glowing within. This glowing extended back out from her heart to the rest of her body and into the air around her. This light reached out toward Holy Man, and when it permeated him, he opened his eyes and smiled.

"You are on a path of healing, Naina. Know it. Own it. And have a safe journey."

Chapter Thirty-Nine

Before she went to sleep that October night in Druskininkai, Naina got an email from Raiya in which he apologized profusely and asked if they could meet. He hadn't seen her in the apartment building and was worried. He also wanted the opportunity to explain what he had done. He didn't have any excuses but he wanted to say sorry in person.

Naina didn't know how to respond. She read the email two more times, to make sure she hadn't missed anything. She shut down her laptop and paced around the room. Her breathing shortened and grew more rapid. Her head felt light, and her body told her she was going to have a panic attack.

She had brought the clary sage essential oil Fiona had gifted her a few days before Naina had left for the trip. Naina hadn't expected to get another visit from her, thinking the kindness Fiona had shown her was a one-time event. But Fiona had showed up with a genuine approach and with a bottle of clary sage essential oil. Naina had invited her in for coffee and digestives, and Fiona had shared she had long suffered from anxiety, and Mimi had been a gift for her.

Fiona had said, "You may need the clary sage Naina, and I would rather you have this than suffer through another attack with nothing to turn to."

Naina had been grateful then, and felt so all over again as she placed drops of the oil onto a tissue and took several deep breaths. She did several rounds of tapping, repeating the affirmation, "I am safe. I can handle this." Soon she calmed down. She placed the angelite and amber in front of her and drafted a response for Raiya:

Hi, I'm really sorry but I can't do it. I have had several panic attacks as a direct result of my stress levels. I am not blaming you for it, nor am I saying you need to worry or care. Alice fired me and then you turned out to be the deceitful person you are, and I couldn't handle it. I had a panic attack a few weeks ago, and after reading your message I almost got one again.

I understand you want to speak to me, and I don't want to hold grudges against you, so I think I will eventually want to speak to you, but not now. When I am ready, and if I am ready, I will let you know. For the moment, the thought of having any type of conversation with you is too stressful.

You say you didn't mean to be hurtful when you said all those things to your friend, but you did hurt me. You hurt me more than anyone has hurt me in the recent past and with all I have shared with you about my upbringing and my father, you should have known better. It's not because what you did was particularly egregious, but because I had grown to care more about you than I had anyone else in recent memory. Your behavior and attitude towards me matters more than other people's behavior and attitude.

Can You Be

So to be treated like you thought so little of me, to hear you say you thought I was odd or weird, was the ultimate sign of disrespect to me because it means you feel like you can say whatever you want, and you think it won't matter as long as you think I haven't heard. It means you feel you can treat me like shit and it doesn't matter ... What I won't know or hear won't hurt me. And that's extremely disrespectful.

I'm sure you were not aware I was listening but that's not an excuse. There's a possibility you'll act that way again, and if you do, it will be the end of us. Although part of me is afraid we have reached the end already.

You may not respect me but I respect myself, and I'm not willing to go through that again. So I'm sorry, but for now, I am happy to have peace on my own, without contact or communication with you.

And you haven't seen me because I have been traveling. I may be in touch when I get back, or I may not. Time will tell.

⁂

Naina woke the next morning simultaneously nervous and excited about having her first ever massage and facial. She had booked a ninety-minute session that included a forty-five-minute full body relaxation massage and a forty-five-minute facial. This would be her chance to determine if becoming an esthetician was a possibility for her. If she experienced a proper facial, she could see if she had it in her to do the same.

Fifteen minutes before the appointment time, she walked down to the hotel lobby and asked where her treatment would be. The front desk agent recommended she get dressed into a robe – one of the ones in the room. Naina thought the treatment would be at a spa, but the receptionist clarified the treatment would take place in a massage room down one of the hotel corridors.

"So it isn't in a separate spa?" Naina asked, realizing it was a redundant question when she saw the expression of annoyance on the front desk agent's face.

"No, we do not have a spa. It is in a treatment room down the hall." He spoke slowly, enunciating every word, and pointed in the direction of the corridor. He spoke in a perfect British English accent.

Naina was ashamed she'd thought the receptionist wouldn't speak English fluently simply because they were in the middle of nowhere in Lithuania. "Where do I go after I change into the robe?"

The front desk agent let out a tight and loud sigh. "You come back here. The massage therapist will meet you here, in the lobby."

Naina ran back to her room, changed quickly, and ran back to the lobby. Not only did she not want to be late for her treatment, she also, somehow, wanted to find a way to appease the front desk agent. She smiled at him as she entered the lobby once again, noting how at ease she felt with smiling. She gave him a small wave, for good measure, surprising herself more and more by these acts of friendliness.

He glanced up at her. "The massage therapist will be here soon."

"So, she's called a massage therapist? Not a masseuse?" She didn't know why she still needed to make conversation with him, but her mouth was working faster than her mind, and it was an unusual feeling.

The agent took a deep breath. "The word masseuse is French for a woman who performs massages and a massage therapist can be male or female, but also implies the person is professionally trained. And this one is also an esthetician. That means she's professionally trained to give facials."

Before Naina had a chance to reply, the massage therapist walked into the lobby and greeted Naina with a smile. She exchanged words with the front desk agent in Lithuanian and signaled for Naina to follow her.

"She doesn't speak English, but she's good," the agent said, as Naina walked away.

"Oh. Thank you," Naina was disappointed she couldn't ask the woman questions, but maybe it was for the best, as it would allow Naina to experience the treatment without having to interrupt.

When they got to the treatment room, the massage therapist indicated to Naina to take off the robe and to lie face down on the bed. She mimed all of this to Naina, and when Naina started to disrobe, the therapist indicated, with her finger, to give her some time. She stepped out of the room, and it was then Naina understood she was meant to disrobe while the therapist gave her privacy.

There was a large purple geode, and Naina kneeled down to take a closer look. Warm tentacles emanated from the crystal, and she touched it to allow some of the warmth to seep into her. When she climbed onto the treatment bed, she was delighted to feel a warm blanket underneath, making the environment warm and cozy. The therapist knocked on the door before walking back in. She draped Naina with a series of sheets and a heavy comforter.

Although the therapist didn't speak a word, it seemed she knew exactly where to place emphasis on Naina's body. She worked diligently to remove the knots on Naina's shoulders and the tightness in her lower back. She asked Naina to turn around on the treatment bed, to face upwards. The therapist eased out the tension from Naina's legs. Naina moaned with pleasure throughout, until the massage therapist tapped her on the shoulder and raised her index finger to her lips.

Blood rushed to Naina's face. This was the day for her to feel embarrassed. She stopped moaning, no matter how good the massage, and eventually the facial, felt. The massage therapist took great care to remove the blackheads from Naina's nose, although there weren't many, but it thrilled her to know her pores would be even more clean. Naina's favorite part was the facial massage. She didn't feel the therapist's nails even once.

When the treatment was over, the therapist once again stepped out of the room and waited for Naina to put the robe back on. When Naina stepped out of the treatment room the therapist offered her a glass of water. Back at the lobby, the therapist asked the front desk agent to translate for her. She was impressed by how smooth and supple Naina's skin was, and wondered what Naina did to keep her skin like that.

"Maybe it's because I don't wear any make up," Naina reasoned.

The therapist spoke some more, and the agent then said, "She said it's got to be more than that. She has never worked on skin as good as yours, and she is asking what your skin care routine is?"

"I don't think I have much of a routine," Naina confessed. Still, she explained the same process she had relayed to Raiya a mere month ago, saying she cleansed her face with coconut oil, wiped off the excess with calendula hydrosol, and moisturized with a mixture of jojoba and rosehip. She used lavender essential oil as a spot treatment.

The massage therapist expressed Naina's skincare routine sounded amazingly effective and recommended for Naina to look into natural skin care product lines, including makeup, to enhance Naina's natural beauty. Naina promised she would.

After the therapist left, Naina asked the front desk agent, "I apologize in advance for the stupid question, but why is she called a massage therapist if she also does facials?"

"Technically estheticians are licensed to do facials, and she is licensed as a massage therapist and an esthetician, but it is a mouthful to call her both, so I choose to call her a massage therapist."

"I see ... there are two more things, if you don't mind?"

"Sure." The front desk didn't appear as annoyed now as he had before she'd had the treatment, but he still didn't smile.

"What was the large crystal in the treatment room? The large purple rock."

"I wondered if anyone ever noticed that, and I'm surprised you did. The geode is an amethyst." For once, his statement sounded like a compliment.

"Do you know why it's there?"

"Amethysts are supposed to be good for healing and stress relief. They can also help awaken the intuition and feel more spiritual connection."

"Oh I see ... And the second thing. I thought I would flatter her by expressing I was enjoying the massage, so I moaned loudly a couple of times. But, she silenced me. Why was that?"

The front desk agent finally cracked a smile. More so, it was clear he was trying hard to contain his laughter. "I can't tell you for sure, but I believe moaning goes hand-in-hand with 'happy ending' massages, and I'm sure she is too much of a professional to associate herself with those."

"What is a happy ending massage?"

The front desk agent dropped his head for a moment before looking back up at her. This time, he let out a short giggle. "'Happy endings' are massages with the aim of sexual pleasure and are not what a professional massage therapist would provide."

"Oh, I had no idea." Naina didn't know if she could handle any more embarrassment. "I hope I didn't offend her."

"I'm sure she's fine and understood you didn't mean any disrespect."

Naina rushed back to her room and when the group checked out of the hotel later that morning, she was relieved the front desk agent was no longer there. Someone else had replaced him.

༈

When Naina sat in the comfort of the van on that morning in almost mid-October, Priidik climbed in behind her. He smiled but didn't sit next to her. He went back to his previous seat.

Naina wasn't going to feel bothered by it. The mortification from earlier still weighed on her, as did Raiya's email. Loss and confusion fueled the all too familiar loneliness that seeped into her. She tried to recall what Holy Man had told her the previous day. He had said she was on a path of healing. Could that be true?

Every time Naina had loneliness creep in, she had come up with a new story for someone she had seen while on a walk around Charleston or someone she had met at the real estate office. She hadn't realized, until that moment, that the activity she enjoyed doing so much, coming up with people's backstories, had been a defense mechanism. She had started it when she was in Candor Boarding School, but she had continued doing it as an adult, seemingly a pro at it.

Dreaming up other people's lives entertained her. Even if a defense mechanism, she enjoyed it, and she did it because it sealed up her dark pockets, squashing away any sadness that dared to rise, dared to disrupt her peace. And what she hadn't been able to fill up

234

with stories, she had compensated for with routines. The constancy of her days had allowed her to feel she had something concrete to hold on to, something stable, something that was hers.

Despite the realization, as Artur drove them to Vilnius, she couldn't deny cracks remained. No matter how many stories she had come up with and no matter how many routines she had devised, the cracks were still there. The more time passed, the more cracks appeared, so many she could no longer ignore them. They were clearly visible.

Naina sank further into her seat, wanting to hide away from the world. She was afraid soon enough, even the sturdiest of the shells around her would crack. The boxed life she had created for herself would soon and surely crumble.

What was the point of keeping all those practices? The stories were innocent, and rather accurate. But she hadn't gained anything from them, other than insights into people's lives. What about the routines? Were they helpful? Did they really provide some type of solace and stability, or were they, as she had increasingly begun to feel, a type of cage?

Chapter Forty

That morning of almost mid-October, they headed to the last stop of the tour, Vilnius. The group still had a whole day together and Naina couldn't believe it would all end so soon. She also worried about Priidik. She would give him until the end of the day, and if he didn't approach her, she would approach him. But what then? Was their connection – she couldn't deny they had one – strong enough to last beyond the tour? Would it wither away as all the other ones had? How would they part?

They didn't stop at a restaurant as they had been doing to make the most of their time in Vilnius, so they had lunch at a gas station. While most bought fresh hot dogs or pastries, Naina opted for a sandwich and chips. She also wanted to have a KitKat and a flat white. For some reason that day she wasn't feeling adventurous.

When they sat back in the van, Priidik said, "There were often different names for the same city or the same place. Much of it is due to the changing ruling ethnicities and countries through the Baltics. The names have caused controversy, and the name currently in use is based on the current local ethnicity. For example, Vilnius was also known as Vilna during the Russian Empire and Wilno by the Polish. Kaunas was called Kovno by the Jews. Tallinn was known as Reval and Tartu as Dorpat or Yuryev."

"Doesn't the river in Vilnius also have a bunch of names?" Pat asked.

"Yes. I'm so glad you were paying attention. The river we'll be seeing in Vilnius is called Vilnelė by the Lithuanians or Wilejka by the Polish."

When they reached Vilnius, the group freshened up quickly and set out within ten minutes of arriving. The weather was perfect, partly cloudy, with the sun lighting up the day but not stinging them. It was a pleasant 52ºF, and Naina shivered in anticipation for what they would see.

They walked across the river and saw a large flower display in support of Ukraine. They continued along the river and up an old Soviet sports center that had been built on top of an old Jewish cemetery. The only reminder of the cemetery was a sign indicating it had once been there. The sports complex was an imposing building, as many of the Soviet structures were, but it sat abandoned, and when they got a closer look, it seemed it could collapse at any moment. Naina was relieved she didn't feel oppressed. Just a sense of sadness and camaraderie for what was abandoned. Some things, though, deserved to be left behind. For the first time, possibly ever, she had the certainty it didn't include her.

They went to the Lukiškės Prison where part of season four of *Stranger Things* had been filmed. After the visit, Naina swore she would do her best never to visit a prison again. Prior to the Baltics tour, she had never been in one, not even to Alcatraz in San Francisco, and she intended to stay as far away from them as she could. They were daunting institutions, and although people needed to be punished for crimes they committed, a better approach would be to reform criminals rather than keep them in such suppressive confinement. It felt inhumane.

They then walked through the Užupis neighborhood, a self-declared independent republic with their own bill of rights. One of the walls in the neighborhood had the bill of rights displayed in plaques in different languages. She read each term slowly and carefully, allowing it to take form within her, as if it were her call-to-action. The Užupis Constitution had forty-one rights. The ones that spoke to Naina were:

3. Everyone has the right to die, but this is not an obligation.

4. Everyone has the right to make mistakes.

5. Everyone has the right to be unique.

6. Everyone has the right to love.

16. Everyone has the right to be happy.

18. Everyone has the right to be silent.

19. Everyone has the right to have faith.

20. No one has the right to violence.

25. Everyone has the right to be of any nationality.

26. Everyone has the right to celebrate or not celebrate their birthday.

31. Everyone may be independent.

32. Everyone is responsible for their freedom.

38. Everyone has the right to not be afraid.

It was written in July 1998 by Thomas Chepaitis (Minister of Foreign Affairs of Užupis) and Romas Lileikis (President of Užupis).

Naina loved them. Maybe she could move to Užupis? This had to be a special place for the residents to come up with such terms for their constitution. Just then, a denser cloud settled overhead with a marked decrease in temperature. No, perhaps she wouldn't move. Instead, maybe she could take a piece of it with her.

She took photos of the constitution. She had to retake a couple because Holy Man appeared in the reflection.

"Can I purchase a printed copy of the constitution?" Naina asked Priidik.

"I am sure you can in one of the local shops."

Naina purchased a copy of one. This might be the first thing she could hang on her walls. The Užupis Constitution was a wake-up call for her life. All she cared for, all she wanted for herself, was captured in forty-one simple statements.

"They're unrealistic," Xavier said, standing behind her.

Naina turned to face him. "They are unrealistic to you because you see the world as closed-in and dark. I find them inspirational because I choose to see the light."

In that moment, the old Naina gave way to the new Naina.

✤

The Vilnius old town captured a similar type of medieval magic of the other Baltic cities, but somehow felt more modern, more integrated with current times, but not as well preserved as the other cities. Still, Naina loved it, thinking she might move to Vilnius, until once again she remembered how much she loved Charleston.

The group had dinner at a typical Lithuanian restaurant. Priidik sat next to Naina and held her hand under the table. She worried someone in the group would notice them, but then, she didn't care. They exchanged anecdotes about the trip, leaving Naina and Priidik's handholding unseen.

Afterwards, Priidik asked everyone out for drinks, but most in the group were too tired. In a reversal from Narva, everyone in the group walked back to the hotel, and Priidik and Naina stayed out. Naina, though, had resolved not to drink. She didn't want to feel hungover again, she wanted to keep her wits about her to make the most of her time with Priidik.

As soon as everyone was out of sight, Priidik leaned down and kissed her.

Naina's heart exploded, an emotion so intense she forgot how to breathe. The mere sight of him made her feel faint, and having him stand so close to her made the world stop. She took in every part of him and laid a hand on his belly, matching their breathing in synchronicity.

She hadn't felt anything like that before, not even with Kevin. Yes, with Kevin everything had been new. She had felt giddy with excitement at the thought of someone loving her. That is, until she realized it had all been a ruse. Until Kevin had flooded her with disappointment and crushed her spirit. Looking back, that first relationship she'd had when she was in college, what she'd felt for Kevin hadn't been love. She'd had an infatuation that hadn't progressed because he had made her believe she wasn't lovable.

But with Priidik it was different. He was expressive, despite his stoic Estonian nature. It had only been a week but it had been a transformational one. And she felt like she knew him. He was patient and considerate with her fellow tourists, answering every question, no matter how petty or senseless or ignorant. He didn't lose his nerve or indicate annoyance. He was gracious and considerate, saying to her once, after she asked if he didn't get frustrated, that he didn't expect everyone to know everything. He wanted to make sure people felt comfortable during the trip in all respects, including feeling all their questions and concerns were addressed, they learned more about the Baltics, and they found a reason to come back, tell others about it, and encourage them to visit.

A warmth in Naina's heart spread to light her entire being. She would be lucky to have someone like him in her life, but then again, she didn't deserve him. But she couldn't help being attracted to him. No matter how much she tried not to, she smiled whenever he was around. He brought so much joy to her, and she would always cherish him, no matter what would come of this.

She had no idea how he felt. Was his consideration for her the same as it was for the other tourists or was there something special he saved just for her? She wanted to believe he did, but in that moment, it didn't matter. He brought her a type of joy she had never felt before. And for now, that was enough.

Chapter Forty-One

"When I was growing up, my favorite birthday tradition was making fairy bread," Gemma said.

Priidik and Naina hadn't slept a wink. They had showered and changed before meeting the rest of the group for breakfast, making sure to arrive separately.

There were no tourist activities planned for the day. Gemma, Caroline, Lou, Pat, Xavier, Priidik, Artur, and Naina were sitting around the breakfast table. They had gathered early for one last meal before everyone flew back home.

That morning, the hotel provided a full breakfast buffet similar to the one in Tallinn, but this time, Naina served herself confidently, spooning large quantities of food onto her plate. She ate with a great appetite.

Gemma explained that although she was from Glasgow, her grandmother had lived in Melbourne. They spent summers in Melbourne and Gemma loved it because she was able to spend time in the city, which upon reflection seemed like Hong Kong. There was a strong Asian influence when Gemma walked the streets, and she felt as if she were in a large cosmopolitan Asian city. Her grandmother had a house in Frankston, which was one hour away from Melbourne, down the Mornington Peninsula. She lived a few blocks away from the beach, and Gemma remembered spending a lot of time frolicking on the long stretch of sand overlooking the Melbourne skyline, albeit from a far.

"We used to have fairy bread as well," Xavier confirmed.

"What is fairy bread?" Naina asked, feeling proud she was comfortable contributing to the conversation.

Gemma explained, "Fairy bread is white bread, slabbed with butter, and covered in sprinkles."

"It sounds like it would be the perfect snack to have as a child. But it wasn't in place of a birthday cake, was it?" Lou asked.

"Oh no! It was just a snack served alongside other food. All the kids loved it. You couldn't have a birthday party if you didn't have fairy bread," Gemma added.

"It sounds like the perfect snack for a child, but as an adult, it's repulsive. The worst part is the white bread isn't toasted and the butter is applied cold. The sprinkles on top make the entire thing taste artificial," Xavier explained.

Naina tried to remember what her birthday celebrations had been like – the ones she'd had when her parents were still with her. She had a vague recollection of candles on a cake and balloons tied to a chair, but she couldn't recall much else. What was the cake like? Had other people been there? Did she have friends back then? What gifts did she receive?

She also wasn't sure if these vague recollections were a result of the only memento she had kept, which was the photo of her as a three-year old sitting in front of a round cake with white frosting.

Her big eyes stared at the camera, but she wasn't smiling. She looked happy, but not overtly so. Her mother and father kneeled at either side and they did smile. That photo was the only one she had of her with her parents, of the three of them together.

"We all just went to the nearby Mickey D's or Chuck-E-Cheese," Lou added.

"Mickey D's?" Xavier asked.

"McDonald's."

"In Australia we refer to it as Macca's," Xavier offered.

"In Scotland it is McD's," Gemma added.

"In Germany it is Mekkes and when I went to Mexico they called it McDona's," Priidik offered.

Although she couldn't remember her birthday celebration, Naina's earliest memory was also her happiest memory. She had been in San Francisco with the Golden Gate Bridge overhead. She had played in the sand as her parents had sat on a blanket. They had packed a picnic but she couldn't remember what they had eaten. She clearly remembered having had a large cotton candy. She didn't have a celebration at a McDonald's, but somehow, her memory seemed particularly special.

"I'm sorry if I've been a downer. I hadn't intended to. I know it takes time to warm to me and for me to warm to others," Xavier said.

"Oh, you've been fine," Gemma said.

The others nodded in agreement.

"I'm a bitter old man, and you are all being too gracious," Xavier said.

"You've been a great addition," Priidik added.

"We've all enjoyed having you," Caroline joined.

"Nah, it's all good. I know I'm grumpy, and I'm man enough

244

to admit it's because I have never known love, and a series of bad relationships have led me to be a person I'm not proud of being," Xavier choked up.

Caroline passed him some tissues.

Xavier dabbed his eyes. "You have shown me more kindness and generosity of spirit than I could've ever deserved, and accepted me for who I am."

There was a moment of silence, after which everyone exchanged hugs.

Naina understood Xavier. "I've been reclusive and awkward for most of my life. I continue to be so, but I've felt more accepted in this group than I ever have before. It's my biggest takeaway from this tour."

The group hugged again.

Naina exchanged contact information with Gemma and Caroline, and they promised to keep in touch.

They left, one by one, and before long it was just Naina and Priidik. Her flight was the last of them all. They sat back down at the table.

"And what now?" Naina asked.

"You have just a couple of hours before your flight leaves, so we can go for a walk or something, perhaps back to the old town we haven't had a chance to explore much of," Priidik said.

"I mean between you and me."

"Let's go for a walk first and decide later."

And so they did. At times, Priidik held her hand, and he accompanied her back to the hotel to make sure she got into a taxi. Naina didn't have the courage to ask him again what would happen between them.

But in parting, Priidik kissed her lightly on the lips. "I will be in touch."

Naina flew out to Helsinki that afternoon with a faint glimmer of hope in her heart.

Chapter Forty-Two

In Helsinki, Naina ordered room service when she arrived. It was late and she hadn't wanted to venture out. The next morning, she had breakfast at the hotel. It was the first time she'd eaten alone since the start of October, but it was a buffet and she reveled in the choices. There were five types of cereals, oats, muesli, seven types of breads and three of crackers, at least eight different pastries, a wide selection of fruit, cold cuts, cheeses, herring prepared three ways, and desserts. Naina sat in the breakfast room for more than an hour, filling herself up.

But she couldn't shake off the feeling she was alone and to dispel her loneliness, she walked around the neighborhood along the Baltic Sea. Naina didn't mind it was raining and although it indicated it was 50°F, the dampness in the air made her feel it was 45°F. She shopped at K-Market before going back to the hotel to eat her lunch in the room. The thought of eating alone in a restaurant was unbearable, unless it was a breakfast buffet. She missed the company of her Baltic Tour group.

Naina joined the afternoon tour at the Senate Square where the guide gave them information about the city. Naina ignored the continued rain, content to cover her head with her hood and go back to being anonymous. She was again incorporated into a larger third-party tour, where she was mixed with people she didn't know and would never know. She was now comfortable to exchange a smile here and there, but the only person who shared their name was the tour guide and, as soon as the woman uttered it, Naina forgot it.

The tour guide shared some interesting tidbits about Helsinki and Finland. The Love Boat was filmed at a shipyard in the city. Alcohol was expensive because it was more heavily taxed than anywhere else. Ice hockey was considered Finland's second religion and they played to beat Sweden. It was a friendly competition, but Sweden seemed to be the better team. Angry Birds was a Finnish invention as were Molotov cocktails, ice skates, and SMS texting. The country was home to Nokia and many app and game developers. Finland had the world's best education system. Literacy was one of the highest, and Finnish students ranked at the top in global test scores. Their approach was about "less is more" because kids started school at a later age, they had shorter school days, and they included daily play and less homework.

Naina was content with the opportunity to learn about yet another place on the Baltic Sea, but she missed the quaintness of the Baltic countries. They had charm and although Helsinki was beautiful, it had a sense of aloofness. The tour guide explained the Finnish weren't particularly expressive, not in emotion or in verbal communication. They were people of a few words and quite direct.

As the tour made its way around the main sites of the city, Naina was the happiest when she saw the areas in Helsinki designed in Art

Nouveau style. They were similar to the ones in Riga, and brought a lightness within her, as if she were still connected to Latvia. In Helsinki, the designs incorporated folk and fairytale animals and beasts. Helsinki had the highest number of Art Nouveau buildings in Europe, given that only 5% of the city was destroyed during wars.

Helsinki was the Daughter of the Baltic because it was where land and sea came together. Nature was always within reach, whether it be trees or sea, with several parks, nature areas, and arboretums scattered around the city. Esplanade Park was the main city promenade. The city included about three-hundred interconnected islands so the sea was always accessible. It was such a part of daily life that in the spring people brought out their rugs to wash away the winter grime in the Baltic Sea.

Despite the city's accessibility to nature, Naina didn't consider living there. Finland was the happiest country in the world, but it was expensive, and far beyond anything Naina considered affordable. Airy substances emanated from the trees in the city, but she didn't feel connected to them in the same way she did to Angel Oak or the forests in the Baltics.

At the end of the day, Naina was relieved the tour hadn't included any prison visits. She couldn't have stomached it. She missed conversing and interacting with others. It was an unexpected reversal from how she had felt in Sweden. She never imagined she'd need people. Now she was certain she needed people in her life.

※

On a mid-October morning, Naina flew back to Charleston. She had been outside of the United States for a full fifteen days. She didn't know how long she had been in India when her parents had taken her as a child, but this was the longest it had been in her memory. It was unbelievable she'd been gone for two weeks.

She was elated and saddened, figuring it must be what people referred to as bittersweet. Bitter because she didn't want it to end, and sweet because she was happy to be heading home. She wanted nothing more than to be back in Charleston, steeped in her own city of history, her own cobblestone streets, her own ancient buildings. They may not have been medieval, but they were significant to her.

She wanted nothing more than to hang on to the exhilarating energy she had acquired during the trip. She wanted to continue to be this new Naina, the Naina who tried new things, the Naina who didn't need her routines to help her make sense of her life, the Naina who didn't worry, fear, and feel anxious all the time, the Naina who spoke up for herself and uttered her thoughts, the Naina who made conversations with others, and the Naina who finally was coming to her own.

Her life had changed so much in those two weeks. It seemed like she had lived an entire life, while simultaneously feeling it had passed so quickly, it had been rather a blur. She had been so nervous when she first landed in Stockholm, not knowing what to expect, and had been much more nervous when she first met the group in the Baltics. Now she regarded them all as friends – at least Gemma and Caroline. And, of course, Priidik. But then again, he was more than a friend.

Gemma and Caroline started a group chat on WhatsApp, and sent updates on their trip back home. The rest of the group created an email group where everyone exchanged photos. Priidik replied to those, sending reference links to the places they had visited. But he didn't send any private messages to Naina.

It was too early to know her feelings for Priidik but what she had felt thus far she hadn't felt before. Her first love was Kevin. But she didn't know if it had been true love. Kevin had swept her off her feet, but it was only because he was the first guy to pay attention to her. He had feigned interest, taking her out on dates, but she had known even then, deep down, he wasn't truly into her. She had grown enamored by him but even then she knew she hadn't really loved him. Back then, it hadn't occurred to her that if she had to question whether or not what she had felt was love, then it couldn't have been. He couldn't have been her first true love. He simply was her first love.

Even so, she tried to forget Kevin was her first love. She tried to forget the experiences she'd had with him. Kevin had told her she was emotionally unavailable. What did that mean? That her emotions were so hidden no one could avail of them? Or that she was of no avail and her emotions were not to be considered?

She hadn't asked and years later she found a quote on Pinterest on eDating that said, "Seeking intimacy with someone who is emotionally unavailable is like talking on the phone without realizing your call has dropped." Had it been like that to be with her? Had Kevin felt he was speaking to a dead line, into nothing? Maybe she had been so focused on making sure he didn't leave her she forgot she needed to give something as well. Maybe she had been too passive.

She searched further. Another quote, this one on *Mind Body Green*, said, "Emotionally unavailable people see a relationship as a source of comfort – something to occupy their time until something better comes along."

When she saw that one, she had to accept she had really been emotionally unavailable. She had known Kevin wasn't going to be her one and only and had spent most of their relationship secretly waiting for it to end.

Naina would no longer be emotionally unavailable. She'd opened up to Priidik and spent two unforgettable nights with him. She would not be as passive as she had been with Kevin, and would question Priidik, including why he hadn't yet contacted her. She wouldn't allow for this relationship, if she could call it that, to float away. She didn't know what the future had in store for her and Priidik, but the feeling she didn't deserve him began to float away. She didn't know yet what she deserved, but she definitely knew she deserved to be treated better than he'd treated her in the last two days.

Naina was finally shaking off the old persona she'd had, and beginning to embrace a new life of her own. She didn't know what shape that life was going to take, but she knew things were going to be different. At least she vowed to herself it would be so.

ॐ

Back in Charleston, Naina was up before the sun rose. Her body still clocked European time. She lay in bed, wide awake, debating whether or not to get out of bed. It was too dark still to go for a walk. She was so awake there was no chance to fall back asleep, so she got out of bed and made herself a cup of coffee. It was a regular black coffee and not her cherished flat whites. She'd have to find a way to get one of those but in that moment, she didn't have a choice but to stick to what she had. It tasted like colored water. And, she only had Special K and digestives in her kitchen. She would have to shop for new options. Yes, she would manage well without her routines.

She thumbed through all the photos she had taken on her phone. She had over a thousand. She was in awe of all she had experienced. The contrast between these images and the starkness of her bare walls made her feel like she had lived in a self-imposed prison. Yes, it was time for her to find a different place to live. A more affordable one, and a livelier one. She wanted to stay in the same building. Perhaps there was a smaller apartment available. She'd have to ask the landlady.

She imagined what it would be like to describe the time she had spent away, in case she went back to speaking to Raiya or had a chat with Fiona. It was hard for her to put it all into words. She had left for her trip without expectations. She had not known much about those countries, especially the Baltic states, other than they were ex-Soviet nations and they were by the Baltic Sea.

Although she hadn't traveled much prior to this trip, she thought other countries, particularly developing countries, would be disorganized and dirty. Even though she hadn't known much about the Baltics, she had expected they would feel like she was in a developing country rather than well-developed ones. And she was extremely impressed at how well organized and how clean they all were. At least 98% of the bathrooms she used, whether in gas stations, restaurants, bars, tourist centers, or anywhere she went, were clean. People were respectful of their fellow users, often lowering the toilet cover before flushing and wiping surfaces down for the next person.

She had learned more during that trip than she had through any other experience in her life. She understood what united the countries: weather, geography, history, some food items, architecture, and landscape. And what separated them: weather (Artur claimed it rained harder in Lithuania, but to Naina it rained equally as much throughout the area), culture, language, certain other foods, religion and beliefs, and the condition of the roads. The

Estonians were lighter in hair color and eyes, and they appeared to be more Nordic looking. Latvians were more disorganized, fun, and darker toned. Although the Lithuanians appeared more similar to the Latvians, the country itself was somewhere in between Estonia and Latvia.

She had learned more about crystals and acquired some. She learned Holy Man could travel. She also learned she liked people, and she could make friends.

She hadn't heard from Priidik, and every time she picked up her phone and didn't see a message from him, her heart broke just a little. She was thrilled he had awakened something in her, making her realize there was more than the weight of the despair she had been carrying most of her life, the deep sense she didn't belong, she didn't deserve, there was no place for her, and all she had was filled with the stench of misery. He had helped her see she was deserving, there was still a light in her that not only wanted but deserved to meet other lights and rejoice in joy, love, and possibility, and feel like there was a place for her. All it had taken was a little whisper in her ear. It was the spark that had ignited her heart. It was all it took for her to be seen, truly seen.

She had left Vilnius three days ago. Her Map app said it should have taken Priidik and Artur seven hours and nine minutes to drive back to Estonia. They should have arrived already. He should have contacted her by now.

She sent him a message asking how his return drive had been.

Chapter Forty-Three

It had been a few weeks since Holy Man had asked Naina a really important question: what would make her heart burst into a billion blazing sparkles? Naina wasn't sure what to answer but was gaining clarity.

On that early morning, after her third cup of coffee, Naina finally got out of the apartment around 6:30am. It was progress, for she had not previously allowed herself to drink that much coffee, and she celebrated the moment. In the past she would have been constrained by going against her self-imposed grain, but this time she felt free, like she was evolving, and strangely so this evolution was allowing her to be more herself.

She turned right on Hassell Street and left on King Street. It was still warm and muggy for a mid-October morning, but early enough she didn't regret the long sleeve t-shirt she wore. She lingered for a few moments in front of Buxton Books. It was too early for the bookshop to be open, but she made a mental note to stop by at a later time. Maybe she could start a book collection, instead of always resorting to library books.

It felt so good to be back on familiar ground, on her own narrow quaint streets, among the gorgeous Colonial era houses. Yes, she had enjoyed her trip, but she was grateful to be back.

She walked to White Point Garden, making a couple of loops around the gravel path. Finally, her stomach growling had spurred her to Harris Teeter. Holy Man leaned against a black Range Rover, eating a burrito. She wondered if the car belonged to him, but didn't ask.

"Why is it that you're always eating?" she asked.

"To make sure you know I'm real."

"I know you're real."

Holy Man asked her about the trip, and having thought about it just a few hours before allowed her to describe her mixed emotions. She didn't make much sense, and assumed he saw right through it.

But Holy Man nodded and smiled through the entire explanation, and rather than call her out, seemingly out of nowhere, he asked her, "What is it you truly want?"

She drew a blank, but later, as she walked the aisles of Harris Teeter, picking up a selection of breakfast bars and biscuits, as well as snack options that weren't digestive biscuits, she pondered the question. She ventured into the ready-made food section and picked up a roast chicken. She had a craving for a roast chicken roll. She had tried one during the trip that had roast chicken, cheese, spicy mayonnaise, fresh red chilies and cilantro, and plenty of chili salt. This too would be a deviation from what she usually ate, and it excited her. She didn't own a sandwich press but would buy herself one later that day.

As she picked up the rest of the ingredients she needed for the chicken roll, her heart and her spirit were guiding her. She would

Can You Be

almost say she was guided by her Guardian Angel – that is, if she truly believed she had one. Her mind told her otherwise, and logic fought against her feelings. It was a battle between facts and what felt right; a battle between her reality and the signs the universe indicated.

Her heart told her she would be able to find a way to stay in Charleston and afford the life she wanted, without having to depend on her father. She knew, in the deepest place of her heart, it could be no other way. She had just started exploring the world, and she would explore more of it, but her place, the city she called home and would forever call home, was Charleston. Yes, she had spent most of her life in the city, but she hadn't really allowed herself to set roots, and now she would. It had been missing from her sense of stability. She needed to get rooted to where she felt more herself, where she felt completely safe, where she felt completely at home, and that was Charleston.

It was the Holy City – her holy city. It had harbored her, as it had harbored others. Charleston was known as the Holy City because since the 1700s, it had been a home for people fleeing religious persecution. A wide range of churches and synagogues dotted the city, the most distinctive of which was the white St. Michael's Church, the oldest religious building in the city. There was also the Greek or Roman circular Congregational Church founded by English Congregationalists, Scot Presbyterians, and French Huguenots in 1681. There were several other cathedrals including the Emanuel African Methodist Church established in 1815, the oldest black congregation in the country. There were also some of the oldest synagogues in the country. The Kahal Kadosh Beth Elohim was founded in 1740 and the Brith Sholom Beth Israel founded in 1854, was the oldest Orthodox synagogue of the South.

257

The city seemed to be sending her signs it would continue to harbor her, she belonged there. On the taxi from the airport, she had come across billboards and advertisements announcing new developments in downtown saying, "Find Your Home In Charleston!" and "Your Haven In This Historic City," and "Settle in the Most Beautiful City in America!" Naina knew they were sent to her from the universe. The signs indicated what she felt in her heart.

She was finally clear about her future career. The treatment she'd had in Druskininkai had confirmed she wanted to be an esthetician, one who would focus on natural facials to help others achieve the same blemish-free complexion she had herself. It was her true passion, and she would do it if she had no obstacle.

Logic, of course, was different. The facial she'd given Fiona had been disastrous. She would soon have to move out of her apartment, despite the money her father had sent, and she didn't know if she had it in her to go back to school. The last time she had studied was in college, which was nearly eight years ago, and during that time she had done the bare minimum. She had gotten very little mental stimulation. She didn't know if she had it in her to study and learn again.

So, how could it be? How could she possibly know or have faith she would make a life for herself in Charleston? Somehow, she needed to gain the courage. Could she really enroll in school? Would she even be admitted? What if she failed? How would she be able to build a business when she struggled so much with people? What if she stayed small and quiet, as she had her whole life until now?

※

Can You Be

Holy Man stood on the promenade just as Naina made her way up the stairs on East Bay Street. She was out on another walk that day, although this time, it was in the evening. She had wanted to stay up as late as possible to fight jet lag.

Unbelievably, Holy Man had appeared twice on the same day. Naina didn't know if he had been standing there all along, watching her make her two rounds around White Point Garden, or if he had appeared just as she asked herself such a poignant question: did she have it in her to live the life she wanted to live?

"Do not give up on love, Naina," he said, in lieu of a greeting.

"Good evening," Naina said.

"Don't pretend you didn't hear me."

"I did hear you. I just don't know what you mean."

"Do not give up on love."

"On Priidik?"

"There are different kinds of love, Naina. Not just romantic love. There is love between friends, between family, and many others. The kind I am referring to is self-love."

"My own love?"

"Yes, love for yourself. Don't give up on yourself before you've given yourself a chance."

"Is that what I'm doing?" She knew the answer. "Am I not loving myself when I don't think I can do something?"

"Aren't you?"

Naina walked towards the railings. Sullivan's Island lighthouse on the other side of Charleston Harbor gave her a sense of comfort. Holy Man stood beside her, looking out onto the ocean. He took a big bite out of a BLT sandwich as a dolphin pod surfaced in the water, its fins dipping in and out of the gentle waves.

"I know you're real now. You know you don't always have to

show up eating something."

"Don't deflect."

Naina let out a breath she hadn't realized she was holding. "Yes, I guess I haven't been good at self-love. If only I believed more in myself ..."

"You have allowed for the love of others to define you for too long, Naina. You are not worthy based on your mother, your father, or anyone else's love for you. You are worthy in your own right. The only love you really, truly need is the love you have for yourself. To do what you set out to do, all you need is to believe in yourself, and that comes from love towards yourself."

"How do I do that?"

"You need to believe in yourself as much as I believe in you. I see who you are, Naina. Who you truly are, behind the unwillingness to break your shell open. I know you are a beautiful and bright spirit who is eager to let her light shine."

Naina smiled, with ease and without concern. She really liked the freedom to smile as she pleased. "I like the sound of that."

"What's stopping you?"

"I feel I have it in me, an inner voice tells me these things are possible. I am possible. I can do anything I want. I just don't know if it's right."

"It is right. You must start listening to your inner voice, the voice that comes from your heart, the one that allows you to feel expansive and light. Don't be confused by the voice of your ego, the one that makes you feel tight and limited."

Naina nodded, allowing it all to sink in.

"How can you be a light to others?" Holy Man put the last portion of the sandwich and, with a mouth full, he gave her a closed smile, and walked away.

Can You Be

Naina walked back to her apartment finally understanding the key to listen to her inner guidance was connecting more within, it was sitting quietly in meditation, especially when she was surrounded by her crystals and when the scent of her essential oils permeated every inch of her apartment. They gave her a sense of peace, spiritual peace, mental peace, and emotional peace.

Logic told her she was limited, in resources, in her skills, in her abilities, but her heart told her she could do anything she set out to do. She was ready for more. She was ready to shed her shell, rip open the box she had built around herself and her life, and set herself free. Her only path was to trust her inner guidance. And the message it had was clear: she was ready.

Chapter Forty-Four

Naina sat down for meditation to gain clarity on what she wanted.

After running into Holy Man outside of the Harris Teeter, Naina had gone shopping. She had bought more than a sandwich press. She had also purchased a small wooden table that looked like a kindergarten desk. On it, she had laid out the lace placemat she had bought in Tartu. On top, she had placed the angelite and amber. She also had a spectrolite she had purchased in Helsinki. She created a small altar in one corner of her living room. If she dedicated time with the crystals on a daily basis, she didn't need to carry them around any longer.

The spectrolite looked like the northern lights of Finland. It was full of bright colors, like a rainbow in the night sky and although Naina had not yet seen the northern lights, she envisioned they would look something like the oval-shaped stone she had bought. The shopkeeper had told her it was a type of labradorite, and it represented hope for the past and for the future. Hope is exactly what Naina needed.

The same day she had purchased the small table, she had walked into Cornerstone Minerals and bought an ametrine, to help her heal, and a lemurian quartz crystal. They were personal investments, the quartz would help her with inner peace and connect her soul with the divine.

She burned incense and palo santo, and sat down on a purple cushion in front of the wooden table and focused on her breath, just like Holy Man had explained to her. She counted four as she inhaled, she held her breath for four counts, she counted four as she exhaled, and she held her breath again for four counts. She repeated the cycle three times and grew more comfortable and at ease. Holy Man had told her this was called box breathing.

Her mind was still running through all her concerns, jumping from one thought to another while she was trying to focus on her breath.

"Be still," she said out loud. And then she focused on a mantra, "I am safe. I am grounded. I am exactly where I need to be." She repeated it ten times. Finally, she got her mind to settle enough to sit with the question: what did she want? After a few moments, the answers began to filter in.

She wanted to have financial freedom and have a house of her own. She wanted to have the freedom to travel where she wished and when she wished.

She wanted to stop feeling crushed. Because she really had felt crushed. Nothing had ever gone her way. She had survived by being meticulous and careful so she wouldn't disappear, so life wouldn't swallow her whole. She hadn't consciously admitted this, but she was aware she tiptoed around her life because she was afraid if she really stepped in it, it would all come crashing down. And if she colored outside the lines, other people would disappear, as her mother had, her father, every one of her friends, Kevin, and most recently, Raiya. So she lived her life, as diligently and quietly as possible, following all the rules and implementing more rules of her own, for she felt this was the only way she would survive, the only way she would remain whole, the only way nothing would fall apart, the only way people would stay in her life.

Except it hadn't worked out. Despite trying to remain small, despite trying so hard to not make a strong mark in the world, despite trying to keep her frailty intact, her world had imploded. Her mother had killed herself, her father had abandoned her, her friends were no longer in her life, Kevin had used her, and so had Raiya. And she was tired of remaining small, of taking little steps, of not creating an impact. She had sold herself short, and her defense strategy hadn't worked.

It had started to turn around for her on the beach in Liepāja. When she had taken a step forward, she opened the door for Priidik. That day Priidik helped her see it was time she did something for herself. His sheer presence gave her a sense of calm. He had explained Priidik meant peaceful ruler in Estonian, and he had definitely brought her a sense of peace.

He had helped Naina see what she wanted most was true love. He helped her feel lovable and loving, like she had something worth giving, and thus, worth receiving. She felt attractive around him and that was a beautiful feeling. He made her laugh and that was more than anyone had done for her in a long time.

She wanted no more games, no more doubts, no more pretending. She wanted clear, genuine, and straightforward communication. There could be a certain amount of holding back until each knew where the other stood. There could be waiting as long as it was because they were scared and didn't know how to deal with their feelings or were afraid of how the other would react. They could be measured until they grew to trust each other and knew there would be no judgment. They could hold back until they knew what they wanted to say and how they wanted to say it. That, she could deal with. That, she could understand. But playing games, no she couldn't deal with that. She couldn't, wouldn't, understand that.

More than anything, she wanted to be with someone who loved her, who trusted her, who respected her, and who supported her. She wanted to be with someone who laughed with her, who enjoyed life with her, and who was a loving and stable support, someone she trusted her life with. She wanted someone who felt like her home and who felt she was their home. She wanted someone to be best friends with. She wanted to be seen, to be truly seen, and loved for it.

She deserved no less.

If Priidik couldn't give her that, she would make sure she found someone who would.

⁂

How could she be a light to others? She had, by now, figured out what she wanted. But all of this was for herself. It wasn't for anyone else. That couldn't be enough for her to be a light to others. She revisited the Užupis Constitution. It seemed to encompass so much of what she valued.

She hadn't yet come up with an answer to the other question Holy Man had posed. Back then, she had no idea what brought her joy, although it had been clear she had not enjoyed her job at the real estate office, and she had never liked Alice. She was no longer at the mercy of her arrogant demands.

But, Alice had been right. Back when Alice had attempted to get Naina to try makeup, and Naina's skin had broken out in little whiteheads, Alice had told her she should look into natural makeup. There was paraben-free and other stuff-free makeup and she needed to discover it. Even the therapist in Druskininkai had mentioned she should find out more about natural products. That had to be a sign.

She needed to search for products that wouldn't make her skin breakout, and she needed to find a way to promote this somehow. Caroline had also had problems with makeup, and it's why she didn't wear any.

A perfunctory Google search, indicated natural makeup was a growing trend, as were natural skincare lines. She had always had a minimalistic approach to her skincare, and the beauty and sanctity of her skin was proof of its effectiveness. That brought her great joy – seeing her skin was soft and supple, taking care of other people's skin, and showing them how to get the same results as her.

Further research indicated Charleston offered a selection of courses in cosmetology. She would need to decide whether or not to do a full cosmetology program or just an esthetics one and after reading further, decided it would be best for her to study esthetics. Would that really make her heart burst?

※

It was less than an hour before the library would close. She ran over, wanting to find as much information as possible about natural skin care and natural beauty products. The books all touched upon aromatherapy and essential oils, but she wanted to learn more. Specifically, she wanted to find scientific books on aromatherapy, books that proved essential oils were effective and therapeutic.

She used lavender essential oil, but selected it only because the lady at Whole Foods had suggested it. It had worked but Naina hadn't fully understood why it was effective. She needed to know what essential oils were and how they worked. She needed to know what else was available to her.

Walking back into the library after so much time away from it, assured Naina she was safe, but she didn't need it as she once had. It was a resource for her, a place of learning, a place of comfort, but it no longer had to be part of her routine.

She found several books on aromatherapy and by the time she finished gathering them, there was no time left to read them at the library. With a few minutes left to closing, for the first time, Naina checked out the books and took them home. She stayed up most of the night and the following day reading.

Naina learned aromatherapy was the therapeutic use of essential oils and other extracts from aromatic plants. Essential oils were administered through inhalation, topical application, or other methods, and they were used for therapeutic or medical purposes, and for overall wellness. Aromatherapy was a fast-growing modality because it improved physical and psychological conditions, and aided in curing, mitigating, or preventing diseases.

Essential oils were used to treat pain, relieve headaches, and reduce anxiety, as clary sage and lavender had indicated.

Naina was most excited to learn that a range of essential oils treated skin conditions, and not only burns and wounds as Gattefossé, regarded as the father of aromatherapy, had discovered, but also acne, rashes, blemishes, anti-aging, moisturizing, tonic, etc.

Following the Druskininkai therapist's suggestions, Naina now knew for certain there was a path for her in natural skincare and beauty.

Reading about all the benefits of aromatherapy brought Naina a great sense of joy. Thinking of herself as a conduit for healing to others, recognizing what she wanted most was to be an esthetician, made Naina's heart burst into a billion blazing sparkles.

Chapter Forty-Five

"**B**ased on the last conversation, we are coming at this from two different places. You seem to think you made some mistakes, and all you need is to appease me, because somehow weirdo was a term of endearment," Naina said.

Raiya had knocked on her door soon after she had come back from seeing the building landlady. She had gone out for a walk earlier that morning, and hadn't run into Holy Man. Two times in one day had been enough, it seemed. She'd had a peaceful walk, still thinking about all she had discovered. She needed to find another place to live, and Naina had gone to see the landlady as soon as she returned to the building. They had agreed she would change apartments at the end of the month. She would move into a studio for half of her current rent. Was she unbelievably lucky? Or was the universe supporting her?

Five minutes after going back to her apartment, there was a knock on the door, and when she had opened, Raiya stood outside. She had let him in, and they were now sitting in her living room.

"I'm saying I didn't use the word weirdo as an insult," Raiya said.

Naina took a deep breath. "You acted like an asshole and don't want to take responsibility for your actions. You're sidestepping the enormity of what you did by pretending I misconstrued you. Meanwhile, the reality is you're the only asshole here."

"Whoa, you're calling me an asshole, now? Aren't you being just a little sensitive?"

"I don't need to be sensitive for this to be an issue. You called me a name and you did it to be hurtful. That was your intention. You were putting me down, minimizing me in front of your friend. You broke what we had with your actions. I didn't break what we had by being sensitive. You were the one who was rude, disrespectful, judgmental, and showed no value or concern for me."

"Come on, Naina. It wasn't that bad. I didn't mean it. I didn't mean to be rude."

"No, Raiya, what you didn't mean was for me to hear you."

Raiya sat in silence. He looked at his feet and then back up at her. "Can we find a way to fix this?"

"What exactly do you propose?"

"To start with, I need you to promise you won't be so sensitive—"

"In my view, what needs to be fixed is not my sensitivity but your actions. Me telling you how I feel served to help you figure out what went wrong with you. But I didn't cause this. We wouldn't be here AT ALL if you hadn't said what you said. You are minimizing your actions, acting like it wasn't a big deal. It takes cojones to admit you've made a mistake. It takes a backbone to admit you've done something wrong. And it takes a spine to admit you're sorry you fucked up and to ask for forgiveness."

"Okay, I'm sorry. Yes, you're right. You are right. What I said wasn't nice, and I'm sorry."

Naina's face got hot. It was the first time she had spoken out so vehemently to someone. "Why did you act that way? What was it about me that made it so easy for you to discard me with the mention of a word like weirdo? How could you act so friendly and happy towards me when we were spending time together and then so easily dismiss me? Why was it so easy for you to make me the target?"

Raiya thought about it for a moment. "You're right. I did fuck up. I'm sorry. I have my own insecurities. I acted like a jerk because I wasn't comfortable being seen with you. It has nothing to do with you, but with me and the image I portray. You are perfect just as you are. By putting you down, by laughing at you, I was somehow making myself feel better. I felt like a loser and thought I would deflect to you. And that's not right. I should never have used you as my crutch. I don't know why I used you, the person I most care about, as a punching bag. I need to deal with that, and I will discuss it with my therapist when I speak to him the next time."

"You took me for granted, and I don't want you to act like you can do what you please, or you can put me down behind my back and think there would be no consequences. If I'm to be your friend, I deserve respect. You have to show you value me. You have to show you genuinely care."

"Please, Naina, please give me another chance. Please let me prove to you I am worthy of your friendship, of your time."

"What I need is for you to accept responsibility for your actions. Small deeds aren't small because you claim they are. What matters is how you make someone feel. And your supposed small action made me feel small, worthless, like I have no value to you. My trust in you is broken. I don't know how we can regain the trust."

"I will figure something out, Naina. I will. I am so sorry for making you feel small. I understand I came across as not valuing you, but the truth is if it weren't for you, I would have nothing. If it weren't for you, I wouldn't have a life here. If it weren't for you, I wouldn't have enjoyed myself so much. I love you. I value you, and I will move hell and high water to gain back your trust."

❄

"I understand you're upset, but from what you've said, it looks like he is repentant," Fiona said. Naina had stopped by later that day to give her the souvenirs she'd bought. Naina had given her lavender essential oil and dried lavender flowers, and she had given Mimi a dog biscuit. Both had been extremely grateful.

Mimi now lay on Naina's lap while Naina stroked her fur. Mimi's eyes were closed and Naina suspected she had fallen asleep. "So you think he deserves a pass?"

"It depends on how you feel. Do you value him and his friendship enough to give him a second chance or not? And do you think you can trust him again?"

"Trust … Trust is a big word." Fiona's apartment had a homy feel. It was cozy and comfortable, like a warm hug. It was the polar opposite to her own. Naina didn't want Fiona's apartment, but she wanted a space of her own that felt like she was wrapped up in a tight blanket.

"Trust is a big word, Naina, but it doesn't mean it's gone or it can't be restored. Everyone makes mistakes. We all make mistakes, and sometimes we act out toward the people we take for granted. I understand he spoke when he thought you weren't hearing but at the same time, he must have assumed it didn't matter what he said to another because your friendship was deep enough it would withstand this."

"I hadn't thought about it that way."

"He may have also not meant to hurt you deliberately, but use you, in a way, to make himself look stronger or better in the eyes of his friend. He may not have been thinking of you at all, which I know sounds bad, but it may also mean he could have used another issue to make himself look better and you just happened to be the victim at the moment."

"It hurts he chose me to be his punching bag. I don't deserve it."

"You don't, Naina. But being a devil's advocate, is it really that bad he called you odd?"

Naina knew she was strange. It was no secret.

"I don't mean to offend you, Naina. You have said you know you are different than most. He was pointing it out, yes in a way that didn't feel respectful, but what if you owned it? What if you said, heck yes, I am odd, and so what? There is strength in being different. You need not want to be normal. Normal is boring. Don't be boring. Be strange and interesting."

Naina smiled. It sounded good to own being different. It sounded really good to be interesting and not boring. And she liked how her face felt when she smiled.

Fiona continued, "You're smiling so I think something sits well with you. Listen, I don't mean to tell you what to do, but I've made mistakes and I'm so grateful I was forgiven. I once got really drunk and told my friend I thought she was just a pretty face. I told her she was lucky she had a brain because most people didn't see beyond her beauty. And I said this to my supposed best friend. Yes, I was drunk, but what I said was extremely hurtful. Thankfully, she forgave me, but I can guarantee you our friendship hasn't been the same, and the thought of what I said and what I did haunts me. I wish I could take it back, but there's nothing I can do other than make it up to her. I don't feel I deserve her forgiveness, but she's a better and bigger person than I am. And I'm better for it. I'm so grateful she's allowed me to stay in her life. Maybe Raiya deserves the same consideration?"

"I'll definitely consider it." How different would her life have been if she had given people second chances? Would there be more people in her life now? Would she have more friends if she hadn't walked away so often?

"Yes, at least think about it. Changing subject, I want you to come over for brunch on Sunday. I make a mean granola or poached eggs on grits. You decide what you want. Or we can do both. Start with the eggs and have the granola for something sweet. Plus I want to know more about this tour guide of yours."

Naina also wanted to know more about Priidik. She hadn't heard from him. "Granola? You make your own?"

"Oh yeah. It's super easy. I put it all in the oven, the oats, nuts, dried fruit, honey, coconut oil, and dust it all with nutmeg and cinnamon. I make a big batch every couple of months or so."

"I've never baked anything."

"I'll show you when you come over. I even have a great recipe for wheat and raisin biscuits that would be way tastier than digestives."

"You don't like them?"

"I do, but I love baking so much I would rather make my own. I'll show you how easy it is."

Learning how to bake seemed like something she would definitely consider.

But she no longer wanted to wonder about Priidik.

⅔

Can You Be

Naina called Priidik as soon as she got back to her apartment. It was six hours ahead in Tallinn.

"Hi," he said.

"Hi," she replied.

"How are you?" he asked.

"I'm fine. You?"

"I'm great. I'm working on the next tour and—"

"Why haven't you replied?" Naina was afraid that if she didn't confront him soon, she'd lose her resolve.

He was silent for a moment. "I'm sorry."

"I deserve better."

"Yes, you do. I'm sorry, Naina. I've been avoiding you."

"Why?"

"I'm trying to figure out how I feel."

"About me?"

"I know I like you. I loved spending time with you. Those nights we spent together were unforgettable."

"Then, why haven't you replied? You got what you wanted from me, and you're done?"

"No, no. It's not like that at all. This has never happened to me before, on any tour. I've never had a personal relationship with any of my clients. Never. I promise you, Naina. I really, genuinely, like you." Priidik let out a sigh. "Let me be honest. I'm afraid we have something good here but no path in our future to make it work. You live in Charleston, and don't have plans to move here. I live in Tallinn, and don't have plans to move there."

"But we had a genuine connection, didn't we? You can't deny that, can you?"

"I can't … Where does that leave us?"

"What do you want from me?"

"I don't know that it's a fair question. Unless you want to tell me what you want from me?"

"I want to feel loved and supported, and I feel you seem like you can be loving and supportive."

"Yes, Naina, I can. The challenge, once again, is you are in Charleston and I am in Tallinn."

"Perhaps we keep in touch? We can remain friends and see where it will take us? If anywhere?"

"You mean be friends, or do you mean have a long-distance relationship?"

"I mean friends. But friends who are honest with each other on where they are in terms of relationships. If you meet someone, you tell me. If I meet someone, I will tell you. In the meantime, we keep in touch. Maybe we commit to speak on a regular basis. We don't need to schedule calls or anything, but we commit to communicating. What are your thoughts?" Naina's voice sounded strong in her ears, as if she had been speaking loudly, but she knew she hadn't.

"Sounds good to me," Priidik said.

Naina was extremely proud of herself. She had explained her needs without hesitation or without reservation.

Chapter Forty-Six

Two days later Naina was out for a walk. Less than a block away from her apartment, before she reached Meeting Street, she turned back. A walk around downtown was not going to cut it. She needed to go to her special place. She needed to go to Sullivan's Island and sink her feet into the brown sand.

And so she did. Holy Man sat on a beach towel by the oat grass, closer to the land than the ocean, as if he wanted to look upon the water but not get close to it. He wasn't eating anything.

Naina was relieved. She sat beside him – his beach towel was large enough for a family of four. The sun was rising, bathing the beach in warm orange and yellow lights. It didn't seem as magical as the sunset in Liepāja had been, but it had its own sense of magic. She closed her eyes and allowed herself to soak in it. "What words of wisdom do you have for me this time?"

Holy Man nodded and smiled. "I see you're getting the gist of this."

"You appear at the most opportune times, as if I had called you, even though I haven't. You're like my guardian angel … or perhaps, like a wise guide who knows exactly when to appear."

"Let's not discuss who I am or what I am to you. Know that I am here for you whenever you need me."

It was her turn to nod and smile. "I'm grateful, you know."

They looked at each other in the eye. Naina wondered if she should reach out to hug him, but restrained herself. "So, what is it?"

"Let me start by asking you: when have you felt the happiest?"

"When I was on the trip in the Baltics."

"How about in your life here in Charleston?"

"When I was with Raiya …"

"That time you spent together was truly special."

"Yes, but it was all a lie. He made a fool out of me."

"It's okay for you to feel angry towards Raiya. He hurt you and you need to acknowledge those feelings. But know no act is unforgivable. Forgiveness is an act of mercy. We aren't all perfect and you cannot expect everyone to act perfectly all the time. We all make mistakes and as long as we are truly repentant, forgiveness is a grace we can extend."

"But what Raiya did was wrong. He treated me unkindly, made fun of me."

"Yes. Forgiving someone doesn't mean you excuse their behavior. It does mean you let go of the anger and bitterness you feel. Do you want to continue feeling angry towards him?"

"No."

"You can decide if you want to let him back into your life. You don't need to. If you let him back in, you'd be extending grace and mercy, but it's not needed to forgive. For yourself, for your own sake, let go of the anger."

"You mean I don't have to be friends with him?"

"Not unless you want to. You can forgive him and welcome him back into your life, or you can forgive him and forever close the door. That is up to you."

"Let me get this right. You're saying if I forgive him, I accept what he did even if I'm not okay with it, but I no longer let it affect me."

"Exactly."

They sat in silence for a while.

"I gather you miss his friendship."

"I do. But I don't want it if he thinks I am some kind of charity case."

"How do you feel after the last conversation you had?"

"I feel he was genuine in his apology, and he really does want to spend time with me, but I don't know if I can trust him again."

"What does your heart tell you?"

They sat in silence again, Naina trying to decide what was in her heart.

"Take a deep breath, inhaling towards your heart. Breathe out slowly. Now ask yourself, what does your heart tell you about Raiya's apology?"

"That he was genuine, and he really does want to spend time with me. I can trust him."

༈

Holy Man nodded and smiled for the second time that day. "You are not alone. Even when you think you are alone, you're not. You may be on your own, but you're not alone. You have me, you have your mother's spirit, and you have God and the universe. You are never alone. You are not forsaken. You have a litany of people who love and support you. It's called your High Frequency Entourage or

HFE. God works through angels, guides, spirits, and other forms of energetic vibration, and these beings help us make sense of our life and purpose. We each have our own. Yours is specific to you, just like each person's is specific to themselves.

"Your HFE guides you, sends you messages, if you choose to see them. You need to open up to yourself and to your inner guidance to see them, and you need to make sure you interpret them according to a meaning that makes sense to you and not according to what you see on the internet. The interpretations are yours. It is good to look up guidance but not to tie yourself to that guidance.

"Your HFE is also who protects you. You are always guided. You are always safe. They make sure they keep you protected through the signs and synchronicities they send your way. Make sure you keep your eyes and ears open, and I don't just mean your physical eyes and ears but your spiritual ones too."

Just then, passing clouds came over the beach in Sullivan's Island. "Where were my HFE when my parents abandoned me?"

"I can't speak for why your parents did what they did. You can't change your past, Naina, as much as you'd want to. You may have wanted them to act differently, but they didn't. You've got to live with that, but don't allow the feeling to define you." Holy Man placed his hand on hers.

The touch was comforting. "I know I need to forgive them as well, but this seems harder."

"What are you grateful for that you learned from your father?"

"How not to be a father. In other words, what not to do. How not to treat your child. How to make sure you don't abandon your child."

"Can't you think of something positive?"

"My father has always been resilient. He's survived and thrived, and although I don't know how to be that resilient, it is something I aspire to."

"What about your mother, then?"

"How not to be a mother. In other words, how to stick around for your child's life. How to make sure you don't abandon your child."

"Where there is a will, there's a way," Holy Man said.

"That has got to be the cheesiest and most cliche statement you've made so far."

"I mean it. You're not alone. Your HFE is with you. You have guidance and protection. You need to focus on what you want and know you will find a way to accomplish it."

"I feel like I have lived in a bubble for most of my life, tumbling from place to place with no direction. I bumped from one place to another without rhyme or reason. And I finally feel like I have a purpose, like I have something to work toward, like I have something to work for."

"That's pretty special, isn't it?"

"I finally have the independence I yearned for. It's ironic I spent all my life depending financially on my father, and his final assistance got me to stand on my own. I realize he could have cut me off cold, and he gave me the greatest gift. In his coldness and his apparently hurtful behavior, he gave me what I had always wanted for myself."

"You did that for yourself, Naina. You took the chances, you made the best of this. You chose not to see the hurt and instead embraced this challenge as an opportunity."

"I've been a spoiled brat. Even when my father cut me off, he still gave me wings to fly."

"Seems like even you consider him as part of your support

group. He may not have been the father you wanted, but he's still a great influence in your life. Naina, for your own sake, I urge you to forgive him. Don't hold on to the hurt and the pain."

"I'll reach out to him. I promise."

"You don't need to promise me. Do this for yourself, Naina."

"I will. I definitely will."

"It sounds to me like my little Naina, has finally grown up." Holy Man had a look of pride on his face.

"Have I really?" She thought about it for a while longer, and realized, yes, she may have finally grown up.

Before leaving, he placed a crystal in her hand. It was a yellow-colored palm stone. "It's a citrine. It's meant to help you feel joy. Happy early birthday."

Chapter Forty-Seven

Naina didn't wait long. The next day, she knocked on Raiya's apartment door. It was after five o'clock, and Naina knew if he kept his previous routine, he would've finished work by then.

When he opened the door, he said, "I'm so glad you're here. I was hoping it was you. Can I make you a cup of chai?"

"That would be lovely."

They didn't say anything to each other as Raiya prepared the chai. When it was ready, Raiya was the first to speak. "I'm so grateful you're here. I was afraid you were going to cut me off and the mere thought made me sad. I really missed not having you here for the last few weeks … I enjoy having you in my life. You were right, I called you a weirdo because I didn't intend for you to hear me. It was an insecure moment I regret. I love you and appreciate you and I promise not to speak ill of you no matter the circumstances, and not because I'm afraid of who will hear, but because I truly value you and moving forward my actions will support my feelings, or more like my feelings are shown through my actions. I don't want to be the person who hurt you. If I could take back the hurt I caused you, I would. I can't, so I hope I can earn your trust once again and show you I really truly treasure your friendship."

Naina nodded and smiled. "I understand being regretful for actions. This trip really changed me. It helped me see change is possible, especially if we are open and we set the right intentions. I think it's possible for us to be friends again because I also miss you. I miss the times we spent together and the bond we created. I thought it was genuine and it crushed me to think it wasn't."

"It was genuine, Naina. All the conversations we had were true and honest. I know I have no way to prove it to you, but the only time it wasn't real was in how I expressed myself during that phone conversation you overheard. It was based on an insecurity, but my friendship and my exchanges with you were genuine. I want to get back to that and have our friendship grow from there."

"I want that too." Naina reached out to Raiya and they stood up and hugged each other.

After they both sat back down, he said, "Do you forgive me?"

"Yes, Raiya, I forgive you."

"What a relief," Raiya exclaimed. He got up and hugged her again.

Naina talked to Raiya about her trip and Raiya told her about how he had spent the last few weeks.

"If you could solve one world problem, what would it be?" Raiya asked.

Naina said, "I would want to clear people's skin."

"Really? That's it? Aren't you being a bit naive?"

"Naive?"

"Well, maybe naive isn't the right word, but isn't there something more significant or impactful?"

Can You Be

Naina thought about it for a moment. "I don't think so. I used to pay close attention to all the people who walked into the real estate office. It helped me realize people, especially teenagers, suffer from anxiety, negative self-image, etc., etc., when they have skin issues which causes hurt and trauma. Hurt people hurt. If you could clear skin, there wouldn't be hurt resulting from shame, and there would be fewer people hurting."

Raiya nodded. It was his turn to be quiet. "That is quite profound."

They sat in silence.

Raiya then asked, "Where else in the world do you long to travel to? You have your passport and have taken the first international trip in your memory. What's next?"

"South Korea. I want to see all the beauty products they have and I want to learn about the culture. Or maybe India. I want to see where I came from, where my family came from."

"You are a good person, Naina."

Fundamentally, she believed most people were good. Despite her father. Despite her stepmother. Despite it all. And the reason was her mother. Love had permeated her mother's eyes, unconditional and never-ending love. Her mother might not be with her in person, but her love was always around Naina. Her mother was hurt and had hurt herself. She didn't hurt others, not deliberately. And that was a sign she was good.

"How about we move in together?" he asked.

Naina struggled to imagine what it would be like.

"We get along well. We're comfortable with each other. We could both save money." His expression was warm and he enclosed her hand with both of his.

"It's generous of you, but I sorted things out with the landlord.

Although I've lived alone for most of my life, I have never created my own space. I want to now, more than anything. I am touched you offered."

In the few months they had known each other, her life had been turned upside down. Her routines were disrupted, she spent more time outside of her apartment than she had ever before. She ate rich and fatty foods and her skin hadn't broken out. Nor had she gained any weight. She had never been happier. She didn't know if the angelite and amber played a role in this, or if the fateful day in which she received the box had sparked all of this change. She had no proof of it, but her crystals gave her a sense of encouragement, unlike anything she had felt before.

Chills ran through her body. It felt good, as if a blanket were snuggling over her. She threw her arms around Raiya, clutching at his neck. It was the biggest hug she had given anyone since her mother had died.

"Raiya, you bring me joy."

Chapter Forty-Eight

Naina would never forget the smell of spices wafting through the door and into the hallway. As soon as she stepped out of her apartment, she knew there would be a sizzling Indian meal ready. When she saw the spread Raiya had created, she knew he was truly remorseful.

Raiya opened the door before Naina had a chance to knock, as if he had been watching through the peephole. Their apartments had no peepholes, so he must have been standing by the door, with his ear to it, waiting for the sound of her approach. Or so she thought.

His apartment smelled of fresh cooking, as opposed to spices that had been stewing for a while and grown slightly stale. No, these aromas were almost crisp, and she tasted the food before even setting eyes on it.

Fiona and Mimi had also been invited and were already there, each holding a present: Fiona a gift card for the spa at the Belmond Charleston Place, and Mimi held a cookie shaped like a dog bone in her mouth. "You can book a facial and see how it compares to the one you had on your trip."

"Will you let me practice on you again? I've learned a few things since the last time. I've been keeping my nails short – really short."

Fiona smiled. "Sure, Naina."

Raiya gave her quartz point to add to her crystal collection. "They told me it was meant to enhance the effect of the other crystals," he said.

Naina's collection of crystals was growing surprisingly fast. It brought her immense joy.

Raiya pulled out a chair for Naina and prepared a plate for her with a little of everything. The dishes were rich. The *aloo tiki* was warm, and it was clear the potato patties had just been fried. They were smothered in a dark brown *cholle*, the spices in the garbanzo so strong, only the sliced onions and cold *dahi* gave her palate a reprieve. Raiya had bought the yogurt, the only component he didn't make himself. The *samosas* were medium sized with a thin and crispy crust, stuffed with potatoes and peas. The tamarind *chutney* paired perfectly, adding a tart sweetness to every bite.

He also prepared a plate for Fiona and told them he had cooked everything himself, keeping his mother on a zoom call to make sure she directed every step. He tasted along the way to course correct when he needed to. It didn't taste the same as his mother's food, but this was the closest to his mother's cooking he'd had in years.

The *tandoori roti* was fresh, and a little thick, but it was smothered in ghee, and that took it to the next level. Raiya had paired it with *tadka dal, masala okra,* and *began bharta,* all of which paired well and were nicely spiced. The okra was dry and crispy with garam masala and a touch of *amchur*. The began bharta was smokey, as if the eggplant had been grilled on a barbecue before it was blended with the onions and potato.

Can You Be

They ate greedily and chatted the whole time, asking questions about their backgrounds and experiences. This was the first time Fiona and Raiya had spent time together, and they were getting to know each other. Any tension had evaporated and there was no chance for it to sour the meal.

The food was sumptuous and delicious and as if it couldn't get any better, Raiya presented Naina with a *gulab jamun* along with a fresh cup of chai. For an added touch, he sprinkled sweetened shaved coconut on top of the milk dough balls, which had been fried until golden and soaked in cardamom and rose flavored syrup. Every bite into a gulab jamun released syrupy goodness into Naina's mouth. She may have even closed her eyes as she ate.

They had birthday cake as well, already set with the numbers three and zero. Naina no longer needed to think of her birthday routines and would throw out the remaining candles she still had. Next year still had to come, and she had no idea what it would be like, but she would make sure it would be nothing like it had been in the past.

"You are worthy, Naina," Raiya said.

"Why are you saying that?" Naina asked.

"We all have something. We all feel we are less than or we don't deserve, and I feel for you, it's about worthiness."

"Do we all really have something?"

"Yes, my therapist and I have identified that mine, for instance, is not feeling lovable."

"I can relate."

"Yes, I know. With you, the feeling of not being lovable stems from not feeling you are worthy of love."

"You may be right, but today is my birthday, and I don't want to speak about anything other than what brings us joy."

Raiya told them his favorite memory was Sunday afternoons with his parents. The servants had the day off and they made a heavy brunch of *idli* and *sambhar* or *methi parathas* with Indian omelet.

"What's Indian omelet?" Fiona asked.

"It's a thin omelet made by browning cumin seed and then browning chili and onion. You then add eggs and fresh coriander and cook it until it's dry. Afterwards, my father would settle for a nap, his snoring setting the rhythm of the lazy afternoon."

"It wouldn't annoy you? The snoring?" Fiona asked.

"Sometimes, but I would watch movies and get so immersed I would drown it out. My mom would read and without fail, her eyes grew heavy and she'd set her book down and settle in for a nap of her own."

"Would she snore?" Naina asked.

"She had an elegant snore."

"What's an elegant snore?"

"You know, the type that makes sound but isn't too loud or too disruptive. Kind of like heavy breathing."

Naina had no idea if either of her parents snored. She had no memory of it. "And you wouldn't nap?"

Raiya smiled. "Not usually. I loved my movies so much I'd relish the hour or so I got to watch without interruption. How I miss those times. I miss seeing both of my parents alive and without a care in the world. I don't know if my mom still naps. She must but I haven't witnessed it in a while."

Naina suddenly remembered the sticky note from that muggy morning in early August. Had the change she had sensed when she got the note, which felt like lifetimes ago, really been ominous? Sure, her life had transformed in a big way and at times the change hadn't been pleasant, but now she was filled with joy. She'd had a birthday unlike any other. It was the first time she remembered celebrating it with such excitement and with others. She was so happy she'd been able to change her routine. The only thing she had still done was to place a small donation, like every year on her birthday, to the Lowcountry Orphan Relief.

Except, of course, she still needed to speak to her father. There was no way of knowing how that conversation would go. He had called her for her birthday, as he usually did, but he hadn't said much other than, "Happy birthday," and "Have you found a job yet?" When Naina told him she hadn't, he promptly hung up the phone. Naina knew she was going to have to be the one to make the effort, but she didn't want to do it then. She didn't want to ruin the most special birthday she'd ever had.

She wondered what had become of the "hey" from those months ago. Had it really been swept away by the hurricane?

※

Fiona left first, and Raiya and Naina stayed up late into the night. Raiya told her of his last boyfriend's affair, swearing him off relationships, at least for the time being. He talked about his happy childhood in Mumbai, an only child, yet ever surrounded by a cacophony of grandparents, aunts, uncles, and cousins who visited constantly. He was two years older than Naina, yet had lived a richer life than she would have thought imaginable.

The longer Naina spent with Raiya, the more she wished she had grown up with her mother, as Raiya had done with his. He called his mother once a day, every day. Naina was with him once when he FaceTimed his mother. Naina waved at her and Raiya's mother called her *beta*, like Naina's mother had once done. Ever since, Raiya's mother had sent blessings to Naina.

For the first time in her life, Naina told another being about how her parents immigrated to the Bay Area from India in 1984. Naina shared with Raiya she was born nine years into the marriage and by then her mother had rejected her new country so fiercely she barely left the house.

She wasn't able to practice law. She would have had to repeat her degree in the US to qualify or study for the bar exam in California, and Naina's father didn't want his wife to work. Naina's mother was overwhelmed by the changes in her life and couldn't stand being alive.

On the few occasions she left the house, she averted her eyes at people stripped down to shorts and tank tops and threw her *dupatta* over bikini-clad women at the beach. She screamed *besharam* at couples kissing. Eventually, she found the liberal nature of the country so unbearable, she couldn't stand living in it.

Naina's father had scattered her ashes into the bay – in the same waters where she had ended her life. But Naina only heard that from her stepmother, years later.

"I have never belonged to anyone," Naina said. She held the quartz in her palm, petting it like a pet.

"You belong to me." Raiya wrapped his arm around Naina's shoulders. She eased into his embrace, feeling safe in his cocoon.

๙

Despite the late hour, that night on her own, Naina was unable to sleep. On the day she'd turned thirty, she'd had a proper birthday celebration with a full cake and a party. The gathering with Raiya, Fiona, and Mimi, which others may consider small, was the largest get-together Naina had been a part of.

She hadn't realized, until she got that box so many months ago, that she needed to open herself up to meet new people and finally find the loving, nurturing, supporting family she had always wanted. It was a now or never moment.

She was learning it was okay to be vulnerable. She was learning to trust again, and to extend that trust to herself. Her self-trust was about realizing she had all she needed. The hurt others had caused her didn't define her. Just because others had caused her pain, didn't mean everyone she met would cause her pain.

It turned out Raiya wanted the same because his family was disintegrating. His father had died and his mother was old and frail. He rejected Naina perhaps as a self-defense, self-sabotage mechanism. When he had felt he and Naina were getting close, he had cut her off before she too would disappear. It's as if they had the same issues.

And now they were friends again, confidants, trusting each other.

Chapter Forty-Nine

The next morning, Naina ran into Holy Man.

He held a box of cupcakes but wasn't eating any. "Looks like you're getting your power back."

"My power?" Naina's stomach growled then, and she eyed the box Holy Man was carrying.

"Yes. You're beginning to understand you are meant to be here. You are a divine being and thus have full rights, just like anybody else, to be here on this Earth at this moment. It is your divine purpose to be born. You are the one who needs to make the best out of this life."

Holy Man and Naina walked in step with each other. She nodded, as if she knew what Holy Man meant. She didn't, but knew he would explain further.

And he did. "I urge you to take your power back. Don't allow your negative experiences to detract joy from you, don't allow the people who have hurt you in the past to continue to hurt you in the future. Your life is magical, if you choose to see it. Magic and miracles are all around you. You are alive and a well-functioning adult despite all that has happened to you – perhaps because of all that has happened to you. Own it. Treasure it. Value it, and harness all the power you have, to push yourself upward and onward."

Naina thought about it for a few moments. It was early still, for a Saturday, and the weekend crowds hadn't yet descended into downtown. This gave her a chance to take in all Holy Man was saying, but she realized her conversations with him were usually so deep, crowds wouldn't have affected their ability to speak to each other. "Raiya said something similar the other day. Sometimes I can see it. Other times I struggle, especially to see the magic. Is magic like what I felt at Angel Oak?"

"Yes, although there are other kinds. The universe will send you the experiences, the signs, the magic, the support you need to make your life happen, but you need to make sure you release worry, fear, and doubt and trust yourself."

❧

Naina continued her walk down Cannon Street, and entered Sugar Bakeshop. She didn't usually indulge in a sweet pick-me-up in the middle of the day, but Holy Man's box of cupcakes were too tempting and her mouth watered. Why not? A nice cold coffee with a sugary something sounded like the perfect indulgence for the day after her birthday.

She scanned the trays of cupcakes and cookie-filled jars. The tantalizing rows of cupcakes were dizzying and she didn't know which would satisfy the perfect bite. Red velvet had become cliche, double chocolate sounded too rich, vanilla too plain, as did almond, but lemon curd sounded like the right amount of tart and sweet. Just as she was going to call someone's attention, she froze in place, hand suspended in the air, as if she were in a classroom waiting to be called upon.

At the head of the line stood Kevin, the only person she'd had a romantic relationship with. Her face and head grew hot, as if someone had turned a spotlight on her. She lowered her hand slowly, feeling an urge to run out of the shop, and she would have if he hadn't turned around and made eye contact with her.

Naina was rooted in place. She'd never expected to see him again. Was the universe intervening to make this happen?

Confusion registered on his face. He smiled awkwardly, the kind of smile you get when you cannot quite place the person standing in front of you. Naina wasn't sure if she was more shocked from seeing him there, in front of her after nearly a decade, or from him clearly not remembering her.

Embarrassment ran through her, the memory of how he'd treated her stinging all over again. She felt small and flat. She had gotten it wrong all these years. She had deluded herself into thinking something catastrophic had happened to Kevin – as it did to the people who disappeared in her life – but it was clear he was in perfect health. His pearly skin was glowing, and she was tempted to reach out to touch his smooth cheek or tussle his beach blonde hair as she had done before. She could no longer deny he had left her, and it had been on purpose.

"Can I have one now, Daddy? Please?" A five-year old girl jumped up and down, her eyes pleading up to Kevin.

Once again Naina wanted to run but was unable to. Her legs were glued to the floor. The universe had to be working its magic.

❧

Naina met Kevin at a mixer on a chilly night while she was in college. She'd been standing in a corner nursing a soda with lime when he approached her. He asked her to dance and she declined, but he didn't move away from her. He stood next to her, taking in the room as if trying to understand the view from her perspective.

Naina was intrigued. She had thought her invisibility was on in full force, but it was clear Kevin acknowledged her presence. "Why aren't you moving on?"

He barely glanced at her. "Why should I? I can see everyone and everything from here. I can see why you've settled on this spot. It's perfect to scope everyone out."

She was surprised he didn't taunt her or deride her in some way. His eyes seemed gentle and the air was relaxed around him, as if he were comfortable to be seen with her. "What do you see?" she asked.

"See the girl in red, the one with the perfect hair, not a strand out of place?"

Naina nodded.

"She's trying too hard. She'd be more attractive if she were more low-key, more relaxed. If I hung out with her I'd be controlled by her."

Naina nodded again, but this time she smiled, as if they were accomplices of sorts. She had been comfortable with smiling back then. She was intrigued there was someone else who liked to come up with stories about people. "She is controlling. She's in charge of the girls surrounding her and she doesn't like it when they don't follow."

It was his turn to nod. "What do you see?"

"I see a bunch of people trying too hard. Too hard to fit in, too hard to be accepted, too hard to be seen. I'm happy not being seen. I'd rather watch than clamor for attention."

"You wanna get outta here?" he asked.

They did. They left the party and walked around downtown, sharing stories they made up about others, making fun of the popular kids and how hard they tried. Kevin wasn't a popular kid either. They walked and chatted, and Kevin dropped Naina off promptly at 9:55pm at the entrance of her apartment building. They exchanged contact information, and he extended his hand. "It was wonderful to meet you, Naina. I hope I see you again soon."

⁂

Naina learned the concept of ghosting once it became a recognizable term. Kevin took her out for a few dates but the moment she slept with him, he never called her back. He didn't return her calls or reply to her emails or messages. She didn't know where he lived, but she searched for him, at every college event she ever attended from that point forward, and never saw him.

He had called her "emotionally unavailable," and she hadn't been curious then to figure out what that meant. It would be years later before she realized he was right.

At that time, she turned to the Charleston Public Library for solace and, strangely, Naina got drawn into reading romance after Kevin. Books had always allowed her to escape, and this was no exception. This was when she discovered Nora Roberts and later J. D. Robb. She also read a couple by Nicholas Sparks, being particularly drawn to stories of star-crossed lovers, dreaming this may have been the case with Kevin. She hadn't wanted to accept he had ghosted her. She wanted to believe something tragic had occurred to him, and that is why she hadn't seen him again. Maybe he'd suffered from amnesia, had been lost at sea, or injured at war.

Yet, she knew reality wasn't like the tales in the books. Love wasn't so easy. The truth was unavoidable. She had lost her virginity to Kevin and he had disappeared.

❧

With her heart thumping in her chest, so loudly she was afraid others would hear, Naina found the confidence in her legs. She was no longer going to let herself be put down. She was different now. Another person. She had nothing to fear, and nothing to lose.

"Do I—" Kevin started.

And so she ignored Kevin, walked right past him and up to the counter. By the time she placed the order for her cupcake, Kevin and his daughter had left the shop.

❧

Holy Man was waiting for her at the corner of King and Hassell. He no longer had the box of cupcakes with him. "The universe seems to be supporting you in your healing, wouldn't you say?"

"Yes, it must be working its magic, conspiring for me to run into Kevin after so long."

"You were finally ready to face him. You're getting your life back."

"I haven't had the best life, though. And even seeing Kevin was hard. It took everything for me not to run away," she said.

"Yes, you haven't had the best situation, but it is beginning to turn, isn't it?"

"Yes, I'm losing my naïveté, seeing people for who they are and realizing it's their loss for not valuing me. Not mine."

"You are a magical being with gifts, talents, and purpose. You're a spiritual being who happens to be inhabiting a physical body at this time. Your life experiences are pushing you to grow and expand

299

and make yourself better, not to bog you down and make you feel depressed. But you have to do that, for yourself. You have to pick yourself up and know and feel you have all you need."

"How do I know when it's the universe who's working to support me?"

"The universe is always supporting you but you have to support yourself. The universe communicates directly through your inner voice. Get quiet and allow for your intuition to guide you."

"I'm trying, but it's hard."

"Naina, you are a child of the universe and you have all you need to move forward with your life. You are loving, lovable, and deserving. Own it."

"I will." And just then, Naina knew the time had come to have an honest conversation with her father.

Chapter Fifty

"**C**lear your blockages," Holy Man had told her.

And now that Naina sat in her apartment, having just called her father, there was no running away from this conversation. She needed to have this talk and let him know she no longer needed him.

"I am clearing myself from you," Naina said.

Her father didn't respond.

"I know I'm a disappointment." There was a heavy ache in her chest, she couldn't take a full deep breath. Yet, she was keenly aware she needed to release the tightness. "I know I always have been."

Naina craved for her father. Her only solace was seeing his name appear on her monthly bank statement. But she wanted to put those days behind her. She wanted to no longer need him.

He spoke slowly, as if he thought of every word before uttering it. "I failed your mother. I didn't want to risk failing you as well. I always assumed you'd be better off in other people's care."

"How can that be true? How can you think I would've been

better off with others instead of you?"

"I don't know, Naina. I simply don't know. But it seems I've caused more hurt than help."

They were both silent. He didn't say anything else, and she didn't add more to the conversation. What else was there to say?

ॐ

"You lost your mother a long time ago, right?" Fiona asked. On a Saturday in mid-November, she had stopped by Naina's new apartment to try some of her baked goods. It was a week after Naina had called her father.

Fiona and Naina had made a habit of exchanging food with one another. Raiya had promised to join them in the future, having awakened to the joy of cooking when he tried it for Naina's birthday. It seemed odd to Naina that cooking and baking for each other had become a nice addition to the friendship blossoming between the three of them. She had spent so much of her life eating the same food, it was strange that sampling new foods was a way for her to bond with others.

"Yes, I was seven years old when she killed herself," Naina replied.

"Why then is all of this coming up now? I don't mean to lack sympathy or empathy, but why, after all these years are you feeling grief over her again?"

"I don't think I felt grief the first time around. I was too young and too bewildered. It has been twenty-three years and I finally feel I'm mature enough to deal."

They stayed silent as they each sampled the homemade granola Naina had prepared to replace the Special K she ate every morning. She had also baked a selection of biscuits and bars to replace the digestives.

Naina used to feel envious of Alice who seemed to be cooking and baking constantly. Naina had often wondered how Alice was able to do it all, have a family, cook, bake, manage a business, and still take such good care of herself.

Naina had asked Fiona how she did it, and Fiona said she simply made time for it. It was important for her to eat freshly cooked meals, and she preferred home-cooked to processed or prepared food. Naina was excited to learn how to do this for herself.

"What was the catalyst for you to enter this moment of grief, then? What's changed?" Fiona asked, breaking the silence.

Naina had clearly been grieving for a while. Her whole life, perhaps. Why was her grief suddenly relevant right now?

Fiona continued. "Can I share something with you? Something I've been reticent to discuss but might help?"

"Yes, of course," Naina said. She adjusted her seat to face Fiona. She even put Mimi back on the ground to make sure the dog didn't distract them.

"I moved to Charleston because I was running away. I was in a ten-year relationship with a man called Philip, but he didn't have the courage to ask me to marry him, or to have children with me, and I didn't have the courage to leave him. I stayed with him because it was easier to do that than it was for me to make a life on my own. It was easier to stay with him than to gain the courage to leave. I had grown comfortable, you see. I had a comfortable job and I had a comfortable home. It wasn't what I wanted, and it took me a long time to wake up to that reality."

"I'm really sorry to hear, but I'm so encouraged you finally did gain the courage … Didn't you? Isn't that why you're here, now?"

"Yes, it is," Fiona said. She leaned closer to Naina and looked at her intensely before continuing. "The reason I'm telling you this is because I had a miscarriage. I hadn't realized I was pregnant, and I went to the toilet one morning after a bad night of drinking. We used to party hard, thinking ourselves as still being college students even though we had long passed the age. But Philip really liked having a good time, drinking and dancing, and I went along with it. I didn't mind, but I also didn't particularly enjoy it. Anyway, this one morning, I had a bad cramp, as if I was getting my period. I went to the toilet and I saw a lot of blood. I assumed I had gotten my period until I heard a plop, like a turd falling into the water – I apologize for the horrid detail—"

"That's okay, Fiona. I want to know." Naina placed her hand on Fiona's arm.

"Well, I realized then it wasn't a period, I was having a miscarriage. I was devastated. It helped me wake up to the reality I wasn't happy in my relationship with Philip and what I wanted most was to have a happy life for myself, and an environment of my own making rather than that of someone else."

"I'm really sorry, Fiona, for the loss of your child. You are so put together, so on top of your life. You're a wonderful example of perseverance."

"Thank you, Naina. What started as grief for a child I didn't realize I'd had evolved into grief for a life I wanted for myself but wasn't allowing myself to have. What I wanted most was to learn to live life on my own terms. I had to get away. I moved from Portland, Oregon to the furthest place I could think of, and that was Charleston. I found a job at the NICU here."

"And the universe has been supporting you, it seems. You are happy here?"

Fiona placed a hand on Naina's and smiled. "I am. Very.

Can You Be

Meeting you and Raiya has also helped. My point is to make you think about why all this is coming up now. I don't deny you are grieving your mother, but perhaps this is about something deeper? Is it possible it's about something else?"

Naina chose that moment to put a spoonful of granola in her mouth.

Fiona continued. "This pain you carry, about your mom's suicide and your father's abandonment, doesn't define you. Don't let it define you. Don't let it become you. Rise above it."

Naina finished chewing. "I see what you're saying. I have to find a way to forgive my father. Find a way to forgive my mother, as well."

"Relationships don't come into your life by accident. You're not meant to be hurt or you haven't brought this upon yourself. But all your difficult relationships are pushing you to consider what you've learned and how you can grow."

What Naina most admired about herself was her perseverance. For most of her life, she had survived, barely making it. Now, she was thriving. She hadn't given up on herself. Others may have, and that was okay. It was their bad, their misperception. Her perception was ultimately what mattered. She knew herself best. Her opinion of herself counted most.

She couldn't change her past, and she didn't need to. But her future was in her hands.

Naina brightened up. "When can I practice that facial on you?"

Fiona agreed to stop by the next day.

※

Naina had just finished the practice facial on Fiona, and Fiona had fallen asleep. She snored softly. Naina took that as a compliment.

Her hands had shaken at the beginning, but as Naina progressed throughout the facial, she had grown more confident. She'd had the facial at the spa at The Belmond Charleston Place, and quietly paid attention to every step the esthetician made, like she had done in Druskininkai, but this time, she had written down notes the moment she had come back home. She had watched many more videos and added to her notes, and she'd kept her notebook next to her as she practiced on Fiona.

"We all have a purpose," the Holy Man had said. "Don't ever doubt that. The universe has a purpose for every single one of us. Even those who suffer. We don't need to understand the purpose. Our souls sign contracts, unbeknownst to us, or rather that we forget when we are born. The suffering is temporary. It's for this lifetime only. And every human suffers in one way or another. Yes, some suffer more than others, but we all suffer. We think of our experience as immediate, but our souls are eternal, and they have many lives to learn the lessons they are meant to learn."

After hearing about Fiona's miscarriage, Naina understood she wasn't alone. Many had suffered, and many had experienced great losses. Some had suffered a lot more than she had.

Fiona's restful expression gave Naina certainty she finally had purpose, a reason why she had been brought to the world. She had more to learn but she knew she had it in her to work as an esthetician, and she was going to give it all she had.

Chapter Fifty-One

That afternoon, Naina went back to Angel Oak, and sat in the comfort of its roots and trunk. She closed her eyes and connected to the tree, the earth, and everything around her. She started by bringing light to every person who had hurt her, used her, taken advantage of her, and/or mistreated her in some way. She pulled out all the energetic cords they enmeshed within her. She pulled out Ellen, Caitlin, Elie, Kevin, Alice, and her stepmother.

She pulled and pulled and pulled some more. Some people had become engrained in her far beyond what she had anticipated. She extracted their claws from her body and gathered them in the space around her. She expressed gratitude to each, for they had each taught her a lesson. One by one – person by person – she lovingly released them. She watched them lift away from her. They no longer belonged with her.

Then she pulled out her father. She pulled some more, just to make sure she was free and clear. Still in her mind's eye, she wrapped him in his own cord and placed him, cord and all, in his own bubble. She pushed away his bubble. He bounced back, and she pushed him away again. She pushed him away as many times as she needed until he was gone, until his bubble disappeared.

There was only one cord she knew she couldn't pull, at least not yet. She lit her inner light. A bright golden flame ignited in her core and spread through her body, reaching every cell and every surface. The light spread beyond her, sinking roots into the earth, tentacles into the world around her, with links up into the sky. She felt strong and courageous. She was invincible.

With this invincibility she cast her past, her old friends, her old coworkers, and took in a reckoning she didn't know she had. She would reinvent herself in her new apartment. And with her new profession after esthetics school, whatever it would turn out to be. Maybe she didn't need to find a job, but she could work for herself. She could rent a space somewhere and work on her own terms.

Naina was aware going to cosmetology school meant she needed to change her ability to engage in small talk. She would need to speak to her clients, and not just about their skin or their lifestyle, but also about everyday trivia and ask them about themselves. She would need to establish a relationship with them because a dry personality wouldn't get her anywhere. She wanted to have repeat clients and she needed to treat them as if she had a friendship with them without actually cultivating a friendship. In other words, she needed to treat them like she had treated the people on the tour, but not to the extent that she had treated Gemma and Caroline with whom she had maintained a friendship. She needed to make sure she was able to maintain a conversation, even though she wasn't going to go out to dinner with them.

Even if she chose to set up her own business, Naina knew she still needed to do more work because the one person she hadn't pulled out was her mother. She wanted to make amends with her mother, but she didn't know how. All Naina could do was open her heart, and hope somehow she connected with her mother's spirit.

Her mother had loved her, and still did, from afar. Naina understood her mother's pain had been too much for her to handle. She didn't kill herself because of Naina. Her father also loved her. He may not have known how to demonstrate it, but she knew he did. Her inner knowing told her this.

Naina knew she also needed to work on forgiving herself. This was a journey she needed to embark on regardless. The time had come to face her truth. She needed to face herself and follow her heart. She was learning to love herself, to understand that in doing so, she opened to give and to receive love, and as she did, that love extended all around her, to every aspect of her life.

Only then, would she be truly boundless.

❦

Holy Man said, "What you put out is what you project and what comes back to you. It's the basis of the Law of Attraction. You need to love yourself, feel worthy, feel lovable because you love yourself, and when you do, you'll start putting that emotion out there for others to see, and you'll attract people who love you for you. But for as long as you don't feel lovable or worthy, you'll attract people who don't see you as lovable and worthy. It starts with you."

Naina opened her eyes. She knew exactly what he meant. The love for herself was far stronger than she had ever felt before. "Are we really connected?" Her voice seemed to be vibrating, almost as if shaking with fear, but she wasn't afraid. The sound from her voice seemed to be reacting to the warmth and reverberations within.

Holy Man looked at her tenderly, as her mother often had.

"What does your heart say?"

She didn't need to think about it this time. The answer came from a place deep within her. "Yes."

"Isn't that enough? Isn't that knowing in your heart all you need? Why do you feel the need to ask for additional evidence?"

A similar translucent airy substance radiated from her into him. Hers was a slightly different hue. When it reached him, he closed his eyes and nodded in gratitude. The substances mixed together, co-existing and actively moving between them. Naina was surrounded by unconditional love. There was no judgment, no criticism, no expectations. She could just be, plain and simple. She didn't need to prove anything or act in a particular way. She was loved, for who she was.

"I don't," she said. "At least not anymore." And she meant it.

A sensation of light spread throughout her being. She felt the connection she had always yearned for, as if she were a conduit between heaven and earth, and energy was channeling through her – and through this man.

After a few moments the warmth started to dissipate. Yet, Naina continued to feel elated. She didn't realize she had closed her eyes until she opened them and stared at Holy Man's smiling face.

"Any time you want to come back to this, chant the name of God. It will activate the energy. Or you can sit once again with Angel Oak," he said.

Without needing to ask, Naina knew that her tree, Angel Oak, was special and mystical. It contained the answers she had always sought. It was glowing, the glittering quality ever brighter. She was honored for having the ability and opportunity to connect with it in such a deep way.

She turned back to Holy Man. "What is the name of God?"

"Any name you use to refer to God. It can be the word 'God,' or any other word such as Father, Lord, Allah, Christ, Creator, Elohai, Spirit, Bhagwan, or any other term you feel comfortable with."

"That's all?"

"Yes, my child, that's all you need to connect to the magic of Angel Oak, the Tree of Life, to the source of the universe, to all there is."

Naina nodded as if she understood. She couldn't articulate it but, oddly, it was a knowing that came from deep within, as if she'd always been aware of this, but hearing him utter these statements had suddenly caused her to "remember."

Holy Man extended his arms and gave Naina a vial with a flower essence. "It will give you the clarity you need to feel you are on the right life path."

This time she was confused, and was unable to hide it.

"You haven't asked for this," Holy Man said, pointing to the vial, "but I know it's hard to keep deep connections when we get into the day-to-day. When you need something more tangible, there are tools you can use. Understand these tools are made available by the universe so we have various ways to connect back to it, and to our oneness. This flower remedy is one of those tools. It is simply a reminder. Not only will it give you clarity, but every time you take a drop, use it as a prompt to be quiet for a few moments and sense the deep connection you have with the earth."

Naina took a drop in her mouth. The bitterness of the flower essence immediately melted away the dissatisfaction. It was as if all her worries came to her on purpose, like they were meant for her someway, and not as a form as punishment as she had always felt, but as an opportunity for her to learn a lesson. She didn't yet know what that lesson was, but she sensed she would know soon. "Is there anything else I can use?"

He handed her another crystal. "This is an opal. It will help awaken the magic you seek. Remember to pay close attention to your dreams."

The opal was polished, one-inch wide with a slightly rectangle shape but not exact. It was mostly light brown, almost orange, but it had iridescent blues and greens throughout. It also had a glittery quality, similar to what she saw on Angel Oak – the Tree of Life.

"What words come to you as you hold the stone?" Holy Man asked.

Naina's mind was blank.

"Don't think too hard. Just say the first words that come to mind. And don't worry, you won't say something wrong. Trust yourself."

"Happiness? Change?"

"Are those questions or statements?"

Naina smiled. "Statements."

"You need to trust your inner voice, Naina." His voice was gentle, without a trace of judgement.

"So I was right?"

"I said you couldn't say something wrong, didn't I? What else came up?"

"I feel it will help me with my relationships, mend them, bring back the faith I've lost ... I feel it will bring me luck," she said, more confidently.

Holy Man smiled. "Indeed, it will. Is there anything else you would like to know at this moment?"

Naina nodded, taking a deep breath. "Where did the 'hey' come from?"

"What do you think?"

"I feel it may have been the tree ..." Naina was doubtful, but the moment she uttered the words, it made sense to her. Yes, the tree had called out to her.

As if reading her mind, Holy Man said, "The Tree of Life is always there for you, it will always help you connect back to yourself and to source. As will trusting yourself. Work on that Naina, learn to listen – and trust – in your inner voice. Use the tools I gave you."

On the way home, Naina was certain there was no way out. She had to accept herself and find her way to forgiveness.

Chapter Fifty-Two

That same night in mid-November, Raiya, Fiona, and Naina had a dance-off. They were celebrating life. Naina had run into Fiona and Mimi while checking her mailbox and they had knocked on Raiya's door, inviting themselves in. He had suggested the dance-off.

They were in Raiya's living room, music blasting. Naina's feelings moved through her body. She started awkwardly and tight. Raiya dance with his eyes closed in pure bliss. His body moved in waves and he wasn't self-conscious. He didn't seem to care Naina and Fiona were also in the room. He was in his own world. Fiona also danced but she moved in sync with the rhythm. Fiona danced as if she had someone else in front of her.

Naina tried to move with the music too, to dance without concern, and closed her eyes. She moved awkwardly and was conscious of lifting one leg and then another. Her movements seemed forced. She stopped and stood still, listening to the music and allowing the tunes to settle in her bones.

Can You Be

Soon, her body swayed from side to side. Her face broke into a smile. The rhythms infused her being, moving through her legs, up her hips, and into her waist. They remained there for a while. She finally understood what it meant to be moved by music.

But then, the notes hit her shoulders and her neck and her arms upraised as her upper body shook. She had no idea what she was doing but she loved the feeling. A feeling of ecstasy took over and the world melted away.

It was similar to what she'd had when she had practiced the facial on Fiona that morning. She felt free, without a care in the world. Naina connected the movement of her hands and fingers with the movement of her body dancing, realizing they were similar. They allowed her to feel free, uninhibited, allowing her to just be.

What would her life be like if she didn't focus on holding back but rather on raising her arms in utter bliss? She would have no fear. She wouldn't be afraid to settle. She wouldn't be hesitant to trust. She would open herself up to love, knowing she was always safe, always blessed.

ॐ

Naina's perfect day prior to letting go of her routines was one in which she followed her routines without interruption. Now, she knew she had to create a new perfect day, one where her routines didn't bog her down. With the start of the new year, she was compelled to start afresh.

She would start her day with a hot cup of something, but it didn't have to be coffee. She would check in with herself before deciding. She could make a cup of tea, or even a pot of masala chai, as Raiya did. If she felt like drinking coffee, she wanted to have flat whites, as she'd had during her travels in the Baltics. She bought a moka pot to make espresso without having to invest in a complex coffee machine.

She stopped having Special K and instead made oatmeal with raisins and cinnamon, or cream of wheat porridge with dried cherries and a dash of cardamom powder. For her snacks, she now had homemade nut bars baked according to Fiona's instructions, and she continuously tried new recipes to ensure she had a variety of options.

She had gotten rid of the pesky Gazelle when she moved into her new apartment. No one had wanted to buy it when she tried to get rid of it, so she simply put it in the trash room. She walked for at least an hour a day and walking outdoors ensured she got fresh air. So, instead of walking to gather her thoughts, she walked to get exercise. Or to do both.

Over the last few weeks, she'd gotten together regularly with Fiona and Raiya. They met at least once a week on a Tuesday so it wouldn't interrupt anyone's weekend plans. And since they all lived on the same floor it was easy. They took turns cooking and hosting, and whoever cooked, hosted. They tried new and old recipes on each other and watched TV series or movies. They had most recently been watching *Game of Thrones*. It wouldn't have been Naina's choice. There was too much fantasy, too much incest, and too much conflict.

"This should be called 'Game of Porn,'" she had commented. There was simply too much sex in it. But she loved those days. She reveled in them. They were the best days of the week.

They also went out together on weekends. Raiya had bought a car, which allowed them to explore the low country with more freedom and flexibility. They sampled all the beaches – Isle of Palms, Folly Beach, and even Kiawah Island – but Naina's absolute favorite was still Sullivan's. It was quieter and less touristy and they didn't mind parking in the residential area as long as they secured a spot close to the oat grass. They took day trips together, and visited all the nearby plantations: Boone, Magnolia, and Drayton. They shopped at farmers' markets in Mount Pleasant, West Ashley, and when they didn't feel like driving, they went to the weekend market on Marion Square.

Naina finally had a family structure.

"Sometimes family is the one you choose, not the one you're born into," Fiona commented once.

And so they had become family. They had even celebrated Thanksgiving with each other. Raiya did fly out to India for New Year's, but Fiona and Naina had each other. And having Mimi was if Naina had a pet of her own.

And thus, the new year had started, and Naina looked forward to starting school in a few short days.

Naina pinched herself every time she thought of how different her life was. She felt free and spontaneous. She never thought she would feel that way. Life made sense to her and she finally understood what she needed to feel joy.

The conversations with Priidik had become longer and more frequent. They caught up about their daily lives but also exchanged thoughts about what made a good story, how songs evoked such strong emotions, and how food brought up vivid memories long thought forgotten. They even spoke about what it meant to discover one's life purpose.

"When we learn to be comfortable to just be," Naina had said. "That's when it means we have accomplished our life's purpose."

Naina's love for Priidik grew stronger, and although they spoke often, they still hadn't discussed the future of their relationship.

Naina wasn't sure how much longer she could continue being away from him. It remained unresolved.

That and her father. Naina didn't want to cut him off, but she wasn't yet sure how to keep him in her life.

अं

"I just don't know who you are," Priidik said over zoom on a morning in early January.

"What are you saying?" Naina straightened her back.

"I'm saying this in the best way possible. You're like a new person, so different from the woman I met a few months ago."

"You're making it sound like it's a bad thing."

Priidik shook his head vigorously. "It's not at all. I mean it as a compliment. You're so different from the quiet woman I met at the beginning of the tour, and I like it."

Naina relaxed her shoulders. "I guess you're right. I used to be a lonely woman who lived a self-imposed sheltered and quiet life, yet I want nothing more than to have a loving, supportive, and nurturing family – and friends. I used to be too afraid to get myself out there to meet this potential family. I've been hurt a lot in the past, but a few months ago, I received a box, a gift perhaps, that somehow presented me with a chance to change my life. I needed to learn to get out of my own way and learn to be vulnerable and trusting. Even though I'm getting better, I'm still quiet, afraid, reserved, and I'm socially awkward. I've lived a self-imposed sheltered life. I'm odd – people have told me so, but I know that about myself, and I own it. I'm weird. I also don't like change. I like to feel the world is soft and cushiony and I want someone who makes me feel that way." Naina's face was hot, and she had started to sweat.

To her relief, Priidik was smiling.

She continued. "I don't like change, but I realized change is good for me. Change brings me what I really want. I've always wanted a family and a supportive network, I've always wanted to be strong and independent, and I finally feel I am. All I needed to do was embrace change, and it brought me new things. I understand, better than anyone, it's scary to take risks, but staying stuck and stagnant are no longer options for me."

"You sound very wise, Naina." Priidik was still smiling.

Naina nodded. She was surprised by the depth she was expressing, and she wasn't done. "The trip to the Baltics really changed me. I felt motivated and inspired by the revolution those people went through. They had so many invaders, so many people who wanted to take over their land, and they persevered. They remained steadfast, even through the worst of times. They were willing to change and adapt and it made them stronger. I can't believe what they endured, and yet I felt such peace and safety when I was there. People were kind and gentle. You were. Artur was. The other tour goers were as well, although they're not from the Baltics, but the entire experience was really good for me. It opened my eyes to how small my life was, how small my mentality was, and how much I needed to change."

"I didn't realize the trip had been so transformative for you, Naina, and touched you in such a deep way."

"Yes, I guess it did ..."

"What else are you trying to tell me Naina? I feel like you're saying so much, yet you're holding something back."

It was Naina's turn to smile. "I'm astonished you live so far yet you've gotten to know me so well." She took a deep breath. "I need for us to be different, Priidik. I feel so connected with you, and keeping in touch has been nice, but I've reached a point where I need to know if there is a future for us."

"I love you, Naina."

Naina was at a loss for words. She knew it wasn't in Priidik's culture to utter words of affection, much less those three particular ones. She knew exactly how she felt about him and had been waiting, in fact, for the right time to express it herself.

"I love you too." Naina was lightheaded and thought she might pass out. Her heart rate was up and she was unable to breathe, but something told her she wasn't having a panic attack. This was different. A warmth spread through her making her feel that she belonged.

"I have some free time coming up, and I want to know how you feel about me coming over for a visit?"

Naina nearly fell off her sofa from excitement. She knew when she told Raiya, Fiona, and even Gemma and Caroline that Priidik would be in Charleston during spring break, they would be delighted for her.

Chapter Fifty-Three

The last time Naina had made a significant decision in her life was choosing the major she would graduate in. Yes, she had considered studying law, but when she had opted not to, she had to choose her major. And it was a cop out, since she opted for something akin to liberal arts, which meant she had flexibility in the classes she chose.

Afterward she seemed to not consider decisions. Perhaps she had decided by instinct. She had seen a "Help Wanted" sign outside the real estate office and, without thinking, had stepped into the office and filled out an application. Alice had interviewed her then and offered her a job on the spot. Alice would often refer back to that incident to say Naina's spontaneity had been misleading. Alice had liked Naina acted on instinct, and it played such a big role in her decision to hire her. Alice had later wondered where Naina's decision making skill had gone, while Naina wondered where the spontaneity had come from.

But that first day in early January, when Naina stepped into the Cosmetology School of Charleston, Naina was certain she had finally made a sound decision. The program for esthetics cost her $12,995 and would require six hundred hours of training. It was more than what she'd anticipated, given she also had to purchase books and a product kit. The program asked the students to consider buying linen and a treatment table so they could practice what they learned and build up to their six hundred hours. For those who didn't have the means, there were treatment room facilities they could use in the school, but Naina wanted to offer facials to Fiona and Raiya, and to Priidik when he visited. She thought she might even offer facials to people who worked in the building, and thus build up confidence and a potential clientele.

Although she enrolled in a payment plan at the school, she needed to supplement her income. She walked into the City Lights Coffee one morning after one of her walks and something told her to take a chance.

"A few months ago, I saw a 'help wanted' sign. Do you still have a job opening?" she asked the lady behind the counter.

"The person I hired just quit unexpectedly. Do you have experience as a barista?"

Was the universe making things happen? "I don't but I'm a quick learner, and I love making coffee. I also live a short walk from here, so I guarantee I'll always be on time and I'll be meticulous in my service and care."

The woman, Samantha, eyed Naina carefully. They chatted a while longer. Samantha then asked, "How about I hire you on a trial basis? For the next couple of weeks, I'll train you, and we'll see how well you learn and how the customers respond to you. After the two weeks are over, I decide if I hire you full-time and you decide if you want to work here."

And so it was. Naina started on a trial basis, working the early shift at the coffee shop. For those two weeks, she opened the shop with Samantha, learning how to get everything set up, preparing and serving the different kinds of drinks, who the regular customers were and their drink of choice, and so much more.

The hardest part for Naina, to her surprise, was not dealing with customers. For the regulars, she was able to remember their names and preferences, and for newcomers, she asked polite questions to create a friendly environment. She had learned by then she had the ability to make conversation with people – Charleston weather was a big and easy topic to discuss. The hardest part was getting the right consistency of milk when steaming it to prepare the right kind of coffee or tea drink. With cappuccinos, she struggled getting foam. But Samantha was patient with Naina and gracefully coached her until Naina was able to make hearts and other dainty shapes on the coffee foam. Thankfully, Samantha hired her full-time.

Naina attended evening classes and worked during the days. It didn't pay much, but it helped cover her expenses while she attended school.

꽃

Two weeks into the esthetics program, Naina set an intention to become the city's first holistic esthetician.

She had started to learn about the physiology of the skin, skin treatments, skin infections, sanitation, safety, consultations, and service protocols. Over the next six months, she would also learn about skin analysis and chemistry, and would learn how to perform exfoliation, extractions, and electrotherapy. She would learn about key ingredients and skincare products and she would get classes in hair removal, waxing, brow work, makeup, as well as state laws and regulations.

And although Naina was certain she had finally made the right decision, she wanted to do more. By becoming a holistic esthetician, in addition to looking at the skin, she would focus on the body, soul, and mind. Various factors contributed to skin health, including hydration, food consumption, sleep, and more. For this, she enrolled in the Institute for Integrative Nutrition and took their online classes alongside her esthetician degree.

Naina knew she was pushing herself, and with the two loads of courses she had little free time. She continued her job at City Lights Coffee, attended courses at the cosmetology school in the evenings, and conducted her work for IIN on the weekends or whenever she found a quiet moment at the coffee shop.

The combination of the studies in integrative nutrition and esthetics was perfect for her newly discovered passion. Naina felt blessed when she discovered that esthetics and healthy living could be combined as holistic esthetics.

She hadn't thought she would have had the skills to work with people and interact with them in such a personal way, but she really enjoyed it. She hadn't done well in real estate because she hadn't been interested in houses. But she was truly interested in skin care and in healthy living and talked about it nonstop.

She practiced on Fiona and Raiya, and they were more than happy to lend their skin. Eventually, the cosmetology school allowed them to practice on clients. These services were offered at a discounted rate, since the facials weren't yet licensed.

Working at City Lights Coffee had given Naina the ease to make simple conversation. Still, her hands trembled with the first customer she had.

"What concerns do you have with your skin?" Naina asked.

The client explained they wanted to reduce the appearance of the pores on their nose and chin, Naina asked, "How would you like to feel after your facial today?"

"Relaxed," the client said.

"How would you describe your food habits?"

Holistic facials considered a complete view of the client. Naina didn't just study the skin but discussed the client's lifestyle.

She would provide skincare product recommendations, as well as practices to improve their health to ensure they had visible results on the skin.

The more practice Naina got, the more confidence she gained. Her routines had been advantageous. She was detailed and meticulous when analyzing and treating skin. She was consistent with her clients. Her favorite part was doing extractions. She got a real satisfaction of pushing puss and debris out of the pores. She was thorough and excelled when she gave facials.

She was finally coming into her own. And yes, she was beginning to trust.

⚛

"It's not enough to want things, Naina. You also need to learn to cocreate with the universe." Priidik had flown in to meet Naina during spring break. She had taken him to all her favorite spots around Charleston. They had walked everywhere, although Naina had long forgotten to count the steps or track the time that it took her to get places. Those times seemed like distant memories. What she hadn't left behind were her ghost stories, and she shared them all with Priidik, who listened intently. He understood why Naina had asked about ghost stories during the Baltic trip.

Now they were walking around the Battery, which was Priidik's favorite spot. He had told Naina he loved to look out onto Mount Pleasant and Sullivan's Island on the left, James Island on the right, and Fort Sumter towards the outlet into the open ocean.

"What does that mean? Cocreate?" she asked.

"Cocreating is when you set an intention about what you want for your life, and you work with the universe to allow it to happen. Cocreation happens in various ways. It starts with yourself, listening to your intuition, following the voice of your inner guidance. You also need to learn to pay attention to the signs and synchronicities."

"You know, you sound very much like someone I know ..."

"Oh yeah? I hope it's someone you like?"

"He definitely is."

"He? Should I be worried?"

"Not at all. He's a guide to me, and I really enjoy our conversations. What you said sounds very much like something he'd say."

"I have my wisdom to share." Priidik took her hand in his.

Naina leaned into him. He was the perfect height for her to fit into the nook between his arm and his chest. "How did you learn all of this stuff? Online?"

"I've developed a meditation practice—"

"So have I. I only started after coming back from the Baltics," she exclaimed.

"I learn something new about you every day. I had no idea you meditated. I started about ten years ago. And no, I didn't learn online. When I rely too much on the internet and on what others say, I miss out on figuring out what I really want and who I really am. The universe sends us messages, but the true message comes from within."

"I'm also learning about you. I didn't know you had such deep understanding of intuition and the universe. I thought you weren't religious, like the other Estonians."

"I'm not religious but I have a deep spiritual practice and it's something I have studied. I pay attention to how the universe communicates with me."

"I've been paying attention to signs and messages, but I still get confused."

"When you see the sign, get quiet, sit with yourself, and the true interpretation will come." Priidik stopped walking and faced her. He leaned down and spoke in a whisper close to her ear, as he had done in Liepāja. "If you don't get a sign, it doesn't mean you'll not get what you're looking for. Often events won't unfold how you want them to but rather how they are meant to."

"Like with us?" Naina whispered back.

"Yes ..."

"It's the first time we're seeing each other in person in five months."

"But isn't this better than anything else we could have wanted?" Priidik kissed her. It was a deep kiss and travelled from her lips to the pit off her stomach and set it ablaze.

When they drew away, Priidik's eyes were sparkling and he was glowing, as if he were feeling just like she was. "I have to be honest Priidik, I want this, and yes, this connection with you, this love I have for you, is unimaginable, but I also want more. I want for us to spend more time together, to really see if we can build a future with each other."

A smile spread on Priidik's face. "I feel the same."

"How are we going to make it work? How will we both cocreate with the universe to make things happen for us?"

"When it comes to two people it becomes trickier because

now we're dealing with two life paths. We both have the ability to cocreate, and we both have our own journey to go on. Our journeys may intertwine but one person doesn't have more control than the other."

"I can ask the universe for us to have a relationship and I don't need to push for it to be more. If it is meant to be more, it will be, but I don't need to force it."

"Yes, exactly. It is essential for you to trust. Do you trust the universe? Do you trust its and your ability to guide you in this life?"

"Yes, I guess I do."

"That doesn't sound convincing."

"I do trust the universe. I trust it supports me and loves me and will deliver what I am intending. I have a hard time doing it all the time though. I go back and forth on my trust. But I also know it's key."

"Yes, Naina, and you also have to trust me. I love you and I want to be with you, and we will make this happen. In the meantime, let's enjoy the journey."

"I feel like we need to be more active. I mean, I have been on the journey when it comes to my sense of safety, becoming a great esthetician, and being financially self-sufficient. I do like it, and I feel I'm on a positive path. I get bothered when I don't see results, especially because I want to have a family, I want to be together with you, and I want us to make a future together. I just don't see a way for us to do this with you being in Tallinn and me being in Charleston."

"I want for us to be together as well, since we've both set the same intention, let's notice signs and synchronicities. I know the universe will lead us. It always has. Always. I trust it deeply." Priidik closed his eyes and placed both of his hands on his heart.

Naina did the same. "I trust, I trust, I trust."

Chapter Fifty-Four

On that day of early July, the day Naina finished cosmetology school, she knew this was the accomplishment she was most proud of. She had been proud when she'd graduated from Candor, again when she graduated from the College of Charleston, and finally when she got her job at the real estate office. She had even been proud when she had come back from her trip to the Baltics. She had felt courageous.

But finishing her cosmetology diploma was monumental because she had finally studied a subject she was truly interested in and she'd discovered this passion later in life. She was one of the oldest students in the program and she did well. She had never been a top student, not even a good student, she had been a barely passing student. For her to finish the degree without struggling was a feat she never thought she would have been able to do, ever.

She was also extremely proud because she was finally pursuing what made her feel meaningful and gave her life purpose. It meant she was learning how to cocreate.

Can You Be

❧

And cocreate she did. Events fell into place as if a series of dominoes had been laid out carefully to be knocked down in complex yet meticulously laid out sequence at the exact time and place.

Priidik flew down ten days after she finished her esthetics program to manage a tour agency in Charleston. He was hired as a specialist and had the option to buy a stake in the company in the future.

Naina had often come across a place called the Healing Gallery on her walks down Queen Street. There was a sandwich board placed outside it, advertising holistic healing, acupuncture, yoga, and other types of therapies, and Naina approached the owner and asked about renting space from her. The owner was expanding and opening another location, and thus agreed to lease a room to Naina.

Naina set it up with a brand-new treatment table and once it was decorated, Raiya told her he would arrange for a *puja* to properly bless the space and ensure Naina was setting up herself and her business to be successful. He found a Hindu priest from Columbia, South Carolina, and made arrangements for him to travel to Charleston to conduct the prayer.

"Hindus fix everything with a *puja*. Or, more likely, everything and every occasion is an excuse for a *puja*. You can look at it how you like. I find it auspicious and in any case, it doesn't hurt."

It seemed faith fixed quite a lot of things and Naina wasn't going to take any chances. So she agreed.

The *puja* cleared out negative energies and created an environment conducive to success. The prayers were in honor of Ganesh, the remover of obstacles, and Lakshmi, the goddess of prosperity. The priest set it up outside of the entrance to the treatment room, in a small courtyard. It had to be conducted outdoors because a *havan* with an active fire was a central focus of the prayer.

Naina, Priidik, Raiya, Fiona, and the Healing Gallery owner all sat on the floor. Naina was in front of the havan and next to the priest, since this was to be her space. Over the course of nearly two hours, offerings of spices, ghee, milk, gur, sweets, fruits, incense, water, and blessings were placed into the fire while the priest chanted prayers in Sanskrit. Naina didn't understand what the priest was saying, but ended every section of prayer or mantra claiming "Swaha." Swaha was a term in Sanskrit meaning "well said" or "so be it."

With every "Swaha", every releasing of prayers into existence, every releasing of expectation for the universe to take care of the rest, the energy in the space shifted. It felt light, joyous, and meant for her. She could really be herself in it.

ॐ

One year to the day after she had received that box outside her door, the box that had changed everything, the angelite that had been her constant companion, Naina began her practice as a holistic esthetician.

Because she was associated with the Healing Gallery, they were able to advertise an opening event, which Naina hosted on that day in early August. She had catered food, coffee, and tea from City Lights Coffee, and set up a table with wine and other refreshments. People were able to mingle and ask questions. Raiya, Priidik, and Fiona were armed with treatment brochures and walked around giving attendees any information they requested.

Alice attended the Healing Gallery opening. Naina had sent

invitations to the real estate office and everyone showed up. Some of them out of curiosity, just to see what the quiet girl had made of herself, and others to offer their genuine support. There were quite a few people in attendance since Raiya, Priidik, and Fiona had sent invitations to everyone they worked with. The gallery owner had sent an email blast to all of her contacts. Samantha and the regular clients from City Lights Coffee also attended.

Naina spoke to as many people as possible, as did the owner of the Healing Gallery, explaining how holistic facials were different. Afterwards, Naina provided mini facials for customers to sample her services. She offered a quick cleanse, short facial massage, and a leave-in mask. For anyone who wanted to, she reapplied mascara and lip gloss, reducing their concern about having all of their makeup removed for the rest of the evening.

Alice had booked a mini facial, and Naina knew it wasn't a coincidence. There was a reason for Alice to receive a facial from her, and Naina was happy to do so. This would bring her closure with Alice, and a sense they had moved past any previous grievances.

Naina was nervous, of course, fearing Alice would be overly critical, but she wasn't. She praised Naina and her touch, saying no one had been able to treat her in the way Naina had. And to Naina it was priceless.

ॐ

Alice recommended Naina to all of the clients at the real estate office. She, along with other women at the office, made standing appointments. Eventually, they worked out an arrangement where Naina gave Alice's clients a discount on their first facial. Often, they became Naina's regulars.

Yes, the universe had conspired to bring them together.

Naina was confident with her clients. She provided insightful recommendations, exceeding the client's expectations. She never confessed she sensed their stories, but she made subtle hints. If someone had conflicts at home, she said, "It would be beneficial if you also focused on your relationships at home and worked on them becoming more loving and supportive. Stress comes in various forms and having a loving environment contributes greatly."

Clients would look at her with knowing and gentle eyes. Sometimes they would open up and discuss their challenges further. At times, they would cry, or other times they would hug her.

She also learned how to determine if a client had energy that wasn't supportive to her. In those cases, Naina would conduct the facial and ask information about the client's lifestyle but stick to what was shared in the questionnaire. She didn't provide additional insights. She was happy to be of service but she was wary not to give too much of herself.

She shared this with Priidik who suggested she use a mantra and kriya practice. The Satanama kriya helps to reduce stress and a variation of it helps to clear and protect the aura. It involves chanting and hand gestures while sitting in meditation pose.

Naina started and ended her workday with this practice. She was present for each client, and she was able to clear herself and feel light when she went home in the evening, as if she were leaving or clearing her energy before each client and then clearing her energy before going home.

She sat in meditation pose and calmed herself with a few deep breaths. She uttered meditations as various tips of her fingers touched. She said "Sa," as she brought her index and thumb together. Then, "Ta," and she brought her thumb and middle finger together. Then was, "Na," where her ring finger and thumb touched, and finally she said, "Ma," and her pinky and thumb touched.

She cleared her aura by moving her arms around in circular motions, while repeatedly chanting "Wahe Guru, Wahe Guru, Wahe Guru, Jai Guru."

If she was nervous for a particular reason, she quickly did a round of EFT. The practice still helped her especially as a quick grounding exercise between clients, if she felt the need.

The results showed. Her clients came back and many set up standing appointments. In their reviews, they mentioned her presence of mind, her ability to look deeply at their lives and provide gentle yet effective guidance, and said Naina was meek in attitude but wise, powerful, and insightful in her approach.

Priidik bought her an amethyst geode, similar to the one she had seen in the treatment room in Druskininkai. She placed it in a strategic spot to ensure the room harnessed its healing energy.

Naina had finally found her purpose, and was headed in the right direction. Looking back at her life she recognized she had been strong, her strength of character had been with her all along. She had persevered, she had survived, and where others, and even herself, had seen her as a weak person, she hadn't been. She was just waiting for the right circumstances to come together for her.

That box had turned things around for her. Holy Man had helped her shatter her previous view of herself. He had helped dismantle the layers of protection she had built around herself. So had Priidik, Raiya, and Fiona. Even Mimi. They had all contributed to the breaking down of her old self and her discovery of who she really was and of the potential she held within. Even Alice had been instrumental in her journey, and not just because she recommended clients for Naina, but also because if she hadn't fired her, Naina might still be at that dead-end job in the real estate office.

⁊

Naina had just had the best day in her new job as an esthetician. She was booked back-to-back, with just enough time between appointments to clean up after one client was done and set-up for the next. She'd had four clients, which was enough. More than that would have left her too exhausted. Every one of her clients bought at least one of the products she had recommended, and one had even bought the $150 serum of pure rose essential oil. It was the most expensive retail item she sold, and Naina was chuffed. She was able to get her products at cost and retailed them at 50% profit. When she counted her treatment earnings, retails earnings, and tips for the day, she had made nearly $1,000. It was remarkable.

On her worst days she had no clients and she spent her time catching up on cleaning, counting inventory, and managing her accounts. She wanted to make sure she stayed above board on all of her expenses and had clean accounting for business and tax purposes. They weren't bad days because she felt productive. She was able to do things for herself and that gave her a sense of empowerment.

Those kinds of days didn't happen often. She usually had at least one appointment each day, and on most days she had two or three. She had many repeat clients and conducted her business mostly through word-of-mouth. Fiona and Raiya – especially Raiya, had helped her with much of the marketing, including setting up her social media. And they provided guidance and templates for her to continue them during her downtimes. Her busiest days were Fridays and Saturdays, but she gave herself the day off on Sunday. She wanted at least one day off a week.

336

That day, on the best day she'd had to date, she closed her treatment room, walked out of the Healing Gallery, and found her father standing on Queen Street.

Chapter Fifty-Five

That day in early September, on the best day Naina'd had as an esthetician, she now faced her father.

She knew why he was there, though. When she had opened her treatment room at the Healing Gallery, she had mailed an announcement and signed, "In case you want to come, you're invited."

They stared at each other. He took two steps toward her and she took two steps back.

Her father was the first to break the silence. "You look good, Naina. You're all grown up."

Naina crossed her arms, resenting the hint of a smile on his face. "No thanks to you."

He hung his head. After a few seconds, he lifted his head and nodded. "I deserve that … I'm here to make amends, not to fight … Is there somewhere private we can go to talk?"

They walked to Bakehouse, which was about five minutes away. Walking to the coffee shop with her father, Naina no longer counted the time or steps she took, not even to help fill the silence.

Her father got each of them a coffee and a chocolate chip cookie. They took the first few sips without saying a word. Neither of them touched their cookie.

Once again, he was the first to break the silence. "Just because I didn't agree to pay for your expenses doesn't mean I abandoned you. I was pushing you to grow up and be on your own."

"No, father. You abandoned me long ago. You abandoned me when I was just a child."

"I was lost. After your mother passed, I would park the car and amble for thirty minutes, trying to remember where I'd left it. I lay curled on the floor in the fetal position for hours. It made no difference when day turned to night and night to day. Thank goodness you were with the Smiths. I wouldn't have wanted you to see me in such a deplorable state.

"It's not that I didn't love you. I loved you more than anything in the world. I still do. I felt the loss of your mother was my fault. I hadn't been there for her. I'd been a bad husband. How could I not have seen how much she was suffering? I guess I did but I thought she'd learn to assimilate in time. I never thought she'd do it. It never occurred to me she would take her own life.

"It was my fault. I shouldn't have doubted her when she told me she wanted to die. I should have taken her seriously. I noticed her sadness but I didn't realize how serious it was. I didn't notice she was suffering from depression. It haunts me … These thoughts still keep me up at night. Why couldn't I save her? Why couldn't I do more? Why couldn't I stop her?"

"I don't blame you for my mother's death."

"You don't, but I do. We fought a lot and she once said it would be easier for me if she weren't here. I didn't believe her. The last thing she said that day, as I walked out the door to leave for work was, 'Take care of each other.' I should have known she was saying goodbye."

Naina scoffed. "Clearly, you didn't follow her wishes."

"You're right, Naina. But I didn't see it at the time. I was riddled with guilt. I was certain if I couldn't care for my wife, I couldn't care for my child. I didn't want the same to happen to you and thought I needed help to raise you properly. When I was able to get myself back tougher, I flew to India, convinced finding a new wife, a new mother for you, would be the solution. When I saw the two of you weren't compatible, I knew I had to send you away. I thought I was doing what was best for you."

Naina remained silent.

"And then time passed and the rift between us was too wide. It grew wider in front of my eyes but I had no idea how to get you back. I didn't know how to breach it. And I know your stepmother hasn't helped ... I have done my best, but I have failed. Please forgive me. Please give me a second chance – the second chance I never had with your mother."

"Dad, it wasn't your fault. She left us. Both of us."

Naina knew a fall from the Golden Gate Bridge took only four seconds and carried a 98% fatality rate. Bodies hit the water at 75 miles per hour, which was the same force as a truck hitting a concrete building. If the impact didn't kill them, it was likely they would die from drowning or hypothermia.

"And I broke us further. I kept you away from me because I thought it was the best way to keep you from getting more damaged. As the years went by, I believed you wanted to be away from me."

"All I ever wanted was to be with you. You're my family."

Her father nodded. "Your stepmother wanted children, but

I couldn't bear to bring another person into this brokenness. I thought I was doing it for all of our good. And yet I have failed. Failed you all. Even myself."

Naina's heart cracked open. She knew what it was like to feel like a failure. She didn't want anyone to feel what she had.

"Forgive me, Naina. Please forgive me." Her father broke down into sobs.

Naina moved to his booth and embraced him. She sank into the comfort of his loving arms and dug her tear-stricken face into his chest. She suddenly remembered how he used to hug her as a child. "I thought my mother had killed herself because of me … and when you left me, the belief was solidified. I've lived my life feeling so guilty."

Her father hugged her tighter. "It was never your fault, my *beti*. Never. None of it."

Naina's heart was full. He had finally called her his daughter. She hugged him back as hard as he held her. "I forgive you, Papa."

❧

Holy Man stood in front of her. He met her outside of her apartment building as she was about to head out on a morning walk.

That morning, he didn't have any food or drink on him. "You may or you may not see me again. I can't tell you for sure. You have a lot of ways to communicate with the universe. Pay attention to signs, numbers, rainbows, crystals, and other messages you come across. You will know they are a sign when you feel they are for you. We can get busy in life and forget to notice. Pay attention, stay alert. When doubt starts creeping in, breathe towards your heart, as I have taught you to do, and you will know what the message is. I am here for you always, the entire universe is here for you."

Holy Man didn't show up after that morning in front of her building. Naina looked for him everywhere, constantly glancing around her, but she never spotted him again.

∗

Naina never figured out where the crystal came from, that angelite she had received the previous year, the one that had spurred her to get to this place, forced her to explore who she could be. She didn't make an effort to search, but it was a question that lingered in the back of her mind.

She couldn't deny it had brought her what the books had promised it would, those books she had read at the Charleston Public Library had been accurate. The angelite did bring her a sense of calm and peace. It had helped her feel less alone. Not only had she met a lot more people since the angelite had come into her life, but she had also learned to feel more self-reliant. It had even helped her connect with the divine. Of that, she was most certain.

She called her father a couple of times since he had come to see her, just to talk. Surprisingly, he shared her mother had worn a gold necklace with a crystal pendant – an angelite. Her mother was so attached to the necklace, she never took it off.

Had her mother somehow sent her the crystal from another realm? Maybe she had even sent Holy Man. Both seemed to show up at pivotal moments, when she most needed support.

She wondered if the crystal and Holy Man had been the universe's way of telling her she belonged, she finally had a place for herself. And she would never be alone. Holy Man had been right. The angelite had been what she needed a year ago for it had sparked so much change in her life. She had thought the crystal orb was an ominous sign, but it had turned out to be anything but. The angelite had allowed her to experience all the magic she had always wanted to experience.

⚹

Naina finally understood she had purpose. To be alive was her purpose. She had her HFE to call upon whenever she needed guidance, and the energy of her mother, her guardian angel, and her crystals.

Her personal development was going to be a life-long endeavor, and she would continually have to release old ideas, fears, doubts, the past, people who had hurt her. Healing occurred in layers and as she healed one aspect, a deeper one would surface. She may even need to heal the same one over and over again, until the wound wouldn't reopen.

She had it in her to manifest her desires. She had big plans and she knew they would become a reality. All she needed was to set her mind and her heart to it, and trust the universe would deliver. She had proven it was so. The resources she needed would come to her.

And she also had people in her life she could count on. There were Priidik, Raiya, Fiona, Mimi, and now she also had her father.

Everything Naina had ever wanted was coming together. She was living with Priidik and they were building a life together.

She was able to make it on her own. She was truly financially independent. The income she earned from her practice was enough for her to cover her own expenses. Sharing these with Priidik was a bonus and enabled them to maintain a savings account.

Her relationship with Priidik was growing stronger day by day. They planned a trip to India with an added stop in Korea for Naina to look at beauty products. Raiya would join them for part of their journey in India. He wanted to show them around his favorite places. Priidik and Naina had started talking about starting a family, and possibly adopting a child, even if they could have one of their own.

She had a deeper relationship with her father and instead of speaking only once a year, they spoke once a week. They FaceTimed and delighted on seeing each other's faces over video. They spoke for twenty to thirty minutes, and sometimes longer if needed. It was their new ritual, and one Naina cherished.

She didn't feel constrained any more by her routines. Any cherished experience had become a ritual. If she was able to keep them, she was happy, but if she wasn't, she no longer thought something was off or there was to be impending doom. It was just a part of life.

Things didn't happen without a reason. Naina had survived turning thirty, and the box with the angelite had led her to shattering the box she had built around herself. She had learned to be who she was meant to be. And she was comfortable with that. To just be.

References

The books I used as reference regarding crystals:

The Book of Stones by Robert Simmons and Naisha Ahsian.

Crystal 365 by Heather Askinosie.

The Crystal Bible by Judy Hall.

The book I used as reference regarding the Baltics:

The Baltic Revolution: Estonia, Latvia, Lithuania, and the Path to Independence by Anatol Lieven.

The books I used as reference regarding aromatherapy:

Aromatherapy Science: A Guide for Healthcare Professionals by Maria Lis-Balchin.

Clinical Aromatherapy: Essential Oils in Practice by Jane Buckle.

Essential Oils: A Handbook for Aromatherapy Practice by Jennifer Peace Rhind.

Handbook of Essential Oils: Science, Technology, and Applications edited by K. Husnu Can Baser and Gerhard Buchbauer.

I also used the following websites:

Atlas Obscura: https://www.atlasobscura.com

Damon Richter: https://www.exutopia.com

Deep Baltic: https://deepbaltic.com

Golden Gate Bridge Deaths: https://therushhour.net/2021/12/15/10-people-who-have-jumped-from-the-golden-gate-bridge/

Kaunas Forts: https://www.kaunotvirtove.lt

Visit Estonia: https://www.visitestonia.com/en/

Visit Kauna: https://visit.kaunas.lt/en/

The mantras and kriyas that Priidik taught Naina in Chapter Fifty-Four were based on the teachings of Kyle Gray, particularly his "Raise Your Vibration" course: https://www.kylegray.co.uk/online-courses

I had a particular affinity to The Užupis Constitution, and I didn't include it in its entirety in the book. For anyone interested, the Užupis Constitution states:

1. Everyone has the right to live by the River Vilnelė, and the River Vilnelė has the right to flow by everyone.

2. Everyone has the right to hot water, heating in winter and a tiled roof.

3. Everyone has the right to die, but this is not an obligation.

4. Everyone has the right to make mistakes.

5. Everyone has the right to be unique.

6. Everyone has the right to love.

7. Everyone has the right not to be loved, but not necessarily.

8. Everyone has the right to be undistinguished and unknown.

9. Everyone has the right to idle.

10. Everyone has the right to love and take care of the cat.

11. Everyone has the right to look after the dog until one of

them dies.

12. A dog has the right to be a dog.

13. A cat is not obliged to love its owner, but must help in time of need.

14. Sometimes everyone has the right to be unaware of their duties.

15. Everyone has the right to be in doubt, but this is not an obligation.

16. Everyone has the right to be happy.

17. Everyone has the right to be unhappy.

18. Everyone has the right to be silent.

19. Everyone has the right to have faith.

20. No one has the right to violence.

21. Everyone has the right to appreciate their unimportance.

22. No one has the right to have a design on eternity.

23. Everyone has the right to understand.

24. Everyone has the right to understand nothing.

25. Everyone has the right to be of any nationality.

26. Everyone has the right to celebrate or not celebrate their birthday.

27. Everyone shall remember their name.

28. Everyone may share what they possess.

29. No one can share what they do not possess.

30. Everyone has the right to have brothers, sisters and parents.

31. Everyone may be independent.

32. Everyone is responsible for their freedom.

33. Everyone has the right to cry.

34. Everyone has the right to be misunderstood.

35. No one has the right to make another person guilty.

36. Everyone has the right to be individual.

37. Everyone has the right to have no rights.

38. Everyone has the right to not be afraid.

39. Do not defeat.

40. Do not fight back.

41. Do not surrender.

Some argue that the last three are mottos, not rights.

It was written in July 1998 by Thomas Chepaitis (Minister of Foreign Affairs of Užupis) and Romas Lileikis (President of Užupis)

Acknowledgments

his book started as a short story called "The Box." Thank you, Sonal Nalkur, for being my first reader and for planting the seed that this could be stretched out into a novel.

Thank you, Cherri Randall, editor from Writer's Digest, who provided feedback on the story when it was still in its short version. Thank you for encouraging me to turn it into a longer manuscript.

It was during National Novel Writing Month or NaNoWriMo, in November 2022, that I finished the first draft of the manuscript. Thank you, NaNoWriMo, for organizing this event. Writing daily enabled me to complete the novel.

Thank you, Atlas Obscura, for organizing the tour through the Baltics that inspired so much of Naina's journey through Estonia, Latvia, and Lithuania. In particular, thank you Darmon Richter and Will Mawhood, the tour leaders, for providing such an impactful experience. Darmon and Will provided much of the knowledge I gained as well as many articles I referenced. In addition, Will, thank you for fact-checking, and Darmon, thank you for being an early reader.

Jim Dempsey, thank for you being my developmental editor in

chief and for telling me the things I may not have wanted to hear but needed to incorporate to improve the novel and get it to where it needed to be.

Eleanor Narey, thank you as well for your edits, and your kind words through the process.

Michelle Weitering, thank you for being a beta-reader, for hearing all of my struggles and ideas regarding this novel, and for providing so much of your love, friendship and support. Of course, you inspired me to include Frankston and our beloved chicken rolls.

Lisa Benson, thank you for being an early reader and catching so many misspellings and errors. Your friendship has grown to be a strong support and I am so grateful.

Kim Roberts, I can't believe we reconnected over writing. I'm so grateful that you took the time to provide your feedback and read an early draft of the manuscript.

Dylan Ingram and the team at Lusaris, thank you for making the cover and the book come to life.

Karen Mc Dermott, thank you for being the alchemist, for making magic happen in all you touch. You're instrumental in all I do in this literary world, and for that, I'm forever grateful. Did you notice that little nod to Perth?

And thank you to Eamer for introducing me to fairy bread!

Thank you to Nieraj and Alesja and to all my friends and family for all your love and support.

Thank you Mama and Papa, for being there for me, always, without question. Thank you for being early readers of this manuscript and for your loving and encouraging support. I wouldn't be able to do what I do without you.

About the Author

Sonee Singh is a Doctor of Divinity, a cross-cultural seeker of deep knowing. She's an award-winning and best-selling author of poetry and stories of self-discovery to encourage people to accept themselves for who they are and live life on their own terms. Her writing centers on the definitive moments on life's journey. The mystical and spiritual are integral in her poems and storytelling, as is her multi-cultural background.

Sonee is of Indian descent, born in Mexico, raised in Colombia, and resides in the United States. When not traveling, reading, or writing, she indulges in meditation, yoga, and aromatherapy.

Sonee has multiple articles published on *Elephant Journal* and Medium.com. Her debut novel, *Lonely Dove,* was released in 2022. Other works include:

Poetry
Soul Seeker Collection:

Embody

Embrace

Embolden

Sonee Singh

Anthologies
Blessing the Page
The Colours of Me
Kali Rising Holy Rage (Coming in 2023)

Follow her:
www.soneesingh.com
@soneesinghauthor

Printed in the USA
CPSIA information can be obtained
at www.ICGtesting.com
LVHW051502131023
760665LV00008B/848